The Mists of Huron Court

Dorothy Bodoin

A Wings ePress, Inc.
Cozy Mystery Novel

Wings ePress, Inc.

Edited by: Jeanne Smith
Copy Edited by: Joan Powell
Executive Editor: Jeanne Smith
Cover Artist: Trisha FitzGerald

All rights reserved

Names, characters and incidents depicted in this book are products of the author's imagination or are used fictitiously. Any resemblance to actual events, locales, organizations, or persons, living or dead, is entirely coincidental and beyond the intent of the author or the publisher.

No part of this book may be reproduced or transmitted in any form or by any means, electronic or mechanical, including photocopying, recording, or by any information storage and retrieval system, without permission in writing from the publisher.

Wings ePress Books
www.wingsepress.com

Copyright © 2016 by Dorothy Bodoin
ISBN-13: 978-1-61309-738-0
ISBN-10: 1-61309-738-7

Published In the United States Of America

Wings ePress Inc.
3000 N. Rock Road
Newton, KS 67114

Dedication

Dedicated to the memory of my brother, Dr. Nicholas Bodoin,
always in my memories, always in my heart.

* * *

<h1 style="text-align:center">One</h1>

Laughter as clear and melodious as a ringing bell floated through the silent autumn-turning world. It was a jarring sound, for I assumed I was alone with my dogs on the narrow country road that led away from Sagramore Lake.

Never assume you're alone in Foxglove Corners.

Misty, the youngest of the trio, a frisky white collie with a tricolor face, froze in her tracks, head tilted. Moment later I heard another sound. A dog barking.

Another dog.

I slipped into alert mode. Was it friendly or aggressive? Leashed, I hoped, although this was the country where dogs ran free, along with deer, coyotes, hares, and other wildlife forms.

Misty whimpered and pulled on the leash. I rejected my initial inclination to backtrack and walked on. Rounding a curve in the road, I came to the source of the disturbance.

Through a light mist I saw a young girl playing ball with her collie in the front yard of a charming Victorian house. Nestled in a stand of maple trees, it was soft pink, fairly small but exquisite with three gables and twin turrets, all adorned with white gingerbread trim. The color had a magical rosy glow.

The scene reminded me of an illustration in a fairy tale book, only this picture was alive with activity. The girl's long chestnut hair blew in the wind. The dog leaped into the air, a flash of reddish-gold fur, sending leaves flying in all directions. The girl laughed. She still held the ball.

"Ha!" she said. "Fooled you."

I stood at the edge of the road, mesmerized by the enchanting interplay between girl and dog.

Neither one appeared to be aware of our presence. Laughter and joyous barking mixed with the rustle of fallen leaves stirred to life by the dog's prancing motion.

Misty yelped her impatience to be acknowledged by one of her kind and the laughing human. Sky and Halley were oblivious, taking advantage of the opportunity to lie down in the leaves. I took a few steps forward. "Hello. What a pretty collie!"

The girl noticed me then, pushed back strands of shining chestnut hair, and moved the dog's ball from one hand to the other. The bell inside the toy jingled faintly.

"Oh, hello," she said. "Gosh, I didn't know anyone was there. We don't get too many walkers on this road."

I was close enough for Misty to greet the other dog who pranced around Misty with unbridled exuberance. I could see the color of the girl's eyes, gray with flecks of green and gold, and the sapphire earrings peering through strands of glossy hair.

"He looks like a puppy," I said.

"She. Ginger's two."

"That's about Misty's age. I think."

I wasn't sure. With the exception of Halley, all of my collies were rescues. A heartless human had abandoned Misty on my porch one snowy Christmas Eve. She was my youngest and zaniest, still more or less a puppy.

"Your collies are beautiful, too," the girl said. "You have one of each color. How cool."

Halley was black, tan and white, known in collie circles as tricolor. Sky was a blue merle with dark marling in her silvery fur, and Misty had a lustrous white coat.

"I have a sable at home and a bi-black," I said. "All together, I call them my rainbow."

"Nice. My name is Violet, by the way."

I would have shaken her hand if my hand had been free. She still held the ball.

"I'm Jennet Ferguson. We're neighbors —sort of. My husband and I live on Jonquil Lane."

"We're pretty isolated here," she said. "This is our little house in the big woods."

I smiled at the allusion to Laura Ingalls Wilder. As a high school English teacher and ardent reader, I recognized a kindred spirit.

"I've never come this way before," I said. "We walked down to the lake and I decided to take a different route. When I came to that fork in the road, I turned right."

"Most people turn left. It's more populated that way."

"Where does this road lead?" I asked.

"To more woods, another lake, and an old cemetery."

Ginger nudged Violet's hand, and the ball fell to the ground. Instead of pouncing on it, she waited for Violet to toss it, which she did. High in the air, over the carpet of leaves into a stand of fir trees. Ginger dashed after it.

Tail wagging madly, Misty tried to free herself from her restraint. In her mind, Violet had thrown the ball for her. I held on to the leash tightly.

"It's good to know about your collies," Violet said. "I thought Ginger was the only one around here."

She couldn't have been more mistaken. It seemed that all of my friends had collies, perhaps influenced by my amazing pack. There were twelve within walking distance of my house, not counting the rescues fostered by Sue Appleton, President of the Lakeville Collie Rescue League.

"Maybe we can go walking together sometime," Violet added. "We can keep each other company."

"I'd like that," I said.

"Ginger!" she called. "Come! Bring the ball."

Apparently Ginger wasn't ready to obey.

"We'll be on our way then," I said, "and Misty..." I laid a restraining hand on her head. "You have a ball of your own at home, baby."

Ahead lay another stretch of woods and more water —and a cemetery. For some reason I was suddenly tired, and Misty seemed restless. She probably wanted to play a game of her own with her own ball.

Saying goodbye to Violet, I coaxed Halley and Sky to their feet and turned around. For me, the brief meeting had been a highlight of our walk, as I always love to meet fellow collie fanciers, to say nothing of their dogs. But it was time to move on.

~ * ~

The dogs were drooping as we trudged up Jonquil Lane to the green Victorian style farmhouse we called home. It had grown warmer and the wind blew leaves in our faces. Misty amused herself trying to catch one.

The sight of my front porch filled with white wicker furniture and the stained glass windows bracketed by twin gables always filled me with quiet happiness whether I'd been away for a day or an hour.

We owned ten acres, but only the section surrounding the house was planted. Long lean coneflowers losing their faded petals and clumps of black-eyed Susans, still bright and cheery. Dark woods on the right giving way to the magnificent yellow Victorian across the lane. Collie faces appeared in the window. Candy and Gemmy, today's left behind ones, were barking behind the glass.

All familiar and so well loved.

Raven, the rare black and white collie who lived in a custom-built Victorian dog house, had chosen not to accompany us on our walk, but she bounded out to the lane to welcome us with a spate of high-pitched barking.

It's time you were getting home, she might have said.

Time. I never had enough of it even on a lazy Sunday afternoon. After dinner I had lesson plans to write, a short story to read, and papers to correct. Speaking of dinner... I peeled potatoes and carrots to accompany the roast and shoved the roaster in the oven.

In about two hours my husband, Crane, Foxglove Corners' favorite deputy sheriff, would be home from his seemingly endless patrol of the roads and byroads. Which gave me a brief respite from household duties.

I called my collie family and passed out biscuits. Halley and Sky were recuperating from their excursion under the dining room table, but Misty and the wild child, Candy, were engaged in a pseudo vicious game of tug-of-war. Gemmy looked on with tolerant boredom. Raven, who had stayed outside, had scant interest in the house or treats, only dinner served to her on her own doorstep.

While the collies broke for refreshments, I drank a cup of tea and thought about the afternoon's encounter.

Strange how Violet claimed never to have seen another collie in the neighborhood. Besides my six, there was Holly, another tricolor who belonged to Camille, my neighbor and aunt by marriage. On Squill Lane, Sue Appleton had three rescued River Rose collies and an ever-changing brood of fosters. Closer to Violet, on Sagramore Lake Road, young Jennifer Marlington had a new collie puppy also named Ginger.

Well, Violet would soon see collies galore. In the past Candy had proved too rambunctious for me to walk her alone, but there were Gemmy and Raven who often trotted along with us. Sometimes we took Holly along.

It would be fun to have an occasional walking companion.

~ * ~

"I made a new friend today," I told Crane over dinner.

He looked up from the salad bowl, an amused glint in his frosty gray eyes. "Do we have a new neighbor?"

"Not quite. She lives near the lake in the prettiest pink Victorian house I've ever seen. It reminds me of a child's playhouse. Well, a large one."

"Where is this?" he asked.

"I forget the name of the road. You head north from Sagramore Lake, walk about a quarter of a mile, and come to a fork. I took the road less traveled by," I added with a smile. "The right one."

"I know the area," he said, "but I don't remember seeing a pink house there. Just woods."

"You can't know every house in Foxglove Corners," I said.

"Maybe not. You said it looked like a playhouse. Most of the houses around here are large."

I drizzled dressing over my salad, thinking. He was right. Whether they were vintage Victorians, built before or around the nineteen hundreds, or newly-constructed in Victorian style, ours was a town of mansions. Or at least two-story structures, which, when compared to my previous home, was a mansion.

In retrospect my comparison might have been an exaggeration. The pink house communicated smallness, inspired fancies of strawberry cream cupcakes. Maybe it had once been an oversized playhouse, intended for a privileged child who lived in a mansion on the property.

One I hadn't seen from my vantage point.

"Tell me about Violet," Crane said. "Was she young, our age, old...?"

"It's hard to tell. I'd say she was in her late teens."

I tried to call Violet's image to mind. "She was very pretty with long chestnut hair. Let's see. She was wearing blue pants and a white top and earrings. She didn't mention her family, but then we only talked for a few minutes. She's going to take Ginger walking with us sometime."

"That's good, "Crane said. "I'll look for the house tomorrow."

Two

Three hours into a blue Monday I felt the first throbbing of a headache behind my right eye. I stole a glance at the classroom clock hung in the back of the room to discourage time-watching.

In fifteen minutes, my fourth hour American Literature students would be storming into the room. That meant I had a short period of relative peace with my good Journalism class. Then I could take a headache pill with a swallow of bottled water in the hope of heading off the pain and prepare for the worst.

This was not how I'd hoped the school day at Marston High School would proceed. But how could I be optimistic? Every time this particular group of eleventh graders came together, the result was an hour of chaos.

Privately I thought of my fourth period as the class from hell. They had thundered into the room on the first day like a herd of stampeding buffalo. Loud, unruly, and mostly incorrigible.

On meeting a new teacher, most groups tend to be on their best behavior, for a few days anyway. Not this one. Ever since that grim introduction they'd been quiet for only fleeting moments. I had a private seating chart with stars alongside the names of the worst offenders.

From the beginning, from the first day, I must have done something wrong, obviously failed to let them know I was in charge.

That was only part of the problem. How could I teach my students anything about the literature of the Puritan age when they refused to listen to me? Furthermore, I couldn't relax when my nemesis, Principal Grimsley, appeared outside my door at unexpected times, his face registering disapproval at the behavior of the class. There must be a way, but I hadn't figured it out yet.

The reprieve ended. The bell's echo faded. The noise level rose, swelled, threatened to drown me. I had to get the class started. Demand quiet. Call attention to the day's assignment written on the board.

"I want it quiet in here," I said.

"What we want and what we get are two different things."

I didn't know who'd said that. Some boy in the back.

At least today's selection should appeal to them. We were discussing a description of the trial of an accused Salem witch, supposedly read for homework.

In the blessed lull that followed the impertinent response, I described the tests designed to determine whether the accused was guilty of witchcraft or innocent.

"That's stupid," Slade Johnston said.

He was a tall, husky boy whose fair-haired, blue eyed appearance belied a demonic personality. I noticed that he was in the wrong seat. He must have moved after attendance.

"They're either guilty or they die," he said and looked to the class for acknowledgement of his brilliance. "They can't win."

I nodded. "That's the point."

"So what kind of justice is that?"

"Salem justice," I said.

I had found a movie, *Three Sovereigns for Sarah,* about the girls who accused their victims of diabolical deeds and thought it might hold my students' interest. For a few days. Add a composition, begun in class, and soon we could leave the unpalatable non-fiction selections of the Puritan era behind and move on to a short story.

Nathaniel Hawthorne, I thought. *Rip Van Winkle.* That was one of my favorites. After Hawthorne, came Edgar Allan Poe with his archaic language and gruesome scenes. Future sessions, I hoped, would be better.

I didn't like to admit it, but I'd found this particular period a deadly bore in college. How could I make it fascinating for students when I disliked it? As I recalled, Doctor White, my most personable professor, hadn't been able to hold my interest with her spirited commentary.

Perhaps fascinating was out of reach.

Try for tolerable, I told myself.

An ungodly screech calling to mind a small creature in its death throes erupted in the back of the room. That could only be Jasmine, a petite, pretty girl with short dark hair who simply couldn't refrain from talking for more than five minutes.

On cue, a shadow fell across the threshold, Grimsley on his pre-lunch patrol. His eyes swept the scene, his signature pasted-on smile missing.

I ignored him.

"What's wrong, Jasmine?" I demanded.

"Slade broke my pencil. He's a bully."

Slade gave me an angelic smile. I countered with one of my most ferocious scowls.

"By accident, I assume?"

"Naah. He meant it."

"Keep your hands to yourself, Slade," I said. "And Jasmine, you're supposed to write in pen. That's an English Department rule."

"Dumb rule," Jasmine said. "Does anyone have a pen I can borrow?"

I'd written four essay questions on the board. Four questions for forty minutes. Writing would take longer than oral discussion. No matter how I tried, I never had enough material to keep this class occupied.

"Is that all we're going to do today?" was a frequent question.

"Now if you'll write answers to the questions," I said. "Support your ideas. Try to write two or three substantial paragraphs for each. In ink."

I estimated that a third of the class began the assignment. The pill I'd taken before they'd tramped in wasn't working yet. Maybe it wasn't going to. My headache was increasing.

Think of quiet, peaceful places, I thought. *Autumn leaves drifting through the smoky air on Jonquil Lane, dim woods, the lake at sunset. Almost any place in Foxglove Corners.*

Any place but here in this classroom in Marston High School in Oakpoint, Michigan. Here in hell.

Pens scratched, a ripple of conversation burgeoned into constant noise. The hour hand on the clock moved slowly, so slowly I could have sworn it was moving backward. That often happened in this class.

Minutes before the bell rang, my reluctant scholars were out of their seats, dropping papers on my desk as they formed an unwieldy crowd in front of the door. Waiting for the bell to ring before leaving your desk was another rule. My own.

"Everybody," I said, "go back to your seats. Sit."

I should have said 'Take your seats.'

Grumbling, a few obeyed me. More than a few didn't. Slade Johnston maintained his position at the door, a defiant sneer on his face.

"Slade! I said to..."

The bell rang. He was gone, they were all gone, and I was left with the feeling that as a teacher I was completely inadequate. I'd had more classroom control during my first year.

Something, I decided, had to change.

~ * ~

I unwrapped my roast beef sandwich with a lack of enthusiasm and poured lukewarm tea from my thermos into a paper cup. At Marston, we had a twenty-minute lunch period with five additional minutes allotted for traveling to the cafeteria and five for the return trip.

To stretch this skimpy period, I usually ate a packed lunch with my friend and fellow English teacher, Leonora, either in her classroom or mine. Leonora had moved to Foxglove Corners sometime after I did, after which we took turns driving the hour-long distance to our school.

Pretty with golden blonde hair, a vivacious personality, and a way of relating to the most recalcitrant of students, Leonora was the most popular member of the English Department, probably of the faculty.

She lifted the lid of a carton of cold fried chicken. Why hadn't I thought to pack a more imaginative lunch?

I pressed my fingers to my temple.

"Another headache, Jen?" she asked.

I nodded, wondering why the roast, which had tasted so good last night, seemed to have turned into thinly sliced wood.

"Did you take something for it?"

"Over an hour ago."

"It's that class," she said. "They'd give anyone a headache —and indigestion. I don't envy you."

"I'm at my wit's end."

That was an odd phrase, clear to any listener but somehow not strong enough to describe the way I felt. And it was only October.

"Sometimes you get a group that can't be handled," she pointed out.

"The computer had it in for me."

This year Leonora had an enviable section of English Literature. Her students were seniors, most of them college bound, and the class was small at twenty-five. The computer had smiled on her.

"I really love literature," I said. "I want to inspire my students to love it too. We have to start at the beginning. A foundation is important even if the early selections aren't particularly exciting."

"You will, Jen. You'll find a way."

I took another bite of my sandwich and tossed it out the window for the birds. I had an oatmeal cookie, but I'd save it until later.

The side of the building had a view of a wooded acre that belonged to the school district but was rarely used except by members of the Ecology Club on nature walks. The leaves were a brilliant mixture of crimson and gold and russet. Sometimes gazing at the scenery coaxed a headache away. I was willing to try anything to prepare myself to cope with the rest of the day.

If only we had a proper lunch hour with appealing food and hot tea. My afternoon classes were agreeable, hence pleasant, for both teacher and student. I had a small section of World Literature and Advanced Journalism followed by a conference hour. Then the long commute home to Foxglove Corners where I would join the ranks of the mentally healthy again.

The bell rang.

Hastily Leonora covered her container and brushed crumbs into her empty lunch bag.

"All you can do is roll with the punches," she said.

Three

About thirty-five miles north of Marston High School, flames leaped to life in the fireplace of a green Victorian farmhouse on Jonquil Road. A beef stew simmered on the stove, and a lemon meringue pie cooled on the counter. Five collies dozed in their favorite resting places on the first floor.

Surrounded by love and familiarity and sweet normalcy, I felt my headache drift away. Finally.

Dinner was going to be late tonight because of a staff meeting. In retrospect, I should have stopped for take-out, but I'd had the stew meat thawing for two days and the vegetables cut.

Crane stepped back from the fireplace and surveyed his work. The firelight gave the silver strands in his hair an ethereal shine. I longed to touch the fine lines that crinkled around his gray eyes and see their frosty sparkle and feel his strong arms around me.

Firelight and romance go together like... Well, like stew and biscuits.

"That should take the chill out of the air," Crane said, smacking his hands together.

Candy, assuming he was signaling her, raised her head, then rested it on her paws, watching him.

It wasn't really chilly, but a fall household can only be improved by a bit of crackling cheer. The sultry autumn day had turned sullen with lowering clouds and distant thunder, but all of the dogs had had their walk. Inside, touched by firelight and candlelight, all was well with my world.

It was as I'd known all along. My home and my family were all I needed to return to a state of mental health.

And it was so blessedly quiet.

Crane joined me on the sofa and draped his arm around my shoulder. "I didn't have a chance to look for your pink Victorian, honey. The lawbreakers were out in full force."

"It's there," I said. "Maybe I'll walk the dogs that way tomorrow after school."

If it didn't rain. The forecasters promised two days of soggy weather which translated into mud and a multitude of muddy paws.

Crane pulled me close for a long kiss. "After dinner..."

From inside my purse the harp notes of my iPhone rippled. I reached for it, frowning at the interruption and the shattered mood.

"Are you busy, Jennet?" Sue Appleton asked.

With a glance at Crane who had picked up the *Banner*, I said, "We're about to have dinner, but it can wait. What's up?"

"I won't keep you then. I'm a little upset. No, more than a little. I feel terrible."

This must be serious.

"What's wrong?"

"I have a new rescue. She arrived today." Sue's voice broke. Had she been crying?

"I'm sorry. It's just..."

Serious indeed. As president of our Rescue League, Sue usually presented a stoic, unflappable side to her fellow members. "Rescuers must remain objective," she often said. "Otherwise we'll never be able to function."

"Tell me about it," I said.

"This woman, a Mrs. Fontaine, brought her collie to me. She was crying, hugging her, putting on quite a show."

So far that was normal behavior when parting with a beloved pet. I waited.

"It was disgusting. Get this, Jennet. Star is nine years old. They've had her since she was a puppy. Now nobody in a family of six has time for her. They want us to find her a new home."

"The poor dog."

Without having seen Star, I felt a piece of my heart break away. My gaze fell on Halley, the oldest of my brood, snoozing by the fire. I'd had her since she was eight weeks old, and I'd never give her away. Not in a million years. I couldn't understand how anyone could justify such cruelty.

"You should have seen Star," Sue said. "She was terrified. When Mrs. Fontaine left, she tried to go with her. She cried... That heartless witch didn't say goodbye to her, didn't even look back."

I could visualize the scene. Gently I pushed it out of my mind lest I lose another piece of my heart.

"What are the odds of finding her a forever home?" I asked, already knowing the answer.

"Very, very slim. She's in good health, but most people want a puppy or a young dog. Star's owner didn't even bring a toy to remind her of home. Just a collar and a leash."

"You'll keep her then?"

"I don't see how I can," Sue said. "I have eight dogs now."

Sue also had horses. She owned a riding stable on Squill Lane and gave lessons to about a dozen aspiring equestrians.

"All of our foster homes are full," she added.

There was no room for Star in her own home, and no foster home could take her either.

"The family was considering having her put down, then they thought if someone wanted her..."

Put down?

I didn't want to believe anyone could be so cold. Owning a dog was a lifetime commitment broken only by death. Sort of like marriage. I reached for Crane's hand. He let the paper fall in his lap and gave me a look of concern and compassion.

"Why are they so busy?" I asked.

"The usual excuses. She has a demanding new job. They want to take a fall vacation. The youngest kids went away to college. I turned her off in mid-spiel."

"What's Star doing now?"

"Lying in front of her dinner bowl. She won't eat. She isn't interacting with the other dogs. Icy tried to interest her in play. It's so sweet. He brought her his yellow reindeer."

Icy had been a rescue himself, a champion blue merle who had lived in the wild after his owner's death.

"Maybe she'll eat later," I said. "When she gets hungry."

"I hope so. If she doesn't eat, she'll die."

That was a sad possibility. I had heard of dogs who had virtually willed themselves to death, refusing food, as they mourned their lost home. Especially older dogs. To lose a home was tantamount to losing life.

"I'll come over tomorrow after school to see her," I said.

"Would you? You have a way with dogs. Maybe you can coax her to eat or at least wag her tail."

I smiled. "I'm not a miracle worker, but I'll see what I can do. Meanwhile I'll look for a toy that isn't being used."

Misty's precious white goat that had turned a dingy shade of gray lay on its side in front of the rocker. I didn't see Misty in the room. How unlike her to be parted from her treasure. The little stuffy served as her security blanket, a symbol of belonging for a puppy who had been cherished since she'd been abandoned on our porch. My dogs tended to like their old toys best.

Had Star been forced to abandon a beloved stuffed friend in her lost home?

I always had toys that had failed to interest my dogs. Some had never been sniffed or chewed or dropped at my feet for a game of fetch. I'd take Star one of them and a few of the cookies Camille made especially for dogs.

"I'll see you tomorrow, Sue," I said. "Tell Star to hang in there."

I set the phone on the coffee table, realized I was still holding Crane's hand.

"I can guess what that was about," he said.

"Can you believe it?"

"Sure. It happens all the time. Dogs give us humans their all and get thrown away when they become a nuisance."

"Not our dogs," I said.

"No, never."

I love this man, I thought.

With Crane at my side, no problem was insurmountable, not even Star's grim dilemma. Certainly not school. Let the class from hell do its worst. I'd conquer them —or not. The semester would end eventually, and next year at this time, my ever-increasing fourth period angst would be a memory.

My life with Crane was forever.

"Now," he said. "Tonight, after dinner…"

He kissed me again. We didn't need words.

~ * ~

The rain began during the night. I didn't have to look out the window the next morning to know it had turned Jonquil Lane into a leaf-strewn swamp.

We sat at the oak table in the kitchen fortifying ourselves with a breakfast of scrambled eggs and bacon before beginning the day. Crane was already dressed in his crisp deputy sheriff's uniform, his badge gleaming in the overhead light. I wore one of my favorite red dresses with three gold chains, hoping to add a modicum of brightness to a dull day.

"You won't want to walk by the lake with the dogs today," Crane said.

"No, not today. I'll take the car to Sue's. I keep thinking about Star."

And, of course, about my fourth period American Lit class and the movie that would grant me the blessing of a quiet hour. I hoped Grimsley wouldn't linger outside my door piercing me with his characteristic disapproving glare. He considered showing movies a waste of class time.

No matter that *Seven Sovereigns for Sarah* was relevant to our study and not readily available to the students. I'd point that out to him if challenged. It wasn't as if I were showing them cartoons.

"Be careful on the freeway," Crane said. "It may be slippery."

"Leonora's driving today."

"Tell her, then."

A roll of thunder crossed the sky, not so distant this time.

"Better hurry," Crane said and scooped up the last of his eggs.

I sighed, no longer hungry. A long commute, a stormy day, a rogue class... Too many hours until I could come home again.

Just be grateful you have a home, I told myself.

Four

The next day one of Sue's River Rose rescues, Bluebell, tore her dew claw, necessitating an emergency trip to the Doctor Foster's animal hospital. Sue left me a voice mail asking me to postpone my visit. Star, she added, was the same, still in deep mourning and refusing to eat. Could I come tomorrow afternoon instead?

I was disappointed as I'd been thinking about Star during lulls in an otherwise hectic school day.

In the summer Crane had spoken about getting a collie puppy. Well, in truth, I had expressed my desire for a puppy, and he'd told me to make out my Christmas list.

Didn't that sound as if he was amenable to increasing our canine family?

I knew we had reached our collie limit with the adoption of Misty, but why would Crane have mentioned a Christmas list if he was dead set against adding a seventh collie to our brood?

Of course I wasn't thinking about a roly-poly puppy at this point but about Star, the collie without a home, the dog I hadn't yet set eyes on. I had a gift for empathizing with dogs, especially dogs in distress. I could imagine how it felt to lose everything and everyone I loved and how I'd feel when I realized that no one wanted me.

If nobody stepped forward to give Star a forever home, could I possibly have her? Should I?

"You're not thinking clearly, Jen," Leonora said as we hurried our way through lunch. "I have Wafer and Lass. Two large dogs are all I can manage."

"Star needs a home, and we have plenty of room," I said.

"You can't keep adopting your rescues," she pointed out. "As it is, the dogs outnumber you and Crane."

"That's true, but nobody has time or room for Star. I can't let her die."

"You'll risk losing your husband."

"Crane loves our dogs," I said, "and he loves me."

"Crane is a paragon, but even paragons have their limits."

I took a sip of lukewarm tea. "I'm just thinking about it."

"Sure."

"Maybe Sue already found Star a home."

I knew she hadn't or she would have mentioned it in the voice mail.

I glanced at the clock. We had six minutes left. Everybody was always glancing at clocks at Marston High School, hurrying to class or wishing the hour would end. I deplored being unable to eat in a leisurely fashion. But in spite of the overcast sky and constant drizzle, I was in a happier mood today.

Once I'd settled the class from hell, they had enjoyed *Three Sovereigns for Sarah* —or seemed to. I didn't have to deal with any misbehavior as the movie's gruesome aspects had hooked them. And for a change today I had a decent lunch, a container of stew that I'd warmed in the school's microwave.

"When will you know about Star?" Leonora asked.

"Not for a few days. I have to see her first and ask Crane if we can foster her."

Leonora cast me a knowing smile. "As English teachers we understand the importance of choosing the right word. *Foster* will take you further than *adopt*."

Leonora was a member of the Rescue League, but she'd never volunteered to open her home to a collie foundling. She wasn't married, although she hoped to be one day soon as her boyfriend, Deputy Sheriff Jake Brown, had been singularly attentive lately. She had an obliging neighbor who loved dogs and occasionally helped her with Wafer and Lass, but she loved to travel. This summer she'd taken her two collies on a road trip out west.

Try doing that with seven collies. Crane and I were still trying to manage a trip to Tennessee to visit his Southern relatives.

"The bell's going to ring in a minute," Leonora said.

Where had five minutes gone?

I broke my cookie in half, setting aside a tiny snack for my conference hour just as the bell shattered our hard-won peace.

"Back to the mines," Leonora said.

An apt sentiment, but the worst class of the day was over. I truly enjoyed working with my afternoon students.

~ * ~

While I'd been teaching in Oakpoint, a brisk wind had dried Jonquil Lane, and the drizzle gave way to warmth and a blue sky. The sun even deigned to make a brief appearance. The woods across the lane blazed with brilliant color. Leaves drifted languidly through the air, tantalizing Misty with their 'Catch me if you can' dance.

We walked to Sagramore Lake, Misty, Halley, and Gemmy, all of us in high spirits, retracing the route I'd taken on Sunday to the pink Victorian house. Huron Court was the name of the road, a ludicrous appellation as it was a glorified country lane bordered by woods and not a house or a court in sight.

We crunched along on a thick carpet of leaves, savoring the clear air and the fragrant scents. Only rustling in the woods and overhead twitterings broke the silence. Oh, sweet woods of autumn... If only the season weren't so fleeting.

I wondered if Violet was home and in a mood for walking with Ginger. If not, well, I'd turn around and head back to the lake. We should have exchanged phone numbers or made definite plans. I didn't know whether Violet had a job or went to school or who lived with her in the pink house in the woods.

Well, it didn't matter. I'd soon find out, and our mutual love of collies was a strong bond.

As we neared the fork in the road, Misty froze in her tracks, tipped ears alert, eyes fixed straight ahead on something I couldn't see.

A fox, maybe, or a deer? Perhaps a smaller creature like a rabbit that feared the intrusion of a human and three canines?

She whined frantically, signaling her desire to keep walking, and I… I took the road less traveled by again, hoping that whatever had caught Misty's attention had moved on. She was still apprehensive, though, still whining.

But why? The animal must be long gone by now.

Laughter rang out into the oppressive silence.

Violet's laugh reminded me of a clear bell, a joyous sound in a landscape that looked suddenly ominous. The lightest of mists lay on the road, so light it might have been an illusion.

Why didn't I hear Ginger barking?

Misty turned her gaze to the sky as if marking the progress of a bird or a ball. She yanked on her leash, causing me to stumble on a rock in the middle of the road. With nothing to hold onto except leashes, I fell forward, skinning my knees on the ground. The leashes flew out of my hand.

Halley and Gemmy circled around me, nudging me with cold noses as I knelt, then rose shakily.

Leashes!

I picked them up, reined in two collies, and looked for the third one. Misty was digging madly at the side of the road, sending up a spray of fine dirt, leaves and small stones. She didn't appear to notice when I grabbed the leash and called her name. Strange. She wasn't usually a digger.

"Misty, Stop!" I said. "Come!"

She left her hole with marked reluctance, growling a little, which was unlike her. Okay, say grumbling then.

I was standing and moving, but the effects of the fall were making themselves known in every area of my body. I must have skinned my arm, too, because my elbow hurt. But nothing was broken. I was reasonably sure of it.

If we weren't so close to our destination, I'd abandon the walk and trudge painfully homeward, but Violet's house was so close now, mere yards, mere seconds away. Just beyond the curve.

Around the curve...

I came to a standstill, trying to process what I was seeing.

The pink Victorian was there with its three gables and twin turrets. At the same time it wasn't.

I hardly recognized the house in the surround of vegetation that overtaken the neat green lawn I remembered. The glowing paint had faded to a washed-out mix of gray and beige. Sections of peeling gingerbread trim hung free from the structure, and shingles lay amidst the weeds where they had fallen. The windows were dull with the dirt of a myriad past winters. Over all surfaces, maple trees had dropped their leaves of crimson.

They looked like a spill of blood.

The enchanting pink and white Victorian cottage reminded me of one of the deteriorating mansions in the abandoned construction on Jonquil Lane.

"What on earth?" I murmured.

What had happened here? I'd seen the house only last Sunday, not twenty years ago. It had been whole and bright and beautiful then. A few days ago.

Slowly I became aware of my dogs. Halley and Gemmy lay in the road panting loudly, while Misty, whimpering, searched the sky.

For what?

A deep coldness wrapped itself around me. I might have been immobilized in ice. In front of the cottage, I stood, unable to move forward or backward, my various pains forgotten, not comprehending.

All I knew was there was no point in looking for Violet or Ginger in this skeleton house.

They were gone.

Five

Then I had the answer.

This couldn't be Violet's Victorian house. It was another house, abandoned by its owner, slowly coming apart, pieces of its walls falling with the leaves. I hadn't noticed it last Sunday. Distracted by Violet's laughter and Ginger's barking, I must have walked past it.

Nothing else made sense, and I was desperate for sense.

Where was Violet's house then? Grasping for a thread of reality, I looked to my dogs.

Misty's behavior puzzled me. She was busy investigating a tangle of weeds where Ginger's ball would have landed on Sunday.

Why *would have landed*? *Had* landed.

I knew what I'd seen. A young girl with long chestnut hair playing ball with a sable and white collie. I'd talked to her, for heaven's sake. Her name was Violet and...

And what?

She was wearing blue pedal pushers the exact color of the sky with a white top. She had sapphire earrings and a musical laugh, and she was friendly.

That was all I knew.

"Misty," I whispered, not really calling her. She must have realized that because she didn't look at me. She was searching for Ginger's ball, searching the ground as she'd watched the sky. In her experience, balls didn't vanish into thin air.

Misty had seen what I'd seen.

Obviously the other dogs hadn't. Halley and Gemmy were as oblivious as they had been on Sunday. They lay in the road waiting patiently for us to resume our walk.

Dear God! Did I have a psychic collie?

No! There had to be an explanation for this inexplicable transformation. A picturesque pink house doesn't turn into a crumbling ruin in a matter of days. For the moment the 'other house' explanation would suffice. There had to be another pink Victorian house farther down the road, then, an earlier version. Violet's house had been built in imitation of the one I stood in front of at present.

Find it, I ordered myself. *Go back to the fork in the road and keep walking, keep looking, until you find it. Just in case you passed it.*

That decided, I breathed a little easier, having no doubt that I would be successful.

~ * ~

The countryside, so lovely in its autumn dress, seemed forbidding as I retraced my steps. It was darker than it had been a scant half hour earlier and had definitely lost its charm. At least the mist was dissipating.

The dogs were confused. Why were we traversing the same area again instead of going forward? This wasn't how a walk should work. Misty was jittery, tugging on her leash, crying, wanting to explore every inch of the road as if a hidden treasure lurked just beneath its surface.

I focused my attention on the land to my right, hoping to see Violet's pink Victorian appear any minute.

It didn't, of course. I came to the curve and found the same dilapidated abandoned structure I'd just left. In the fading light it looked dull and lifeless.

On an impulse, I kept walking, passing woods and fields and a green pond whose stagnant waters almost touched the road's edge.

When I'd asked Violet where the road led, she had said, "To more woods and another lake and a cemetery."

Finally I gave up and walked the dogs back to Sagramore Lake.

I had to accept the facts. There was no other house to find, no pink Victorian, its gables and turret glowing as if freshly painted, no white gingerbread trim.

No Violet. No Ginger.

"Why are you surprised?" I said, not realizing I'd spoken aloud until Misty pinned me with a curious stare.

I was no stranger to supernatural phenomenon. I'd seen ghosts before —skating across a lake, wandering down the corridor of an old inn, treading lightly over snowy winter fields. Foxglove Corners was quite literally a hotbed of psychic activity.

This time was different though.

Not once had I interacted with a spirit. I'd never discussed the collie population in Foxglove Corners nor agreed to go walking with somebody who wasn't there.

Something else was going on here, and that frightened me.

By the time we reached the Sagramore Lake, the sun had all but disappeared, and my blue cardigan offered little protection against the dropping temperature. At one point, I remembered my fall which was why walking had become such a painful chore.

I was halfway home before I remembered the laughter.

~ * ~

Laughter as clear and melodious as a ringing bell. I'd heard the laughter today but hadn't seen the girl and her dog.

What does that tell you?

Once again I had wandered into the realm of the unknown. I had come to a fork in the road, taken the path less traveled by, and stumbled into one of the eerie mysteries that flourished in the region.

What I needed was a cold dose of reality.

The walk had taken longer than I'd anticipated. I had dinner to prepare and all I wanted to do was to soak in a hot bath and take a couple of pain pills.

Impossible with six dogs and a husband to feed. I settled for medication and a glass of ginger ale.

When Crane and I were married, I had promised myself that every dinner I prepared for my husband would be special, served by candlelight. I'd use the heirloom candlesticks that had belonged to Rebecca Ferguson, Crane's Civil War ancestress and by mutual agreement we'd ban serious or distressing conversation. There would be roasts, steaks, chops, and hearty stews and always a dessert, usually pie. I'd become proficient in pie making.

Tonight?

Having neglected to plan ahead, I took a dozen frozen meatballs (my own) out of the freezer and opened a box of spaghetti. I'd make a salad. There was no time for pie. Frozen blueberry-banana bread would have to do. I set the loaf on the counter to thaw, then reached for the canister of dog food.

And all the time, every minute, one thought played through my head, incessantly, as clear as ghostly laughter.

I had wandered all unaware into the other world again.

What now?

~ * ~

Crane's love for me, his pride in me, were all important. I didn't want him to think the woman he'd married was delusional. To that end, once I'd kept a secret from him. Long after a fatal shooting in my classroom, I'd begun hearing the sound of gunfire at odd times, in unusual places. Not sharing the experience with Crane had been a mistake, and I'd resolved to be completely forthcoming in the future.

That night, after dinner, when we were sitting quietly in front of the fire, I closed the book I'd been trying to read. "Did you ever look for the pink Victorian I told you about?"

He looked up from the *Banner*.

"Sorry, honey. It slipped my mind. It was another busy day out there."

"Don't bother," I said.

That captured his attention as I knew it would. Against a background of crackling flames, I told him about the shocking end of my walk with the dogs.

"Where I saw the cottage, there was a falling down shack. Okay, it was a Victorian shack, but still it wasn't the same place I saw on Sunday. It was run down and not even the same color," I added.

He didn't speak for a while.

Say something, I pleaded silently.

"And you think you went back in time?"

"Or forward. No, I hadn't thought that. I wonder…"

"It seems obvious to me," he said. "It's easy to get disorientated in the country. After a while, every tree looks the same. You took a different road. Naturally you saw a different house."

"But that didn't happen," I said. "We followed Huron Court to the fork. There was a curve in the road. On Sunday we came to a beautiful pink Victorian house. Today… We didn't."

He squeezed my hand. "I've gotten lost myself a time or two, and I know this country like the back of my hand. These byroads can be confusing."

"I heard somebody laughing," I added. "It sounded like Violet."

"Could it have been a bird call?"

He didn't believe me. That wasn't like him.

"I know the difference," I said. "Misty was acting weird, too. Dogs have a sixth sense."

"Mmm. That's the first time she's revealed it."

"This is serious, Crane," I said. "I'm worried. I never communicated with a ghost before, and there was nothing ghostly about Violet."

"All right, honey," he said. "Tomorrow I'll go with you. If there's a Victorian cottage in the vicinity, complete with a girl named Violet and a collie named Ginger, we'll find it."

He picked up his paper again.

"And if we don't?" I asked.

"Then I guess we have another mystery," he said.

Six

Fortunately supernatural phenomena didn't follow me to Marston High School. The problems associated with fourth period American Literature were rooted in the real world —which didn't make them easier to deal with.

Screaming students, countless requests for hall passes, textbooks forgotten, a paper airplane flying through the room. Insubordination, disorder, chaos.

I wondered if the tormented children of Salem had been so disruptive.

"How's it going this morning, Mrs. Ferguson?" Principal Grimsley asked as I stepped outside to close the classroom door.

Didn't the man ever stay in his office?

"Fine," I said.

Well, no one was attempting mayhem. We had two more days to watch *Three Sovereigns for Sarah*; then it would be back to the war zone.

"They're so loud," he said, glowering into the room.

No one saw fit to curtail their conversations. Well, it was good to know that even the mighty principal couldn't affect them.

"They're lively," I said. "It's almost Homecoming Week"

When all kinds of craziness become the norm.

"That's true, but that's no reason to forget why we're here," he said. "Carry on."

I closed the door. What could I do but carry on?

"Are we going to finish the movie today?" Megan asked.

"Tomorrow." I picked up my seating chart. "Please take your assigned seats," I said to a thunder-rumble of complaints.

Slade Johnston didn't move.

"If you're not in the desk assigned to you, you're absent."

"You can't do that," Slade yelled.

I wished I didn't have to resort to threats. They were empty threats, of course. I couldn't mark a student absent if he was present. I hoped Slade didn't know that for certain. At any rate he moved to the second desk in the window row with a maximum of muttering. It was, I figured, too close to the front of the room and my own desk for his comfort.

"Now let's have it quiet," I said.

"Everybody, shut up!" The voice came from the back of the room.

I turned on the DVD player, and it transported us back in time to a bitter winter day in colonial America. Soon the only noise was on the screen.

~ * ~

The promise of interesting after-school activities always makes the day go by faster. This afternoon I was finally going to see Star. Later, after dinner, Crane and I would walk over to Huron Court.

It would be a moment of reckoning.

What if...? I simply had to torment myself. What if we saw the pink Victorian cottage where I'd seen the disintegrating ghost version of it?

That would be good, wouldn't it? It would mean I'd imagined the cottage's derelict replacement, that Violet and Ginger were real.

I'd still have to explain the ghost house, though, because I *had* seen it. Either way I would still have to question my grip on reality.

Speculation was futile. We would find what we'd find. What was important to me was Crane's presence. He'd said 'us', not 'you'. Any burden grows lighter when it's shared with a loved one.

~ * ~

Our house and the yellow Victorian were the last inhabited dwellings on Jonquil Lane. Farther up the lane was an abandoned development of French chateau style mansions slowing falling apart in the shadows of a half-forest.

They would have been exquisite if the builder hadn't gone bankrupt and fled the state, leaving unfinished houses to deteriorate into an appalling and dangerous ruin. They were dark and gloomy, a temptation for dogs and ne'er-do-well's alike.

Past the ruins, the lane continued, woods on either side with red and gold leaves falling like raindrops. Eventually it ended on Squill Lane. Turn left and you'd come to an historic yellow cottage and a cornfield, the cottage usually untenanted. A right turn led to Sue Appleton's horse farm where equines and rescued canines enjoyed a comfortable life.

I turned right and soon found myself at Sue's horse farm. I hoped nothing was wrong. Usually on a perfect autumn day like this she would be outside with her horses or playing with the collies.

Sue opened the door, whipping off a bright orange apron that clashed with her strawberry blonde hair. Two gorgeous blue merles greeted me with excited barking and a prodigious amount of tail wagging. They were Icy and Bluebell, she of the damaged dew claw. I could hear the other dogs barking in the kennel.

"Come on in, Jennet," Sue said. "I'm making chicken soup."

"For dinner?" I asked.

"For the dogs. I'm hoping to tempt Star. She's only had a few bites of kibble all day."

"She's eating then? That's an improvement."

"A small one."

Star was in the kitchen lying with her head on crossed paws. She didn't get up, only surveyed me with solemn dark eyes.

I wasn't the one she waited for.

"Hello, Star," I said softly, offering her my palm to sniff. Her tail never moved. I longed to touch her, to pet her, but knew enough not to make the first move. I took the chair Sue offered me and studied the dejected collie, trying to look into her mind.

She had been beautiful —was a beauty still with a thick dark sable coat, a blaze, and white fur around her eyes.

A fool once told me that the only way one can tell whether a collie is happy is to observe his tail. Otherwise they all look alike.

What a stupid notion! Dogs had many expressions. I could tell when they were smiling —yes, smiling —when they were agitated or fearful or bored or plotting mischief. Star's expression was easy to read. I'd never seen loss and despair so deeply etched on a collie face.

She made me think of a large stuffed toy, fluffy and colorful but lacking the faintest spark of life.

Sue made a show of stirring the contents of her stockpot. "Yummy chicken with celery and carrots floating in the broth. Are you hungry, Star?"

Star looked at her, then looked down at the floor.

"Because if you are, I know where to find a nice piece of chicken with your name on it," she added.

"It smells delicious," I said.

"It does. I may have a piece of chicken myself."

Icy who had followed us into the kitchen, licked his chops and lay down beside Star.

"Did you find a foster home for her yet?" I asked.

Sue shook her head. "No luck. Our members have all the dogs they can handle. We need more members willing to open their homes to rescues."

"I was thinking... I might take her."

"That wasn't why I wanted you to see her," Sue said quickly.

I doubted that. Just as quickly I said, "I'd have to talk Crane into it. He thinks we have enough with six."

"She wouldn't be any trouble," Sue said.

No trouble, except for breaking your heart every time you looked at her.

"Her owner said she has a sweet disposition," Sue said. "She isn't afraid of thunder and doesn't bark. Well, not much anyway. I've only heard her crying."

"What will happen if you can't find her a forever home, let alone a foster home?" I asked.

"She'll stay here with me, I guess."

"Has her owner expressed any interest in how she's doing?"

"Her?" Sue scoffed. "I haven't heard a word. I didn't expect to. Out of sight, out of mind."

"It's so terrible," I said.

Icy had known that his owner, Rosalyn Everett, was dead. Star knew her family had abandoned her. But I suspected she still waited for her owner to come back, still hoped. Probably she would go on hoping until the day she died.

How would she ever accept a new mistress? And still, I wanted her.

Without ever having met Star's previous owner I despised her. To raise a dog from puppyhood only to throw her away when she got old was unforgivable.

"Let me talk to Crane," I said. "I'll see if I can persuade him."

Seven

After dinner we set out for Huron Court with Candy, Gemmy, and Misty. I held Misty's leash and watched her closely as we neared the fork in the road. She seemed calm enough so far, trying to catch leaves and insisting that we all stop at each enticing new scent.

The crisp air held a hint of smokiness, carried to us on a mild wind. Somebody was burning leaves, an activity no longer legal in cities like Oakpoint. Here in Foxglove Corners homeowners could burn whatever they liked or, more often, let the leaves lie where they fell or blew. It was the country, after all.

But who would burn leaves with the wind blowing? Maybe I was smelling something else.

"Up ahead is the fork in the road," Crane said. "You said you turned right. If we went the other way, what would we find?"

"Houses or horse farms, I guess," I said. "Violet said it was built up. I didn't go that way."

"I don't see a sign post."

"We'll call it Huron Court West."

"Let's check it out," he said. "I thought there might be a third fork, a road running parallel to the one you took."

"The road diverged," I pointed out. "If there's another fork, I didn't see it."

What I *did* see was an autumn wonderland. Woods unleaving under a cerulean sky. Vibrant color, mainly dark red and gold, everywhere. Fallen branches and rocks and what looked like a bird's nest in the middle of the road. A patch of wildflowers that I couldn't identify and didn't remember seeing on my previous walk.

"Like I said, these roads can be confusing," Crane said.

Suddenly Misty froze as she had before. Ears alert, she focused her attention on the sky.

"She's looking for Ginger's ball," I said.

"Or a bird, a plane, a hot air balloon... It could be anything."

Even an odd-shaped low lying cloud. There was no evidence of an object in the sky that shouldn't be there, and the other dogs didn't react.

"Heel, Misty," I said in a sharp voice.

She obeyed with grumbling reluctance.

"Violet's house is just beyond that curve," I said.

For a moment I felt like freezing as Misty had. Utter foolishness. I wanted to know what lay ahead. I had to know. That didn't mean I couldn't dread it, whatever it was.

It occurred to me that I didn't hear Violet's musical laughter.

We came to it then, the deteriorating cottage whose paint had faded to a disheartening beige-gray color.

"That house has attractive bones, but it's seen better days," Crane said. "I wonder who owns it."

"Somebody who doesn't care."

Misty began to whimper, nosing the weeds. Looking for the invisible ball?

"It isn't here, Misty," I said.

Neither was Ginger. Nor Violet.

"They must be ghosts then," I said. "That beautiful pink Victorian exists on *another* plane. I had a conversation with a spirit."

"Not so fast, honey. Let's walk on for a while and see if we can find that parallel road."

"What parallel road? The one in the other dimension?"

"We'll just see what's out there."

"I did go farther the other day," I said. "It's just more woods. There's a small lake. No other houses."

"Humor me," he said. "We don't want to spend too much time wandering around these woods. It'll be dark soon."

I estimated we had about an hour of daylight left, but we still had to walk all the way back home.

The wind blew. Leaves sailed through the air, swirling around my face and landing on Misty's head. She growled and pawed at an enormous catalpa leaf.

We didn't find Crane's parallel road and eventually turned around.

What if, on the way back, we found Violet's pretty pink house?

"Hello, Violet," I would say. "This is my husband, Crane. Do you still want to go walking sometime?"

It didn't happen, and I had to admit that the decrepit shack was the only house on this stretch of roadway.

When we returned to the fork in the road, Crane said, "Are you positive you didn't turn the other way, Jennet?"

"We went right. I remember thinking I took the road less traveled."

And that has made all the difference.

I couldn't keep the disappointment out of my voice. "I'm left with another out-of-this-world experience, Crane, and I'm not in the mood for one, not with school and Star and..."

He reached across Candy for my hand.

"It doesn't look like it's your call, honey, but don't give up. If I have a chance, I'll come back tomorrow in the cruiser. Maybe there's still a simple explanation."

"Maybe," I said.

But unlike Star, I wasn't going to allow myself to hope for a different outcome.

~ * ~

To my surprise, Crane didn't require persuading. On the contrary, he seemed to anticipate my request.

He said, "I think it's a good idea, honey. It's not like Star was a puppy."

"It's just that she needs me," I pointed out. "Her owners didn't have time for her. Rescue doesn't have room. Someone has to help her."

For the first time in days I was thinking about something other than the pink Victorian and my rogue American Literature class.

"It won't be like having a new puppy underfoot," I said. "Raven lives outside. Halley and Sky are perfect little ladies. Gemmy never gives us trouble. That leaves Candy and Misty."

"A double handful if I ever saw one."

"It'll be like having three collies in the house, not seven."

"You have a way with math, honey." Crane laughed and poked at the paper he'd tossed into the fire. "I said yes, Jennet. I've never seen Star, but I trust your judgment. She needs a new family and we have one to offer."

And you seem to need her, he might have added. *That's good enough for me.*

"Don't you want to see her first?" I asked.

"I'll see her when she comes home."

I dropped a kiss on his head. "Did I ever tell you I love you?"

"Many times, but you can say it again."

I did. He sat beside me, and pulled me close. I let the warmth, from the fire — that is — surround me. All was well in my life. All was very, very well.

Suddenly I noticed that Misty had left the spot by the sofa coveted by all the collies. She was staring out the bay window into the darkness. Rather at her own reflection.

That was what I chose to believe. She couldn't still be looking for the ghost collie, Ginger.

Ghosts tend to haunt their own territory. Therefore, we'd left Violet and Ginger playing a never-ending game of fetch on that other plane where the pink Victorian glistened like pink and white frost and leaves drifted down from the ghost trees.

The living room seemed to have grown perceptibly colder, even with Crane's arm around me.

Eight

Foxglove Corner's renowned horror story writer, Lucy Hazen, lived on Spruce Road in a house appropriately called Dark Gables. A long driveway bordered by towering evergreens provided all the privacy a reclusive writer could desire.

Here Lucy lived with her blue merle collie, Sky, and wrote stories that delighted and terrified her young readers while she waited to learn whether one of her books, *Devilwish,* would be made into a movie.

I always came to Lucy for advice when I wandered into the realm of the inexplicable. She was a good friend whose talents ranged from tea leaf reading to an uncanny ability to glimpse into the future. She did not do this on demand. Still, who better to share the story of my latest otherworldly experience with?

I had planned to pick up Star after school, but once again Sue had a vet appointment sandwiched between riding lessons. We agreed that I'd stop by on the following day. That would give me a chance to buy a welcome gift for Star, a toy of her own, assuming Candy and Misty respected her ownership. The alternative was buying new stuffies for all the dogs. Maybe I should do that.

The next day I dropped Leonora off at her house and drove to Dark Gables, knowing Lucy would welcome me at any time with or without a prior phone call.

Her black skirt billowing in a sudden wind gust, Lucy held the door open. She dressed the way she imagined a horror writer would, all in black, brightening the look with gold jewelry. Sky, more patient than my rambunctious brood, stood at her side, wagging her tail slowly.

Lucy said, "You look troubled, Jennet. What happened?"

"Does something have to be wrong for me to visit you?" I asked with a smile.

"I know you're busy with school, but... I sense confusion. A kind of gathering darkness."

Lucy spoke the way she wrote, more than a little melodramatic with at least one Gothic image.

"You're good, Lucy," I said. "I hope my students didn't pick up on it. I try to project serenity."

"They won't have. Come in. We'll have tea, and you can tell me all about it."

Sky and I followed Lucy to her favorite room in the house, a sunroom furnished with white wicker furniture where green and flowering plants flourished. The French doors offered a view of fall color, but inside summer bloomed in all seasons.

Over tea and chocolate chip cookies —store bought but nonetheless delicious —I told her about my latest foray into the supernatural.

"It was so detailed, Lucy, so real. I even saw the color of Violet's earrings. They were blue, sapphires probably. I talked to her. We agreed to walk our dogs together. Then to discover it was only an illusion... On another day I saw the house the way it would be in twenty or thirty years if no one maintained it. The experience threw me into a tailspin."

Lucy was unfazed —and fascinated. "You refer to it as an illusion. Is that what you think it was?"

"I don't know. I forgot to mention. Misty, my dog, was aware of it, too, but neither Halley nor Sky batted an eyelash. Crane mentioned the idea of time travel."

"Then he believes you first saw the house at some point in the past? It's possible, I suppose, but I don't think that's the answer. Traveling through time isn't one of your gifts."

"I'm leaning toward a simple old-fashioned haunting," I said. "The second time I walked on that road, I heard laughter. Only..."

"Only what?"

I took a sip of tea. It was still too hot to drink quickly, but my throat was growing drier by the minute.

"As you know, I've seen a spirit or two, but I never actually stepped into a haunting. This time I felt like Alice through the Looking Glass. I was a part of it."

"Then it may be something else," she said

"What?"

"At the moment I can't say."

"I'd like you to go with me the next time I take that fork in the road."

I nibbled at my cookie, mindful that it would only make my throat drier.

"I was thinking," I said. "If I never went that way again, I wouldn't have to deal with the phenomenon."

"You won't be able to do that, Jennet. I know you."

I sighed. "You're right. It's going to haunt me. Uh, oh, wrong word choice."

"Not at all," Lucy said. "Drink your tea. Drain the cup. The last time I read your tea leaves I saw a key. Or was it a door? Maybe both. Anyway it was a good fortune."

"It may be. This is just a speed bump."

"I have a few ideas," Lucy said, "but I want to see the house for myself first."

"I didn't hear the laughter when I was with Crane, but Misty did, I think," I added. "Are you free this weekend?"

"All weekend."

"How about Saturday morning then? That'll give me a few days with my new collie."

"You have another dog?"

Lucy was incredulous. She hadn't seen Star in my future.

"It's another story," I said.

~ * ~

On days like this when I came home later than usual, I relied on take-out dinners from Clovers, a little restaurant on Crispian Road. They specialized in comfort food and the most delectable baked goods in Foxglove Corners.

Annica, my young friend and enthusiastic detecting partner, worked part time as a waitress at Clovers while she studied English literature at Oakland University. With her red-gold hair and flair for dressing to match the season or the day's specials, she was the polar opposite of Lucy whose stock in trade was all things mystical.

I saw her at the back of the restaurant, waiting on a large party that consisted of several children. She wore harvest colors, an orange dress trimmed in brown. Even from a distance I could see whimsical scarecrow earrings swinging out from strands of red-gold hair.

While she finished serving her customers, I stopped at the dessert carousel, admiring the pies and cakes. Today delicate bow ties sprinkled with powdered sugar rested in a large leaf-shaped dish. There! I'd found my dessert, *kruschiki*.

"Did you give up cooking now that school started?" Annica asked, as she escorted me to my favorite booth with a view of the Crispian Road woods, all decked out in autumn splendor.

"Just on super busy days. What's good today?"

"Stuffed pork chops."

"Keep going."

"Turkey pot pie."

"Mmm. Anything else?"

"There's always meatloaf and mashed potatoes."

One of Crane's favorite meals. Mine too.

"That's what I'll have, and a couple of *kruschiki* for here with coffee and a dozen to go. I need cheering up."

"What's wrong?" she asked, jotting my order down on her pad.

"Teaching. I have a challenging bunch of juniors this year."

The class from hell.

"I've decided to add a new collie to our canine family."

As I told her about Star's plight, she exclaimed about the inhumanity of an owner who could abandon an aging dog. Then I asked about Angel.

"She's a little doll," Annica said. "She already knows 'sit'and 'shake.' We're working on 'stay' and 'come.'"

"Those are the important commands," I said.

"She wants to learn. I just love her. I have pictures on my phone…"

I smiled at Annica's enthusiasm. At first I'd wondered how a puppy would mesh with her busy life. I needn't have worried. The fit was seamless.

"In my spare time, I discovered another haunted place in Foxglove Corners," I said. "Last Sunday I met a girl named Violet and her collie, Ginger, on a wooded road near Sagramore Lake."

"Were they ghosts?"

"I don't know. Tell me what you think."

For the second time today, I told the story. To say that Annica was intrigued would be an understatement. Her eyes lit up with that special gleam they had when she heard about a new mystery.

"If I didn't have to work, I'd like to drive out to Huron Court," she said. "Now."

"To see a ramshackle old cottage?" I asked. "Because that's what's there."

"No," she said. "I want to see Violet and the dog and that pretty pink Victorian house you describe."

"So do I."

"Maybe they exist in a parallel world?" she said. "Or is it an alternate universe?"

"Another dimension?"

Strangely I didn't feel so haunted now that I had shared the experience with Annica. To her, it was a lark, although she would never use that word. Moreover, I realized something about myself I had never suspected.

I wanted to find Violet's world again, if only to prove to myself that it was real. That I wasn't once again flirting with delusion. That there was some specific reason this had happened to me.

I simply had to find the way back.

Nine

My life in Foxglove Corners was the essence of tranquility, even when an ordinary walk with the dogs ended in a supernatural phenomenon. Even when I was about to add a grieving collie to my household. In contrast, life at Marston High School moved at a frenetic pace at best. At worst it plunged me into a maelstrom of noise so intense I could scarcely think.

Hell. Damnation. Demons shouting. Fiery exchanges. Two boys tottered on the brink of a fist fight and backed off as the new assistant principal, Austin Greaves, glanced in at the class through the open door.

Time to start class. Past time.

"Quiet!" I said. "Take your seats."

I glanced at my seating chart. Everyone was present. Six students had made their own seating arrangements, and Slade Johnston was perched on the windowsill.

"Your *assigned* seats," I said.

Something was wrong. My throat, slightly scratchy this morning, was sore. I swallowed. Yes, sore.

What abysmal luck. I needed all of my faculties, particularly my voice, to manage this class.

"To clarify," I said. "The seats you were assigned."

Everyone except for Slade moved. He remained glued to the window sill.

"Mr. Johnston," I said. "That includes you."

He remained on his perch, carrying on a conversation with a girl who was properly seated.

"Why do we have to sit where *you* want us to?" he demanded.

Because I'm the teacher!

"Class rule," I said.

"And why are we in alphabetical order? That's so lame."

I chose not to respond.

The comparative peaceful days of *Three Sovereigns for Sarah* were over. Today's lesson involved writing an essay on topics suggested by the movie. I'd written their choices on the board and planned to discuss them, after which they would begin writing their rough drafts in class. As soon as they were quiet.

If that glorious state ever arrived.

The more I talked, the more conscious of my sore throat I became. *Get through today*, I told myself. *Take a sick day tomorrow.*

"Quiet!"

How many times a day had I said that? How many times a week?

Patty Olmstead sashayed up to my desk. "Can I get a drink of water?"

How many times over the years had I been asked that question?

The principal had warned us about signing unnecessary hall passes. "Save them for genuine emergencies," he'd said.

"Not at the moment," I said. "The bell will ring…"

Dear God. In thirty minutes?

"Soon," I said.

"The fountain is just outside the door."

Patty's irritating whine was more suitable for a third grader than the sophisticated junior she aspired to be.

"I know where it's located," I said.

She mumbled something that sounded like witch but probably wasn't.

If I had a throat lozenge or life saver, I could slip it in my mouth surreptitiously.

As I reached for my shoulder bag, I noticed the seating chart that should be lying on top of my grade book was missing.

Where on earth? And when? And how? I'd been watching the class the entire time.

Well, I could recreate the chart. Maybe. Their names were in the grade book.

When at last the bell rang and the thundering herd moved on to greener pastures, I found the chart torn to pieces on Slade Johnston's desk.

Wrap up another failure, I thought

~ * ~

Lunch with Leonora was a brief respite from the insanity.

"It was Slade," I said. "He isn't the only one who objects to his assigned seat, but he's been the most vocal."

"It sounds like he's your culprit. Is your throat better?"

"No."

"For older students, I let them choose their own seats," Leonora said. "Then if I have any problem, I move them."

"I guess that might have been better," I said.

Not feeling like drinking tepid tea from a thermos, I'd made a cup of coffee in the teachers' lounge. That, plus a meatloaf sandwich, should fortify me for the rest of the day. The worst class was behind me.

I took a long drink of black coffee. Not my favorite beverage but it soothed my throat —for an instant.

"Did you see the absence list?" Leonora asked. "A lot of the kids are sick. There are seven subs in the building. Grimsley is fuming. It's standing room only in the front office."

"We can't help getting sick with all the germs floating around," I said.

"I take extra Vitamin C and drink a glass of orange juice every morning. I also believe in keeping the doctor away with an apple a day."

Leonora was the picture of good health with lustrous golden hair, bright eyes, and a complexion that fairly radiated.

"I'll have to try that," I said. "I'm bringing Star home today. I have to feel better."

"With all those dogs, you're lucky you have Crane. If I get sick, I still have to take care of Wafer and Lass. I wish I had a husband."

"I wish you did too."

"Not just any husband. It's Jake I want."

"Is there any chance of that happening?" I asked.

"I think so, yes. Maybe."

Leonora could have any man she desired. At Marston alone, Coach Adam Barrett had been her faithful admirer for years. But she'd set her heart on a handsome dark-haired deputy sheriff, Jake Brown, and no other man would do. Such is true love. I could sympathize with her.

"When I get married, I'm going to retire from teaching," she said. "I'll stay home and cook wonderful meals and make a happy home for Jake."

"That's what Crane would like me to do."

That was what I should do. Why didn't I then? Who wouldn't trade hell for heaven?

The problem was that all of my classes weren't like the rogue fourth hour. There were two sections of Journalism, for example, a class I truly enjoyed. There was the camaraderie of the staff. I'd miss that. There was... Always something to keep me coming back to the high school in Oakpoint where I'd taught for most of my career.

No matter how impossible a group was to work with, they were only together for one semester.

As the bell rang, I finished the last of my coffee, wishing I had more and more time to drink it. I'd probably be teaching at Marston until hell froze over because I just couldn't make the decision to quit.

~ * ~

The first time I'd seen Star I'd thought of her as a stuffed toy, beautiful but lacking any spark of life. She hadn't changed.

Sue attached the leash I'd brought to Star's collar. "Go with Jennet, Star," she said. "To collie heaven."

Star rose, dark eyes projecting resignation. Go, stay —it didn't matter to her. I wasn't her owner. She might as well wait in another place as this one.

"Good luck," Sue said.

"I'm hoping one of my girls will befriend her. Sky, maybe. She's the quietest, most sensitive one, and Halley has taken many a foundling under her wing."

"She'll have a good home with you," Sue said.

That was true.

In the car I had a newly-purchased plush toy, a star, each point a different color, and a bag of stuffed forest creatures for the other collies.

"She ate a little dinner," Sue said. "It's a good sign. I brushed her. Doesn't she look pretty?"

"She does indeed." I ran my hand along Star's rib cage and let it rest on her velvety head. Did her tail move just a fraction?

"I'll give her more. Kibble with crushed meatloaf from Clovers on top. Come, Star."

She came and we went outside into the wind and the flying leaves. She levered herself into the back seat of the Taurus without prompting. A good beginning.

Was Star the new enterprise Lucy had seen in my teacup?

More likely she was one of many.

Ten

After the requisite canine meet and greet on neutral territory, in other words, in our back yard, Star joined Sky in her collie cave under the dining room table. When I fed the dogs, she ate the crumbled meatloaf from the top of her food dish and left most of the rest. She sniffed at her star toy, then ignored it.

I considered this a good beginning.

After dinner, Crane said, "Let's see if she'd like to go for a little walk."

At the mention of one of her favorite words, Candy flew to Crane's side, jumping on him, which was forbidden, and barking as if to say "It's about time!" Crane was her official walker since he had decreed that she was too wild for me to handle.

Next he called Gemmy who rose and stretched languidly, then said, "Star?"

She looked at him, her head tilted.

"Do you want to go for a walk?" he asked.

I saw it then, the life spark in her eyes that had eluded me before. But she didn't come to him. Nor did she object when he attached the leash to her collar.

"Don't go too far," I said. "She's not a puppy and may not be used to walking."

With her busy former owners, I considered that a reasonable assumption.

"Just to the ruins and back," he said. "Do you want to come with us?"

I swallowed. A good hot dinner had failed to banish my sore throat. "Not tonight," I said.

I watched them from the kitchen window as they walked out to the lane. Star showed more enthusiasm than I'd seen to date, sniffing at new scents along the way as any canine would.

No one could resist Crane, unless it was a miscreant he was arresting. Maybe Star would come to accept her new home with a minimum of longing for the old one.

The last glimpse I had of her gave my heart a strong wrench. She was wagging her tail.

All would be well. I hoped.

But during the night I heard an unusual sound, a plaintive whining. It must be Star as the other dogs were usually quiet once they went to bed.

I should get up and go to her. Soon. In a minute. I meant to, then I heard the shrilling of the alarm clock. I had fallen asleep.

Well, I was awake now, and darn it, feeling no better. Crane's side of the bed was empty and an irresistible aroma of bacon wended its way up the stairs.

I was in a good mood, though, having decided to call in sick.

~ * ~

I couldn't pay much attention to Star that day because I really was sick. Once the dogs realized I wasn't leaving the house, they decided to nap the hours away with intermittent bouts for play. That was more or less what I did.

Star lay quietly in the dining room next to Sky and the star toy I'd placed at her side. I drank countless cups of tea and hot chocolate, interspersed with cans of ginger ale. The day couldn't have been longer.

I missed my classes, the good ones, and wondered if my fourth hour had made trouble for the sub. There was no point in wondering. Of course they had, and, of course, their behavior would reflect on me. Fortunately I had left enough work in my sub folder for two hours. One of the principal's main complaints was inadequate sub plans.

"An idle mind is the devil's workshop," he liked to say, pretending the idea had originated with him.

The next day I felt marginally better and went to school. After that I returned to normal, and on Saturday morning, Lucy and I set out for the house on Huron Court. We left the car at Sagramore Lake and walked.

The day was glorious, all vibrant color with a blue sky and warm winds, but the leaves were falling at an alarming pace. Soon they'd all be on the ground, the trees bare, and the warmth a pleasant memory.

We came to the fork in the road.

"Right?" Lucy said. "Is that correct?" She pulled her black cardigan tighter around her shoulders.

I nodded, listening for some sign that we were walking into the Twilight Zone. Laughter, a dog barking, the thud of a ball landing on the ground... But I heard only rustling overhead and the sound of crunching as we strode through the leaf fall.

Therefore I wasn't surprised when we rounded the curve and saw the Victorian, the future version of Violet's house with its peeling beige-gray paint and glaring evidence of an owner who didn't care about his property.

"It's a depressing sight," Lucy said. "I can visualize the place as it must have been years ago—gables and double turrets and gingerbread trim. It could be beautiful again. I wonder how much land goes with the place?"

"Maybe all of it. It's the only house in sight. I should have brought Misty. I'm sure she senses..." I broke off. "Lucy. What's wrong?"

She had stepped forward, reached out to grab a leaning porch post, and held on to it as if it were an anchor in a disintegrating world.

"Lucy!"

"It's all right, Jennet," she said. "I felt a little unwell for a second. A little faint. It's nothing."

But her face was pale, her eyes haunted.

"Are you going to be okay?"

"I —I think so. It's getting cold, don't you think?"

I didn't. To me the temperature was perfect, scented with the sweet fragrances of autumn. This was perhaps a different kind of cold.

"We'd better go back to the car," I said. "Or better still, I'll get the car. You wait here."

"Alone?"

"Sure, alone. I don't think you should walk that far."

"I can try."

She glanced at the post, let her hand fall to her lap, and surveyed the area—so isolated, lonely, and strange.

Suddenly I saw the place through Lucy's eyes. What would happen if I drove back to the house to find Lucy gone, whisked away to that other plane where Violet played a perpetual game of ball with Ginger? *No, we'd better stay together. I don't want to leave her alone.*

"We'll go slowly," I said, helping her up, waiting until she buttoned her cardigan. "You can lean on me."

"Whenever I leave Dark Gables, something bad happens," Lucy said.

"Nonsense," I said. "You go out to dinner with Brent all the time and to the library. This house is different, that's all."

"I thought I heard laughter," she said as we began the walk back to the car. "Just briefly. It was musical as you described it. Happy."

"I didn't hear anything today."

"Maybe it was the power of suggestion," she said.

Or not. I didn't know. But it was clear. Lucy shouldn't come near the place again. I didn't think she'd want to.

By the time we reached the fork in the road, though, her spell —or whatever had taken hold of her —seemed to have passed. Her color was better. But she was shaken, and I didn't think she'd told me everything she had experienced.

When I dropped her off at Dark Gables, I said, "What else did you feel at the house, Lucy?"

"I sensed a darkness about the house and the entire area. I'm sure Violet and Ginger exist somewhere, but I think that darkness is dangerous for you. It's removed from reality. It's hungry. You should keep your distance."

"Then I'll never know what's going on there," I said.

"It's just a suggestion."

"I won't walk this far in the winter anyway," I said. "But I'd like to see what I saw before again. It was like a glimpse into another world."

"That's exactly what it was."

"Kind of like a crack in the world. I saw something I wasn't meant to see, and the opening closed."

"That's one way to describe it," Lucy said.

"Chances are it'll never happen again."

But I didn't believe that, and I knew, though I didn't tell Lucy, that I'd return to the house as soon as I could.

Eleven

The fine October weather continued. On Sunday my appetite returned, a sign that my spell of ill health was over. I glanced at tomorrow's lesson plans —all set and viable —and dismissed school from my mind until Monday morning. The next day would be here soon enough.

The glorious fall day drew us all out to the porch. I had a roast in the oven and a Gothic novel in my lap. I'd read Dorothy Eden's *Ravencroft* before. Still I was so involved in the travails of the sisters-in-peril in Victorian London that I didn't realize we had company until the dogs set up a clamor.

The sleek yellow automobile pulled up behind my Taurus, crunching down the leaves that had drifted over the drive. It looked like a vehicle from outer space with its long white fins that seemed to go on forever. Plymouth Belvedere, circa 1959. Why didn't they make cars like that today? I'd trade the Taurus for one in a heartbeat.

Our visitor was Brent Fowler, Foxglove Corner's flamboyant millionaire, fox hunter, entrepreneur, and Lothario. The list went on and on.

As he stepped out of the Plymouth's shadow, the sun splashed light on his hair. It was an unusual shade of dark red, reminiscent of a certain kind of maple leaf in autumn. He swung a shopping bag decorated with bones out of the back seat.

I closed my book, leaving Eden's beleaguered heroine, Bella, in the hands of a white slaver.

The dogs crowded around him as he took the stairs two at a time and dropped heavily into a wicker chair. All except Star.

He set the shopping bag on the round table. "They're from the new bakery in Lakeville. They sell dog treats. Cookies and everything. I got flavor bones."

Usually he brought flowers for our table, wine, or candy. This was a pleasant departure. At least the collies thought so. Several pairs of eager dark eyes were fixed on the bag.

"Hello, pooches," he said. "Here's Candy and Misty. Halley, Gemmy... Sweet Sky... And who are you?"

Star sat at the fringe of the tail-wagging crowd, her ears flattened.

"That's our new girl, Star," I said.

I told him Star's story, all the time watching her. She didn't seem cowed by him which was encouraging. But she hadn't rushed up to sniff dog treats or solicit pats either. That was all right. Give it time. Brent could be overwhelming, but he loved dogs and horses; and they loved him.

"It's unbelievable what some people will do to a dog," he said. "A dog is for life. Are you going to keep her or is she up for adoption?"

"She's home," I said.

"That makes seven. You now officially have a kennel."

"Seven is a lucky number," I said. "Will you stay for dinner? We're having a standing rib roast."

"What's the occasion?" he asked.

"I'm celebrating getting over a cold."

"You won't have to ask me twice. I just came from Dark Gables. Lucy tells me you're seeing things that aren't there again."

"That doesn't sound like something she'd say."

"I paraphrased, sort of."

"I *did* have a strange experience last week," I said. "I saw a pink Victorian house on a wooded road near Sagramore Lake —and a girl and a dog."

"And?"

I told him the rest of the story. Because we were both Lucy's friends, I added yesterday's visit and Lucy's reaction, together with her warning to me to stay away from the place.

"I'm worried about Lucy," Brent said. "About you, too. You both take these anomalies so much to heart. What does the sheriff think?"

"Time travel, the Twilight Zone, yet once again. An apparition, complete with scenery... None of us know what to make of it."

"I do. Foxglove Corners strikes again."

I nodded. Foxglove Corners *did* appear to welcome psychic phenomena. Spirits returned to the scene of their death. Ghosts walked, and insentient objects cried out their distress. I had first-hand experience of many an inexplicable happening.

"Hasn't Crane warned you to keep your distance?" he asked.

"Not yet. I don't think he sees the danger."

"Is there danger?"

"Who knows? Maybe. Lucy thinks so. It's just that I don't like to leave an incident like this unexplored. If I delve deeper into it, maybe..."

Maybe the crack in the world would open again. I could step through, just a few baby steps, leaving myself room to retreat.

"Lucy's all for pretending it didn't happen," Brent said. "Out of sight, out of mind."

"It did."

"Can I see the house?" he asked.

"Sure you can see whatever's there on any given day."

"You'll go with me?"

"If you like, and we'll take Misty, my psychic collie. I'm sure she saw what I did."

"Good. I'll take my camera."

Misty was lying in front of me, her head resting on my foot. She raised her head when she heard her name.

It was a marvel that the denizens of Foxglove Corners took ghostly apparitions for granted. No one said, "Really? You must have imagined it."

I had kept my last supernatural foray a secret. That had been a mistake, chipping away at my wavering hold on reality. Finally I'd confided in Crane. This one? I might as well shout it from the treetops. My husband and closest friends knew about it, and two of them wanted to see what Annica called 'the Pink Illusion' for themselves.

I found it touching that everyone wanted to be a part of my otherworldly experience. That was all right. It was far better than wandering alone in Twilight Land.

~ * ~

By the time Crane came home and we moved inside, Star had warmed up to Brent. She went so far as to lie down near him as he settled into the rocker. Near Sky, that is. Sky had claimed the coveted spot for her own.

This could be because Brent had opened the shopping bag and passed out biscuits to all of the collies, two for each, including Raven who had joined us in the house, no doubt smelling the roast which was almost done.

I'd made an apple pie, too, feeling that I'd subsisted on invalid food for weeks instead of days.

Crane's arrival threw the dogs into another barking frenzy. They rushed to the door, falling over one another to be the first to greet him.

Once again, all except Star. She took advantage of the other collies' change of focus to steal Sky's place closest to Brent.

"Hey, Sheriff," Brent said. "Are you going to let your wife challenge a ghost again?"

"What ghost is this?" he asked as he locked his gun away in its cabinet.

"The one who plays ball with her dog in Never-never Land."

"Jennet told you about that?"

He kissed me, a bland, chaste kiss as we weren't alone, sat on the sofa, and gave Candy a rough pat on the head.

"I was watching a movie the other night. This woman touches a stone and travels back in time to the eighteenth century. She finds a new husband there."

"That sounds like *Outlander*," I said.

"Something like that."

"I don't think that'll happen to Jennet," Crane said.

"While you two discuss my adventure, I'll set the table," I said.

And light the tapers in the heirloom candles that had belonged to Rebecca Ferguson. They had come to us through the generosity of Crane's Aunt Becky in Tennessee. I considered them a good luck talisman, shining blessed light on our home.

I added an extra place setting and napkins and brought a platter for the roast out of the credenza.

Wouldn't it be an adventure, though, to be hurled back to Civil War days? Before my marriage, I'd often dreamed of Crane as a Confederate soldier. Of course, if I was transported to that time, I'd still be in Michigan, far from the battlegrounds.

What was Lapeer County like during the war years? I wondered.

Woods and lakes. Wilderness. Camille's yellow Victorian wouldn't have existed then. There would be no Jonquil Lane, no green Victorian farmhouse.

"You wouldn't want to risk losing Jennet," Brent said.

Crane agreed. "I don't intend to."

"You'd have to give up these fantastic dinners."

"And so much more," he said.

I smiled. Crane's priorities were straight. Well, I knew that.

Setting fantasy aside, I brought the roast out of the oven and started turning potatoes and carrots into serving bowls while Candy and Misty supervised hoping I'd let a tasty morsel fall to the floor.

It was all well and good to wonder about past times, but I was happy in the present with my loved ones and our friend.

~ * ~

Sometime in the middle of the night I heard whining. Star?

I turned on my left side. Darn. What time was it anyway?

Loath to leave the warmth of our bed, I decided to wait.

The whining continued. Plaintive, impervious.

Come, I need...

...you...

Maybe she'd stop, go back to sleep. She was in her own home, no doubt lying near Sky. Dreaming about her previous family? Crying for them? I hoped not.

I meant to get up. I truly did, but once again I drifted off on a high wave of sleep, neither knowing nor caring if the whining continued.

Twelve

There was a disheartening sameness about my fourth hour American Literature class. I could count on a disorderly noisy entrance, students who balked at sitting in their assigned seats, too much time needed to settle down, too many conversations continuing after the bell. And the impertinent comments directed at me. Don't forget them.

In other words, dealing with this rowdy class was a constant struggle. I always felt as if they were slipping out of my grasp, leaving me stranded on a far-flung shore, a sadly incompetent educator.

It was always the same, and one would think by now I'd have found a way to manage them. Obviously that wasn't the case.

Anything for a distraction. Anything for a delay. "Can I go…? Fill in a thousand different destinations. I was heartily tired of that query. So tired that I either ignored it or answered with a brisk "No." For at the other end of the spectrum was a directive from Administration: "Keep them in class."

Today it was taking me twice as long as it should to fill out the attendance sheet. Three people drifted in late. Four were excused for a field trip. I had to remind Slade to sit in his assigned seat twice, and all the while the noise intensified, minute by minute.

"Sometimes you get a group that can't be controlled," Leonora often said.

But I suspected my students would behave differently for her.

Be that as it may. This was my class until January, not Leonora's, and today we were leaving the grim Puritan era in favor of more palatable fare. Washington Irving and *Rip van Winkle.*

Who doesn't like Rip van Winkle? Who doesn't like a story? Surely they must be familiar with Irving's *Headless Horseman,* if only in cartoon form?

Our textbook even had an interesting illustration, a photograph of a statue of the bearded Rip in Irvington, New York.

This assignment would be a piece of cake.

I'd written background material on the board which they were required to copy in their notebooks. As an incentive to keep these notebooks up to date, I allowed the students to use them when taking quizzes and tests.

"Rip," Slade Johnston said with a smirk. "What kind of stupid name is that?"

"It's a dog's name," announced Matt Ferris. "Here, Rip. Down, boy!"

The class roared their appreciation of his humor.

It's a Dutch name," I said, wondering how they would react to Hendrick. "Please get the notes copied so we can begin the story."

For this class I tried to organize every block of time: ten minutes to copy the notes; five to ten minutes to clarify and discuss them. Twenty minutes or more to read the story aloud as a class. The rest was to be assigned for homework.

A piece of cake, I thought. *What flavor? Chocolate? Devil's food?*

The door opened and Principal Grimsley strolled in, his signature smile in place. Without acknowledging me or saying a word, he walked over to an empty desk in the row alongside the windows and sat down, eyes fixed on my notes.

An eerie silence descended on the room. Eerie because it was so unusual. A novelty.

I heard myself talking about folklore, about Hendrick Hudson, his lost ship, the Half-Moon, and the perpetual game of nine-pins played by his ghost crew.

Babbling.

It was well enough to make snide remarks about Grimsley when he was elsewhere. Not so easy when he sat at a student's desk, watching me.

If this had been my year to be observed, the principal's presence in my room would have made sense. As it was…

Too many glimpses through the classroom window when passing my room had aroused his curiosity? Why was this class always in turmoil?

A sweep of the room told me that roughly half of my students had finished copying notes and were waiting to start the story. A few fidgeted.

An idle mind is the devil's workshop.

Throwing the stragglers and do-nothings under the train, I picked up the heavy textbook.

"Please turn to page one hundred and fifty-one," I said. "I'll read the first page, then ask for volunteers. We'll read as much as we can today. You can finish the story for homework."

Homework! A groan. The rustle of pages turning. The thud of a fallen book. Books… I noticed that several students hadn't brought their textbooks to class. They always complained about how heavy they were.

I swallowed. How could I read out loud when it felt as if I had filled my mouth with sand?

I had no choice.

Making a valiant effort to ignore Grimsley whose pasted-on smile had slipped off, I began:

"Whoever has made a voyage up the Hudson must remember the Kaatskill Mountains. They are a dismembered branch of the great Appalachian family and are seen away to the rest of the river…"

I paused to catch my breath. Not the most attention grabbing of openings. Still better than a Puritan sermon.

With a quick glance at the class, I plodded on, pausing briefly to visualize a tall glass of cold water.

I tried to communicate encouragement. *Wait. It gets better.*

Lorraine's hand went up. "Why don't you just *tell* us what happened, Mrs. Ferguson? Summarize the story for us."

"Yes!" someone agreed.

"Yes! We want a summary!"

Before their dissent turned into a chant I said, "Before writing a summary, someone had to read the original story. That's the business of this class. To read the complete work as Irving wrote it."

Oh, no. How stuffy. Of everything I could have said...

I read on, vaguely conscious of Grimsley when he rose and strolled out of the room with studied nonchalance. But I was relieved. So very relieved, but also puzzled.

What was that about?

~ * ~

"That was weird," I said.

We were eating lunch in Leonora's room. She had a pedestrian meatloaf sandwich embellished with two kinds of lettuce, and I had the more imaginative creation —a container of frozen stew that I'd warmed in the microwave in the lounge.

"I wish I knew why he honored me with a visit," I said. "I wonder if someone complained about something I did or said."

"You never can tell. But Adam tells me the coaches swear all the time."

"They're men. They let them get by with it."

Or so we thought, Marston being one step away from a Good Old Boys' club.

"I never swear," I added. "If somebody complained, you'd think Grimsley would tell me about it."

"Well, not in front of the class, he wouldn't. You may find a note in your mailbox."

"Oh happy day."

I'd considered the possibility. A summons to Grimsley's office rarely led to anything good.

"He may just want to familiarize himself with what's going on in our classes," Leonora said. "In case someone asks him."

"I don't like it," I said.

I spooned up the last of the carrots, thankful that my mouth and throat had returned to normal with Grimsley's departure. I'd had a temporary relapse brought on by nerves.

Even though... What did I have to be nervous about? I was a tenured teacher. He was an unpopular principal. He couldn't crush my career in his hands.

"I think I handled it well," I said. "I just kept going. For once, the class was quiet. Thank heavens for *Rip van Winkle.*"

The bell shrilled an end to our painfully short lunch period. Two more classes, then my conference hour. As soon as I was free, I intended to check my mailbox for a note from the principal. If there was one, I'd have about twenty-four hours to worry about a phantom grievance.

If not, I was home free. Maybe.

~ * ~

My mailbox overflowed with junk mail, the kind I could glance at and throw away. The principal's office door was closed with the lights off inside. He must have left for the day. So far, so good.

Back in my room, I finished reading *Rip van Winkle*, a story I must have read over a hundred times during my teaching career, but I never relied on memory.

As I read, unbidden thoughts of the pink Victorian floated around in my mind, not as I'd first seen it with glowing color and gleaming white gingerbread trim, but the deteriorating version of the cottage. The one Violet and Ginger had left years ago.

From there my mind took an unwelcome turn. What if Violet, like Rip van Winkle, returned one day to her house to find the dilapidated ruin I'd seen with Lucy and Crane?

What if...?

What if one day I came home to my green Victorian farmhouse to find it falling apart? Fallen roof shingles on the ground, the stained glass window broken, paint faded to a bland gray. Everyone and everything gone because, while I'd been otherwise engaged, twenty years had gone by. All without benefit of an enchanted brew that threw me into a decades-long slumber.

Good grief, Jennet, get a grip.

I could use some of that emotion to describe Rip van Winkle's state of mind for the class tomorrow. I could... Here was a thought. I could depart from the strict survey of American literature and have them write a short story.

What if a similar experience happened to them?

Yes! They loved science-fiction. I had come up with the perfect way to make an archaic story relevant to my group of rebels. Afterward, I'd read the best stories in class.

I jotted the idea into my lesson plan book and waited happily for the last bell to ring.

If Grimsley criticized me for today's lesson or some other murky misstep, I would counter with a description of this brilliant, relevant idea.

Thirteen

I didn't find a note from the principal; nor did I see him roaming the halls. It appeared that his visit to my class was destined to remain a mystery, one to be revealed to me in his own good time, if at all.

I was curious but decided that no news was good news. In the meantime, my American Lit students welcomed the opportunity to write stories of their own instead of wading through long sentences and archaic language.

Little did they know that Nathaniel Hawthorne lay in wait for them. Shades of Puritans, darkness, good and evil, and an antiquated writing style.

Consequently the next three days with fourth hour were relatively easy, and on Saturday Brent picked me up in his wondrous vintage automobile, and we drove the short distance to the pink Victorian cottage.

This time Misty and Sky came along.

The Plymouth plowed through fallen leaves, sending them airborne. Brent had opened the windows. From inside the car we could hear them rustling and crackling and smell the sweet scents of autumn.

"At they're rate they're coming down, it won't be long now," Brent said.

"I wish autumn lasted longer. At least as long as winter."

"No use wishing for that in Michigan."

We came to the fork in the road.

"Two roads diverged in a yellow wood," I said.

"Huh? Yellow? I see red and brown."

"It's a poem by Robert Frost," I said. "I thought of it that day."

"Oh, poetry. Which way? Right or left?"

"Right," I said. "The one less traveled."

In the backseat, Misty gave a little growl. Sky was silent.

I had taken the dogs for a reason, wanting to see if Misty would react to an untoward element in the environment and if Sky would be oblivious again. The closer we came to the last curve in the road, the more agitated Misty grew, pacing in the confines of the Plymouth's back seat and whining.

"What's wrong with the pup?" Brent asked.

"She senses something."

"A coyote, I'll bet. Or a deer."

Or an invisible ball sailing across the landscape in another time.

"I should have brought my rifle," Brent said.

"We'll be all right. We have two dogs, for heaven's sake."

We rounded the curve and Brent brought the car to a stop. "Holy Jehosephat!"

We were looking at the falling down version of the pink Victorian house, the one I thought we'd see, all but buried in leaves.

He helped me out of the car and reached for Misty's leash. She tried to drag him toward the porch. He put on *his* brakes. "Hold on, girl!"

"Hold the leash tight," I said. "What do you think?"

"I'm impressed. The house has good bones."

"That's what Crane said."

"I agree with him. It has sharp, clean lines and striking features. It's much too good to be rotting away out here in the middle of nowhere."

"The middle of nowhere could describe most of Foxglove Corners," I said. "You're right. The owner is letting it fall apart."

But we hadn't come here to look at a house.

Misty's whining reminded me of our purpose. It grew louder, almost feverish. She sniffed the ground frantically. In my mind she was looking for Ginger and Violet and perhaps the ball that had vanished.

"Who owns the property?" Brent asked.

"I have no idea."

"I'm going to find out. If it's for sale, I might be interested if the price is right. Could we go inside?"

"I don't think so. I'm sure the doors are locked. Anyway, we don't want to do that. We'd be trespassing."

"Look around, Jennet," he said. "Do you see anybody spying on us?"

"No, but..."

"There's no one around for miles."

Still, I felt as if someone were aware of our presence, as if an unknown person were watching us, waiting to see what we were going to do.

"It's still trespassing," I said.

"Since when are you so concerned about bending the law a little? The sheriff won't know unless you tell him."

"That's not the point."

Leading Misty, Brent advanced to the dilapidated porch, pushing leaves aside with his boot. He tried the door, going farther than Lucy had. I remembered the enigmatic glance she'd given the porch post. Remembering her reaction to the cottage reminded me of everything that had transpired on my last visit.

"Locked," he said.

"Well, it would be."

He moved to the window, tried to open it. When it didn't budge, he peered inside. "Those look like hardwood floors. The room is empty. I wonder what condition the rest of the house is in."

"I'd guess it'll take a lot of work to make the place livable," I said. "More than the average buyer would want to take on."

But Brent wasn't the average buyer.

"Why would you want to buy this place?" I asked.

"I've been thinking about opening another inn. The Spirit Lamp Inn is doing so well. Why not have one in another part of Foxglove Corners?"

"Another haunted inn, you mean," I said.

"You know me too well. The Spirit Lamp ghost has been quiet lately. It's just an idea, but I'm going to do some investigating."

"I wish you could have seen it before," I said. "When Violet and Ginger lived here. It was beautiful."

I wondered. If Brent bought the place, brought in his team of renovators and carpenters and painters, would this invasion put an end to the phenomenon?

What phenomenon? I might never see the pink Victorian in all its glory again.

At the moment, there didn't appear to be anything unusual about the house. Misty was lying on the porch at Brent's feet, panting heavily but no longer whining. On the other end of the leash Sky had been quiet and docile ever since we'd left home, the way she always was.

And I didn't hear the sound of laughter I'd been listening for.

"I can see it now," Brent said. "We'll have it painted pink with white trim, just the way you described it to me. And I'm going to let you name it."

"We can call it Ginger's House."

What?

From what shadowy recess of my mind had *that* come? I hadn't even taken a second to think about it. It was as if the response had been on the tip of my tongue waiting to be voiced.

"Not Violet's House?" Brent said.

"No, Ginger's House."

"Oh, I see. For the gingerbread trim."

"And Violet's dog."

"I've seen enough," he said. "I'm going to take you home as soon as I take a few pictures. I think Lucy is right. I know you don't like anyone to tell you what to do, but I'm going to do it anyway. Don't come back here alone."

As we drove away from the cottage I suspected that I had to return alone if I wanted to see Violet and her dog and Ginger's House as it had once been again. The presence of other people kept them away.

~ * ~

We took the dogs back to the car, and Brent returned to the fork in the road and from there to Sagramore Lake, a blue mirror of a waterway sparkling in the sun.

"I'll treat you to lunch," he said. "Clovers okay?"

"I should get home."

"What's the hurry? You have to eat."

"True, but I don't like to leave the dogs alone in the car."

"Tell you what. You stay with them. I'll go in and get take-out. Cheeseburgers all around?"

Misty gave a yelp. Not her ghost alert sound. I think she understood the magic word, *cheeseburgers*.

"All right. Thanks and Clovers is always okay with me. It's not like I never left the dogs in the car while I went into a restaurant," I added, "but I always made sure I can see them through a window. Clovers doesn't have a view of the parking lot."

Besides we would be leaving three irresistible prizes at the mercy of a possible thief: a gorgeous blue merle collie, a rare white, and a pricey vintage automobile.

"If Annica's working, ask her to call me," I said.

She wanted to see the pink Victorian, too. The Pink Illusion. Well, we'd go together, but I'd also plan a solo trip. I didn't mean to visit the cottage entirely alone, of course. I'd take Misty with me. After all, she'd been there in the beginning.

After a while, Brent came back with a bag full of food and two drinks. "The dogs can drink their water," he said. "For us, there are root beers and fries. Oh, Annica's not working today."

"Are you sure you want the dogs eating in your car?" I asked. "Misty could make a mess."

"Then I'll have it cleaned. I'm hungry now. I'll bet they are too."

But he'd spread a green throw over the back seat, I noticed.

"Eat nicely," I told them as I unwrapped their cheeseburgers.

They were gone before I'd taken my first bite. Food always tastes better when eaten in a different place. Hence, the popularity of picnics and vintage Plymouths.

"I'll have to give the other collies a special treat of their own," I said.

Brent broke two pieces of his burger and turned to feed them to Sky and Misty. Presently he said, "Do you think Misty is aware of that other plane you talk about?"

"Something unsettled her. It's strange, though. You'd think I would have seen signs of her talent before."

"She acts just like your other dogs. A little zany, maybe, but she's still a puppy."

I thought about Misty's babyhood. Aside from her appearance on our porch during a snowstorm, she'd been an ordinary puppy, perhaps a bit more mischievous than some.

"There was her attachment to her plush goat," I said. "At one time it was missing in the house for weeks. Then one day she had it. I never figured out where it was."

"That's not the same as being tuned in to the spirit world."

"All dogs have a sixth sense," I said. "In some it's stronger than in others. Just like with people."

"Where did you read that?"

I shrugged. "I always knew it. Anyway, I'm not sure Violet is a spirit. Something else may be going on."

"What?"

"I wish I knew."

We gathered the napkins and wrappings, and Brent stashed them in an orange plastic bag covered with pumpkins.

"Whatever it is, I agree with Lucy," I said. "There's something dangerous about that place, and yet you're thinking of renovating it and opening it up as another inn."

"The danger is for you, not me," he said.

For the second time today, he sounded like Lucy.

Fourteen

I didn't plan my next visit to the pink Victorian for fear something would happen to prevent it. I simply decided to go quietly and without fanfare. On Sunday, after saying goodbye to Crane, I leashed Misty, Sky, and Halley and set out for Sagramore Lake.

This is just a run-of-the-mill walk, I told myself. *I'm not expecting to solve any mysteries this morning.*

Therefore, no matter what happened, or didn't happen, I wouldn't be disappointed.

My always vigilant inner voice warned me not to delay. Brent might already have set his plans for Ginger's House into motion. Once the house was a legitimate inn, renovated and furnished, I suspected I could say goodbye to its mystic properties.

Also, Brent might say something to Crane about his worries. The two men had become confederates, often banding together to oppose me. I didn't need Crane to slip into his stern deputy sheriff persona and order me to stay away from the pink Victorian. If he did, I would be compelled to resort to subterfuge, which was, in my estimation, a last resort.

We left the lake and walked on to the fork in the road, savoring every step. Myriads of leaves flew like crazed winged creatures in the gusty wind. Misty was in ecstasy, wanting to catch them in her mouth or roll in them, sometimes both at once. I allowed myself to be optimistic. Maybe today the fissure in time would open again.

First you'll hear the laughter.

Then you'll come across Violet throwing the ball for Ginger.

Then...

The wind continued to blow. We walked into a swirl of russet leaves so thick that it reduced visibility for a moment. Then I could see clearly again.

Suddenly Misty froze. She let a leaf fall from her mouth, stared at the road ahead, and howled.

Nothing was there, nothing I could see, that is. The curve beckoned. The road almost glowed. I felt my heart racing. I sensed something ahead, lying in wait.

In an instant sound ceased. It was as if an invisible hand had pushed the button of a sound effects machine, throwing the world into an all-encompassing silence.

I stopped and pulled back on the leashes. "Stay!"

Misty howled again. As the eerie keening faded, I heard laughter. That remembered melodious laughter from the first time.

Stay? Go back? Forge ahead?

Ahead, I decided. This could be a prelude to the manifestation for which I'd hoped. The reason I'd walked the dogs in this direction.

We rounded the curve, and I saw the house —looking more dilapidated than it had before in its surround of wild vegetation and drifted leaves.

I looked away, looked back, thinking to see walls of pink and flowers and a girl playing ball with her dog.

I didn't, of course.

But I heard the sound of laughter again, and, in its wake, the rustle of leaves and the never-ending sigh of the autumn wind and the dogs panting and my own breathing. Heard every whisper the earth had to offer.

I couldn't have said when sound had come back to the world or why it had ceased. All I knew was that I was standing on a lonely country road in front of a faded Victorian house that had seen better days.

And I was exhausted.

~ * ~

The feeling of exhaustion appeared to be connected with the manifestation. I remembered being tired that first time but had attributed it to the weather or the longer distance we'd walked. Not that I'd experienced a proper supernatural manifestation. There was only the laughter and Misty's wolfish howl which I interpreted it to mean she'd heard it too.

The fringe of the manifestation then.

By the time we reached Sagramore Lake I felt more energetic. Practically energized. Misty was her usual frisky self, trying to pull me to the water's edge. As appealing as that would be, I had other plans and was anxious to implement them.

At home, I made a cup of tea and sat at my desk, re-reading the manuscript of my unfinished 'Spirit' book.

Every inexplicable experience I'd had since moving to Foxglove Corners had its own chapter, beginning with the appearance of the phantom Christmas tree in the old white Victorian next to the Foxglove Corners Animal Shelter and ending with the woman in bridal array — Rosalyn Everett, I believed —who had wandered the snowy fields of her home-in-life, River Rose.

It was time I added a new chapter.

I wrote slowly, taking care to include every detail of my first meeting with Violet and Ginger. Violet's sapphire earrings, Ginger's ball. Violet's remark about not seeing collies in the area which, in retrospect, made sense, as all the collies I knew had come to Foxglove Corners at another time. I added the way the house had appeared to age and decline into a dilapidated relic of itself between my first visit and the second.

I wrote about the laughter and Misty's behavior: "It was as if, like Rip van Winkle, I'd been away for twenty years while the house fell slowly apart in my absence. But I'm going to find it again."

With that resolve, I turned my attention to dinner with no more idea of what I was going to make than of how I was going to accomplish my goal.

~ * ~

Steaks were always a good choice when I'd neglected to plan ahead. I took two Porterhouses out to defrost and made a salad. Rice and rolls were easy. I needed a dessert.

"What kind of pie should I make, Candy?" I asked.

She tilted her head. She'd never tasted pie, only smelled it baking.

Chocolate meringue, I decided, and gathered ingredients from cupboard and refrigerator.

As I rolled dough, my thoughts returned to the pink Victorian. A logical way to find Violet would be to trace the past occupants of the house. The problem was that Violet hadn't mentioned her last name. At the time, I hadn't noticed the omission.

I frowned, fitting the crust into a pie plate.

Are you sure she didn't say, "My name is Violet White or Violet Smith or Violet Whatever?

I didn't believe she had, but now that I thought about it, I wasn't sure.

The house which might have been built as early as the eighteen nineties, might have had one owner or several. Brent had said something about trying to find out who had lived there in previous years. I'd check with him.

Suddenly I thought of another way to learn the house's history.

Miss Eidt at the Foxglove Corners Public Library had an extensive collection of books dealing with all aspects of the supernatural. In the past I'd consulted a volume devoted exclusively to the ghosts of Foxglove Corners.

If Violet was a ghost.

Somehow I couldn't see her as a spirit, mainly because we'd had a very ordinary conversation about collies and other houses in the area, the kind you'd have with a person you've just met. That wasn't how interactions with spirits were supposed to proceed.

No matter. Whether Violet was a spirit or something else, surely I wasn't the only person in Foxglove Corners who had seen the pink Victorian that Violet called home.

One day after school I'd make time to visit the library. Maybe Leonora would come with me. One way or another, I'd find Violet.

~ * ~

School. Always waiting at the end of a weekend ready to drag me back to reality.

I'd forgotten that Monday was the first day of Spirit Week until I walked into the building and saw a jumbo-sized poster announcing the theme for each day of the week, culminating in the Homecoming dance and the big game on Saturday. Today was 'Twin Day'.

"What on earth is that?" Leonora asked.

"You and a friend are supposed to dress like twins, I guess. This is going to be a wild week."

"What do you know? We're both wearing red dresses."

"Coincidence."

"No, let's pretend we did it on purpose," she said. "It'll give our classes something to talk about."

"Only if we stand together. Otherwise, no one will notice."

"Good point. I'll step into your room once during each class, and you can visit me."

"That's one way to liven up a blue Monday."

"And it's just the beginning," Leonora said. "This goes on all week. Are you and Crane coming to the Homecoming dance?"

I hadn't even thought of it. "No."

"Adam and I are going. It's important for kids to see you taking an interest in their activities."

"I suppose so, but Crane's sure to be working."

"Come stag."

"I don't think so."

"Well, I'm going to get a cup of coffee. I think I'm going to need it. I just wish it could be a vanilla latte."

"Do you want me to check your mailbox?" I asked.

"Sure, if you will."

We both had quite a lot of mail, including yesterday's attendance sheets. I gathered Leonora's first, then mine. On the top of my stack, I saw a yellow slip, folded in half.

Oh, no. Please. No!

I glanced at it. "Mrs. Ferguson, See me in my office at your earliest convenience."

It was signed G. Grimsley.

<h1 style="text-align:center">Fifteen</h1>

The walls of Grimsley's office were painted an icy shade of blue, inspiring images of icicles and igloos and organisms kept away from the sun. Sort of like the man who sat behind the desk in a bland suit, hands steepled together, signature smile pasted on.

I couldn't decide whether the suit was taupe or gray. Anyway it didn't matter.

He came right to the point. "You're having trouble with a class, Mrs. Ferguson." He glanced at a page covered with handwritten notes. "Fourth period American Literature Survey."

Admit nothing.

"It's a difficult group," I said. "I do my best to... Do my best."

"I'm sure you do, but maybe you can do more."

I sat still, waiting, studying the glass paperweight on his desk. What was it? A rock? I wondered how heavy it was.

"Where there's excessive noise, I find there isn't much learning going on," he said.

What to say? I couldn't deny that my class was noisy. But to say they weren't learning? That was a blatant lie.

"That's not necessarily true," I said. "Noise can be indicative of a lively nature. Of creativity."

"Or chaos. You need to work on a faster start to class. Don't give them a chance to begin conversations. Assign penalties if they don't bring textbooks and materials to class. You have English Department Rules posted on your bulletin board, but I don't see you implementing them. Eight students were tardy. That's way too many."

I'd decided ahead of time to agree with any reasonable observation. Not to argue. After all, what would be the point? Grimsley was in charge of the school. To him noise equaled chaos. In a sense I agreed. But for the rest? How could he know I didn't assign penalties? And how could I make sure students were in class when the bell rang?

He consulted his notes. "You describe the group as difficult. Jeff Elandt in Biology has many of the same students. He doesn't have a problem keeping them on task and quiet."

Jeff was six feet tall, husky and a charismatic assistant coach. Of course he wouldn't have problems.

But I couldn't possibly say that. Any response would sound pathetic. So I didn't respond.

"Also, I don't believe you should read to juniors," he said. "They're not in kindergarten."

"You're right," I said. "To a point. But oral reading is a way to keep them engaged and make sure they *do* read the material. If I assigned the entire selection for homework, I can't be certain they even looked at it."

"Your job is to make them want to do the assignments," he pointed out. "Get their interest and keep it."

Sure. Nothing easier. Especially during Spirit Week when the entire school's attention is focused on elections for Homecoming kings and queens and what to wear to the dance.

"From what I see, there isn't enough work for them to do in your class," he added.

"Wait a minute!"

I'd sworn I wouldn't do anything to prolong this session, but I couldn't let that accusation pass unchallenged. I told him about my short story assignment inspired by Rip van Winkle. I'd already read some of the rough drafts. They were good.

"That's all very well," he said. "But how does writing made-up stories further their understanding of the literature of early America?"

"It's a way to make the class relevant," I said. "It adds to the variety, to the fun."

He slipped the notes back into a file. *My* file?

"Yes. Just remember that your thirty-three students aren't in your class to have fun. They're there to learn."

He rose.

"I'll be back in a week or so to see how the class is doing," he said. "That'll give you time to make some changes."

I nodded and let myself out. Outside his office, it was twenty degrees warmer, and it wasn't my imagination.

Wasn't I doing anything right?

~ * ~

Changes?

I returned to my classroom to wait for the last bell to ring.

My heart sank. What changes could I make? What could I do that I wasn't already doing? And why couldn't he have visited another one of my classes? Why zero in on the worst class I'd had in years?

I couldn't have said that either. I supposed I'd handled that agonizing half hour as well as I could have.

I was still brooding on the difficult situation I found myself in as I navigated the freeway on the way home to Foxglove Corners. Home where I could recover from the threat to my career and the blow to my self-esteem.

"Grimsley should try to hold the interest of a rowdy group of teenagers," said Leonora, the ever-supportive. "He used to teach Woodshop. How hard could that have been?"

"That kind of class is totally different. It's an elective. It attracts kids who like to work with their hands."

I passed a slow-moving Saville and had the lane to myself as far as I could see.

"He has a hard time connecting with kids when he addresses them in assembly, and he's the principal."

"My short story assignment is my best so far," I said. "I wish we offered Creative Writing again."

I had taught it one year and enjoyed my days and my students.

"Well, the powers-that-be consider Creative Writing an unnecessary frill. I'm surprised they still allow art and music."

"Sometimes I don't think I belong in education. Not anymore."

"What would you do? Start a P. I. business?

I laughed. "A psychic P.I. business. I wouldn't get rich, but as long as I have Crane, I won't starve."

"When I get married, I'm not going to teach."

Leonora had voiced that sentiment before. I didn't think she was serious. She was an excellent teacher, charismatic like Jeff Elandt, and she had very few discipline problems.

My exit rose out of a late afternoon haze. Another half hour on country roads to Foxglove Corners where I could concentrate on mundane issues like cooking a dinner that would hold the interest of my husband and on warding off another kind of threat to my sanity.

~ * ~

"You don't have to stay at that school," Crane said that night after dinner. "We talked about you going back to college for your doctor's degree. You could teach older students who want to learn. Maplewood University is going to need English teachers next fall."

I'd considered that. My sister, Julia, had changed careers in midstream. At one time she had found and arranged props for soap operas on the west coast. Some time ago she'd come back to Michigan and gone back to school to earn her doctorate. She was now in England, doing research on her area of expertise, Victorian literature.

I had followed a different path and for the most part was happy. Grimsley and an always-changing collection of recalcitrant teenagers were the only shadows on my life.

"You didn't marry a college student," I said.

"I married *you*."

I smiled at him. "So you did."

In a way, I was sorry that I'd mentioned my visit to Grimsley's office, except I didn't like keeping anything, good or bad, from Crane.

"This will pass," I said. "Maybe Grimsley will move on."

To the superintendent's position when elderly Mr. Hastings retired. Better still, to another state.

"Nothing lasts forever," I added. "Besides, I have a few ideas for changes I can make."

Group discussions. I would have them form themselves into groups of five and assign a topic to each group. The group members would elect a leader to take notes. At the end of, perhaps, fifteen minutes, the leader would share the results of the discussion with the entire class. This would result in noise but good, productive noise. It would allow them to move out of their assigned seats —which they hated —for that brief period of time.

My role would be to monitor each group, making sure the conversation didn't stray from the topic.

I could do this once a week. On Friday, which tended to me the most unsettled of days.

Not this Friday, of course, because classes would be shortened for the pep assembly at which Grimsley would announce the kings and queens for each class.

There was no reason why this wouldn't work. Now to come up with a list of topics.

Enough work for them to do.

How long would I keep hearing Grimsley's words in my mind?

My other idea was a hands-on project related to the Colonial period, one done out of class. One akin to a wood-working assignment. At present my ideas were vague. A replica of Rip van Winkle's house? Action figures playing a game of nine-pins?

Well, I'd work on it.

Crane's hand on my knee brought me back to the present.

"I have faith in you, Jennet," he said. "Whatever you decide to do, it's fine with me, but that school has been dangerous for you in the past. Remember the shooting."

As if I would ever forget that horrible event or its aftermath.

It was far away in the past, far removed from this cozy living room with flames crackling in the fireplace and my collies snoozing, even Misty and Star.

I went back to my Gothic novel, confident that tomorrow's lessons were ready, workable, and well thought-out, and Crane went back to the *Banner*.

As long as I had my husband and my canine family, I knew I'd be all right.

Sixteen

That night I awoke from a dream of classroom chaos to hear one of the dogs whining —again. It was the most pitiful sound a dog could make, quivering with need and incessant.

Determined not to fall back asleep, I left the bed quietly, pausing to shine a small flashlight on the alarm clock.

Midnight. A cry at the witching hour. What a perfect title for a Gothic novel!

What a bother for an exhausted high school teacher.

I reached for my slippers and robe. It had to be Star. She had seemed to blend into our canine family so seamlessly, bonding with Crane and to a lesser extent with Brent. She'd appeared to be happy, and I'd stopped worrying about her.

Perhaps that had been a mistake.

Slipping the flashlight into the pocket of my robe, I stepped around Halley, who liked to sleep in the doorway, and made my way downstairs, dodging shadows. Strange how my familiar home took on an alien aspect in the dark of the night.

Abruptly the whining stopped. I paused to listen but didn't hear a sound. As soon as I went back to bed, I knew it would start again.

I continued walking carefully down to the first story hall, holding on to the railing. Crane would tell me to turn on a light, but I didn't want to wake him or disturb the dogs lest they decided they needed to go outside. Even though we lived in the country, I didn't want to annoy Camille and Gilbert or Doctor Linton's family with dogs barking at night.

By the way, why couldn't Crane hear a dog whining?

I found Candy stretched out in front of the fireplace. Gemmy slept near her, upside down in classic collie fashion, her front legs leaning on the rocker. I shone the light into the dining room. Sky was beneath the table. The searching beam revealed the white tip of her tail. Star? I moved the light back to the living room.

Star lay on the sofa, undeniably the softest bed in the house. Her head rested on the armrest, and she showed no sign of distress. On the contrary, she looked like a dog who had been in a deep and peaceful sleep.

Was I mistaken? I'd been so certain Star had been crying for her lost family.

She watched me as I moved into the dining rooms looking for Misty.

I didn't see her. You should be able to see a white collie in the dark.

She must be in the kitchen. Or maybe upstairs? She had to be somewhere in the house.

She was lying at the side door, one snow-white paw flung over her toy goat, and she was awake. Giving a soft yelp, she rose and stretched.

Is it morning already? Time for a walk?

"Hush," I said. "Lie down. Go back to sleep."

She padded up to me and nudged the hem of my nightgown.

So who had whined?

No one came forward to say, "I did."

Obviously none of the dogs needed to go outside, which was good. Still, I wanted to know which one of my collies had uttered that piteous whine.

Don't look for trouble, I told myself. *Go back to sleep yourself.*

But first... I drank a glass of orange juice, then went upstairs leaving my sleeping beauties to their slumbers. All except for Misty.

She padded up the stairs after me, carrying her goat in her mouth. While I rejoined Crane in the human bed, she settled down at its foot.

Episode ended. Inconvenience averted.

~ * ~

Tuesday. Day Two of Spirit Week was Green and Gold Day, those being the school colors.

Forcing myself into the spirit of school fun, I slipped on a Christmas-green turtleneck sweater and added a long gold chain and my gold bracelet. Getting carried away, I brushed green frost shadow on my eyelids.

Never let it be said that Jennet Greenway Ferguson of the English Department didn't play the game.

Green and gold crepe paper festooned the hall, creating a festive air foreign to Marston on a typical Tuesday morning. Early arrivals, all wearing something green, if only a headband, milled around the vending machines and tables.

"This is kind of fun," Leonora said as we passed the cafeteria.

She also wore green, a wool jumper with a splashy faux emerald brooch pinned to an old-fashioned white blouse. With her bright blonde hair, she didn't need a gold accessary. "I hear the dessert today is a double chocolate brownie with green sugar."

"Left over from last Christmas, no doubt."

"No doubt, Scrooge, but sugar doesn't lose its zing. Our cafeteria ladies don't let condiments go to waste."

"I guess I'm not in the best of moods," I said.

After the midnight disturbance, I'd slept fitfully. Because it was Leonora's week to drive, I'd been able to doze in the car. Consequently, on arriving at Marston, I felt as if I had just rolled out of bed.

"I'll bring you a cup of coffee from the lounge," she said.

"That'll help."

I liked to be in my classroom before the first bell rang to organize my desk which would become a jumble of books and papers by mid-day. As soon as I opened the door, kids would begin to wander in. I supposed they liked to be organized, too.

In the brief respite before the first fourth hour students stormed into the room, I wrote an assignment on the board:

Write an original one-sentence definition of 'spirit'. <u>Don't</u> repeat the word 'spirit'. Due today. In ten minutes.

I added, *Due tomorrow: Short stories.*

A few of the stories had already come in. I'd have to add a reading assignment for those who were finished. I'd ask them to read the introduction to the next unit.

I stood back to read what I'd written on the board to make sure I hadn't left out any words. The mini-assignment didn't relate to our course, but I thought it might be a way to get the work of the class started more efficiently —before conversations and mayhem took hold.

"What does a definition of spirit have to do with Colonial American Literature?"

I could almost hear Grimsley's voice edged with ice. Fortunately it was locked in my mind. I didn't have to give him an answer.

That wasn't true with my class. Objections bombarded me until I felt as if I were the victim of a witch hunt.

"A whole sentence?"

"I can't do it."

"Can we look the word up in the dictionary?"

"We're still working on our short stories. How can we do both?"

"Spirit is Hendrick Hudson and his crew."

That last wasn't quite what I had in mind, but at least one of my students, Jasmine, was paying attention.

Slade Johnston was the most vocal. "Hey, this isn't a writing class, teacher, or didn't you know?"

"It's a question for Spirit Week," I said. "Show your school spirit. Write your definition, then you can work on your stories. If anyone wants me to read what you've written so far…"

Apparently no one did.

"We'll read some of the stories in class tomorrow," I said.

Which meant I'd have homework to do this evening.

The minutes passed. They didn't fly by but didn't exactly crawl either. I thought the class was a little quieter. Naturally I didn't see Grimsley's face framed in the window. It wasn't rowdy enough. If only I didn't have to go back to the syllabus.

At the end of ten minutes, I collected the definitions and walked up and down the rows, monitoring their progress. Not everyone was reading. A few claimed to be finished, but when I asked them to show me their work, they claimed it was at home.

"Read the pages on the board then," I said at least a dozen times.

The bell rang, I joined Leonora for lunch, and the afternoon classes passed without incident. At the end of my sixth hour conference period, when I gathered the materials I always took home, I couldn't find the folder in which I'd stashed the completed short stories.

I might have put it in one of the desk drawers...

It wasn't there. It wasn't anywhere.

Could someone have picked it up by mistake? Unlikely. The average student didn't keep work in a manila folder.

I was trying to think of another place to look when the last bell rang and moments later, Leonora appeared at the door, ready to leave. I was ready to leave as well. My raincoat was already lying across my chair.

Maybe the folder was with the stack of materials I was taking home, although I couldn't see it.

Home?

Oh, no. I'd said we would read some of the stories tomorrow in class.

"What's wrong?" Leonora asked.

I told her.

"It'll turn up," she said. "Lost stuff always does."

I chose to believe her. It was better than tearing the room apart looking for one lone manila folder that looked exactly like every other manila folder in the world. If it didn't, I'd build a lesson around definitions of 'spirit'.

Always be flexible. That could well be a teacher's motto.

But wait! The folder *had* to turn up. I couldn't lose students' work.

Worry about it tomorrow, I told myself. *You don't need another sleepless night.*

Seventeen

"I'd rather hear a laughing ghost than a crying ghost," Annica said. "As luck would have it, I didn't see any ghost at all."

"When was this?" I asked.

She handed me my take-out country rib dinners and slipped into the chair across the table from me. We each had a cup of coffee and a slice of pumpkin pie. In honor of the season, Annica's earrings were tiny smiling gourds.

"When I drove out to Huron Court Road yesterday," she said. "I had a morning free and couldn't wait to check out the house."

"What did you see?" I asked.

She stirred sugar into her coffee, three heaping teaspoons. "The old house you described. Don't you adore those two turrets? It must have been so pretty at one time, kind of like a castle. The owners let it fall apart at the seams."

"Did you hear anything unusual?" I asked.

"Just a lot of birds singing, but there's a weird feeling about that place. A kind of miasma."

"Can you describe it?"

"Not very well. It made me aware of how alone we all are, and how vulnerable we are to the ravages of time."

That surprised me. It didn't sound like anything the breezy, lighthearted Annica would say. To be sure, it was true of the Victorian house on Huron Court, but to apply that idea to life?

We are alone, I thought, *even in the arms of a loved one, and we all grow old. No one can outwit time, not even Doctor Faustus.*

Those grim reflections were incompatible with pumpkin pie and whipped cream.

"Oh, I almost forgot," Annica said. "I took Angel with me. She dug up a bone."

That got my attention. "A human bone?"

"No, a marrow bone. The kind you make soup with. It looked like it'd been in the ground for years."

"Ginger," I said. "Violet's dog must have buried it."

"Don't jump to conclusions."

"What did you do with it?" I asked.

"Took it away from her and threw it in the woods. She snapped at me. I should have named her Devil. She's going to have a temper."

"She'll grow out of it," I said, "but you shouldn't try to take a bone away from a dog."

"Brent says he's going to turn the house into an inn," Annica said. "He'll fix it up, like he did the Spirit Lamp Inn."

"I know. When he does there won't be room for weird feelings."

"Well, it hasn't happened yet. In the meantime, that has to be the most depressing place in Foxglove Corners. I don't think I want to go back, even to see a ghost."

That also surprised me. Annica was always eager to chase a mystery, especially if it had a spirit in it.

"I don't think the girl I saw, Violet, was a traditional ghost," I said.

"What is a traditional ghost? A bony, bloodless creature wrapped in a white sheet? A shape made of mist?"

I smiled, thinking of the graceful skater who haunted the frozen lake in which she'd drowned and Rosalyn, the lady in the bridal gown who traversed snowy fields without a coat. Those two spirits had looked like living people. From afar, that is. I hadn't seen either one up close.

"The girl I saw, Violet, was as real as you are," I said.

"Now wait a minute!"

"I talked to her, just like I'm talking to you. We discussed collies —and other things."

"We'd better find her then. Find out what's going on."

"I thought you didn't want to go back to Huron Court."

"I'll go if you go," she said. "Let's do it before Brent gets his hands on the cottage, while it's still ours."

"It's a date. We'll find a time that works with both our schedules."

"Before the snow flies," Annica said. "Just think how desolate it will be then."

~ * ~

At home I transferred the country ribs to large casserole dish and put them in the oven, after which I rifled through the work I'd brought home from Marston along with my grade book and plan book. I had four manila folders of papers to correct, but not the one with the American Lit stories. Nonetheless I looked through each one in case I'd shoved the papers in the wrong file.

The folder had to be in my classroom then, probably mixed in with other materials.

Don't worry about it tonight.

Tomorrow instead of reading stories, we could discuss their spirit definitions —which would amount to fifteen minutes of class time, if that. What else should I do?

I had promised myself to pretend that every day was the day Grimsley would choose for his second visit, to be in a constant state of preparation.

Should I start a new unit midway through Spirit Week?

And what was tomorrow? I couldn't remember. We'd had Twin Day and Class Colors Day. Thank heavens I didn't sponsor the group responsible for coming up with Spirit Week ideas.

Back to tomorrow. What else could I do in Fourth Hour?

Introduce the idea of group discussions? Encourage the class to brainstorm topic ideas.

Anything with the word 'storm' in it would be noisy.

Candy leaped off the sofa, barreling into the magazine stand as she led the way to the side door to welcome Crane home. "Hey!" I cried, but she paid no attention to me.

I restacked my school work, shelved the problem of filling an entire hour of work for American Lit, and joined the crowd to greet my husband.

~ * ~

After dinner we sat in the living room with a roaring fire and our collies grouped around us. I told Crane about the mysterious midnight whining.

"Could you have been dreaming?" he asked, petting Star who lay closest to him.

"No," I said. "I was wide awake when I heard it."

"What's the mystery?" he asked.

"This isn't the first time I've heard whining in the night," I said. "I thought it was Star missing her other family."

Hearing her name, Star lay her head on his knee and gazed at him with... Could it be adoration?

"I think she's accepted us as family, honey. You were right to adopt her."

She left him and padded over to me for additional attention.

Yes, she'd come a long way from the apathetic collie who refused to eat. She got along well with the other dogs, especially Sky.

I supposed I shouldn't waste time wondering which dog had whined a few times when all of our collies were happy in our home. When I had so many other problems to solve, among which was the ongoing ordeal of my class from hell.

Forget about it, I told myself. "*And if you hear whining in the night again, move a little faster.*

It was a good plan, and that night, I slept until the alarm clock woke me.

~ * ~

Wednesday was October Fools' Day.

We saw the posters on the windows as we walked through the cafeteria to the front office.

"What on earth is that?" Leonora asked.

"I'm only guessing, but maybe it's a version of April Fools' Day. Like Christmas in July."

"They're getting desperate," Leonora said. "What idiot came up with that idea? Who wants kids joking around in class?"

"Not me," I said. "But we're forewarned. Take everything with a grain of salt. Fourth hour should be fun today."

"Said with a grain of salt?"

"Said with sarcasm," I said.

It seemed as if the students were as confused by the day's theme as we were. As we walked by a small group of students congregating in the cafeteria, I heard Meg Carter say, "Bart Anderson asked me to the Homecoming Dance."

Bart was the captain of the football team, a popular senior who was almost certainly going to be crowned Homecoming King.

Her friends shared her excitement.

"When?" Ally wanted to know.

"Lucky you!" Janie turned to practical matters. "What are you going to wear?"

"October Fools!" Meg announced.

"Lame!" Ally shouted.

I glanced at the clock. It was going to be a long day.

Eighteen

Before the first hour bell rang I searched for the missing folder in every drawer, in the closet, and even on top of the desk. I didn't find it, and finally there were no other places to look.

I considered the wastebasket. An old trick involved sliding an item off the teacher's desk to the floor, or even better, into the nearest receptacle which was unfailingly the basket.

I recalled the time my gradebook had been stolen and tossed into the dumpster of a local business. That incident had a semi-happy ending, semi because the gradebook, when retrieved, was in no condition to use.

Well, if my folder had ended up with the trash, it was too late to do anything about it. I'd lost students' work. How could I solve this problem? I ran my hand across the desk one more time.

There was no way to fix this, except to explain that the stories had gone missing and give away automatic A's. Unfortunately I had no idea who had handed their work in. No doubt that was the point.

The bell rang. It was decibels higher than usual. It seemed to drill into my brain. I felt a sinister pressure behind my left eye, signaling the arrival of a headache.

What would Grimsley say if he knew that I'd lost student papers? And he would know. That was a given.

I didn't want to deal with this day. I couldn't.

But of course I did. Taking my cue from Grimsley I pasted a smile on my face. My students were tenth graders, and we had a good story to read this morning, an excerpt from *A Dog of Flanders*.

For the next hour, I pushed the case of the missing folder to the back of my mind.

Between classes, however, a random, redeeming though insinuated itself into my grim reflections. I was assuming I'd lost the folder. I won't say I never misplaced papers. Everyone did, but they always turned up; and I was careful to keep track of my property.

What if one of my fourth hour students had stolen it?

For what purpose?

That was obvious. To claim that I'd lost a paper that had never been written. It would be like killing two birds with one stone. Get the teacher in trouble and get out of work. Exactly the kind of plan a diabolical mind would conceive.

I didn't guard the contents of my desk nonstop. Yesterday I'd circulated through the class offering help when it was needed. Anyone could have wandered up to my desk and relocated the folder when I was looking the other way.

That's what must have happened. What if it did? The fact remained that the folder was gone, and fourth hour was rapidly approaching.

~ * ~

I kept my pasted-on smile in place even though by now my entire head was pounding.

"I thought you were going to read our stories today," Slade Johnston said, when I announced the change of plans.

"I was. But I thought we'd talk about your definitions of spirit. After all, it *is* Spirit Week."

"I get it," he said. "It's an October Fools joke."

"No. It's Spirit Week."

"You're the teacher," he said with an unpleasant smirk. "I guess."

Someone laughed.

He was the only one who objected. To my surprise the spirit discussion gobbled up most of the period. The class was marginally more civilized, probably because nine students were absent. The hour hand on the classroom clock seemed to move a little faster. Still my headache persisted.

Before the bell rang, I collected the rest of the short stories and definitions. I now had two sets of papers, and I planned to guard them with my life. In other words, they would stay in the locked closet until school was over, and I'd take them home with me.

Thank heavens it was time for lunch. I joined Leonora in her room and took two aspirin. I wasn't really hungry but would be later if I didn't eat now.

"I still don't know what to do about the missing stories," I said.

Leonora passed me the homemade brownie she'd brought for me. "You can't accuse anyone without proof."

"I don't intend to, but with over thirty kids in the room, one of them must have seen something and would be willing to tell me what happened, privately, of course.

"I wish I had some advice to give you."

"I got through today with spirit definitions, but there's tomorrow."

"One more weird day, then it's Dress-up Day," she said. "When kids are wearing nice clothes, everything goes more smoothly."

"And their minds will be on the Homecoming assembly."

I nibbled at the brownie, hoping the extra ration of sugar wouldn't make my headache worse. I was getting too many headaches lately.

"All I can do is tell them that the folder with their stories is missing," I said. "Honesty being the best policy."

"Wait till next week when this Homecoming madness is over. It still may turn up."

"I can do that," I said.

And I'd pin my hopes on the as-yet-unknown informer. My gradebook had been returned to me, thanks to the intervention of a student who disapproved of underhanded methods to obtain passing grades.

But I hated working in an atmosphere of distrust, hated being constantly suspicious, having to watch every valuable thing. I wasn't in a high school classroom; I was under fire.

By now I was convinced the folder had been stolen. I could hardly wait for the school day to be over. The air in the building was dry and stuffy, the heat stifling. I longed to walk on a country road in a fresh wind while there were still leaves on the trees to rustle and whirl and crunch underfoot.

I could only do that at home in Foxglove Corners.

~ * ~

It was inevitable that when I returned home, I took Halley, Sky, and Misty and set off for Huron Court. I had the fresh wind I'd craved and bright leaves flying through the air. Misty considered them toys to catch in her mouth. To me they were a crunchy layer to tread upon. But they were falling too fast, rushing the season's end.

Slowly, surely my headache subsided.

We came to the fork in the road, and almost immediately an unnatural silence wrapped around me. I walked more slowly, listening to the rustle of leaves, aware when it ceased, aware when the wind quieted. Even aware when errant mists began to swirl above the road.

Déjà vu.

Misty sniffed the air, her gaze fixed on the curve ahead. Halley and Sky appeared to be unaware of any change in the environment. Halley waited for the brisk pace to resume, and Sky gave an impatient little whine.

Musical laughter rippled through the air.

Violet?

Picking up speed, I led the collies around the curve and beheld the Victorian cottage in all its glory. Soft pink walls glowed in the mellow sunlight. The gables and the turrets reached for the sky. The white gingerbread trim gleamed, and the windows had a freshly-washed sparkle, all bathed in light mist.

The house was young again, the yard neatly maintained, albeit draped in fallen leaves. But where was the one who had laughed? Where was Violet?

Could she be inside the house? The ghost house?

I couldn't say why, but I didn't think anyone was at home. Certainly not a collie who would bark at the invasion of a human and three canines in her territory.

That laughter... I'd heard it clearly, but where did it originate? Not in the house. Closer to the road, only higher than ground level.

In the air? Embedded in the mist?

While Halley and Sky seized the opportunity for a mid-walk rest, Misty pulled me close to the porch, wagging her tail.

Remembering Lucy's reaction when she realized that she was leaning on the porch post, I thought it best not to touch the house. Not to knock on the door.

Wait a minute! How else would I know for certain that no one was inside?

I looped Misty's leash over my wrist and mounted the steps to the porch, rapped on the door softly, and waited. Then I rapped more loudly. Then I pounded on it, all the time thinking of the questions I wanted to ask Violet.

Are you aware that you aren't always on this piece of earth?

Where do you come from?

Where do you go when you're not here?

What year is it?

I couldn't ask them. I'd probably never know the answers.

But there was something I *could* do. If I'd remembered to bring my cell phone... I shoved my hand into my jacket pocket.

It was there!

Tapping 'Camera' I moved back a few yards, brought the entire house into focus, and took the picture.

Now, I thought. *They'll have to believe me. I'll have to believe me.*

I pulled up 'Camera Roll' and stared in disbelief at the image I'd recorded.

It was the pink Victorian all right, but in its aging, deteriorating state. The peeling paint was a faded, dismal beige-gray. Shingles had detached themselves from the roof, glass littered the ground beneath a broken window, and the porch stairs were crumbling.

They had been whole when I'd climbed them only moments ago.

This was the picture my cell phone camera had captured while my eyes beheld the same structure in its prime.

Rapidly I took six more pictures. I now had a half dozen additional images of the old falling-apart house that everyone else saw and one view of a Victorian beauty.

Incredible. Impossible.

Terrifying.

Get out of here!

I grabbed Halley's and Sky's leashes and led a loudly protesting Misty back to the road.

A ripple of melodious laughter followed me.

Nineteen

That was terrible.

The tea kettle whistled. My hand trembled as I reached for it. I steadied my grip, poured boiling water over the loose leaves, and let the tea steep.

What had happened was clear enough. I saw one image. The camera saw another. Cameras don't lie. Something was wrong with my perception. Or with me.

No, you're seeing a supernatural manifestation. This isn't the first you've wandered into the Twilight Zone.

But this manifestation was so different.

Where were the ghosts?

I sat at the oak table, stirring the tea leaves idly, watching them settle at the bottom of the teacup.

Why was I seeing this?

I needed Crane with his down-to-earth outlook. I needed to talk to Lucy. What I had at the moment was Misty, her soft warm body pressing against my leg, her eyes searching mine.

Had she also seen the pink Victorian as it had once been? Had she heard the laughter? I felt certain she'd seen and heard what I had, and the eerie experience united us.

I rested my hand on her head. "I don't know, Misty. I don't know what happened."

She whined and left my side, returning a while later with her toy goat.

I had hurried away from the house on Huron Court as if pursued by devils and never looked back, all the time remembering Lucy telling me the house was dangerous for me. For her, too, although she had no plans to return.

I took a sip of tea. Finally cool enough to drink without burning my throat, it helped. Tea always does.

I'd thought that when and if I saw the pink Victorian again, I would also see Violet and was disappointed that I hadn't had a chance to talk to her.

And what was the meaning of that ghostly laughter? It no longer seemed pleasant and melodious.

You may never know, I told myself.

I finished my tea and started making dinner. A chicken to roast, potatoes to boil, a salad to make... Supernatural manifestations come and go, but a homemaker's chores are forever.

~ * ~

Crane took a dim view of the afternoon's misadventure. He was missing the point. It was my fault. I hadn't explained the significance of the pictures, only given him my cell phone turned to 'Camera Roll'.

"When I took those pictures I was looking at the older version of the Victorian cottage before it started to fall apart," I said. "The camera saw something else."

"I see now why you're upset," he said slowly.

"What do you think?"

"That you've managed to find another haunted place in Foxglove Corners. I don't know how you do it."

"Walking the dogs," I said.

"I walk them, too."

"You're not a ghost magnet."

"I've been driving down Huron Court every day," he said. "I've never seen anything but that old ruin."

He set the cell phone on the oak table. "I thought you were going to stay away from that place."

"I don't remember saying I would. Anyway, after the day I had, I needed a long walk by the lake."

"Fowler thinks it's dangerous."

"He lets Lucy influence him. I don't see how it can harm me."

I didn't add that I had no intention of returning to Huron Court at present. Alone, that is. I might, of course, change my mind, especially if Brent purchased the house.

"Maybe it can't hurt you, but you look stressed out," Crane said.

"Ah, that. It's a school problem. A folder of students' stories is missing. I suspect it was stolen."

"This happened in your class from hell?"

I nodded.

"I'd like to have your job for a day," Crane said. "I'd put the fear of God into those delinquents."

"You couldn't take your gun into the school."

"I wouldn't need it."

He smiled, but I wished I hadn't attempted to inject levity into the discussion. The mention of a gun in connection with school set a grim parade of memories in motion.

"I'll handle it," I said, "and it won't happen again."

We had strayed from the discussion of the house. Maybe that was best, as I had no idea what was going on in my new haunted place and couldn't imagine what my role in the phenomenon could be.

~ * ~

Thursday was Flower Day at Marston High School. Whoever was so inclined could purchase a "Spirit" carnation with a message to be delivered to a person of their choosing.

"Now that's civilized," Leonora said as we drove to school. "And tomorrow is Dress-up Day. What are you going to wear?"

"A dress, like always."

"I'm going to go through my closet and find something special. Maybe a blouse with lace."

Tomorrow classes would be shortened, and school would be dismissed early, after the Homecoming Assembly. I'd already made plans to visit Lucy. Before that, though, I had to deal with the lost stories.

I told the American Lit class what had happened at the beginning of Fourth Hour. By then I had a collection of red and yellow carnations, enough for a vase, and a stack of messages, all from students. I looked to the flowers for assurance that I wasn't a complete failure as a teacher.

"I've searched everywhere for the folder," I said. "I think it dropped into a black hole."

"What about our work?" Slade Johnston demanded.

I had thought of that. "If you handed in a story, write a short paragraph describing it. Include the length. That's what I'll grade. I have the stories turned in after the folder went missing."

"Why should we have to do more writing because *you* lost our stories?"

Slade again. He was the only one who objected to the plan.

"It's just a paragraph, I said. "I'm not asking you to rewrite your whole story."

This seemed more than fair to me. I didn't expect everyone to be honest, but that couldn't be helped. Slade, for example. I'd be surprised if he'd written a story, based on his past lack of participation.

"I'll give you time to write your paragraphs now," I said. "Then we'll talk about the next unit. Some good stories are coming your way."

"Try not to lose *those*."

I couldn't hear who had said that and decided to ignore the remark. It didn't make sense anyway. How could I lose Hawthorne or Poe?

I was glad Grimsley hadn't chosen today for his return visit. So far I didn't think he knew about the lost folder. I only hoped he never would.

This setback had ended well, although no one had come forward to tell me what had become of the stolen material. Perhaps that would still happen. In the meantime, the carnations on my desk scented the dry air with a hint of fresh spice. They filled me with an unaccustomed sense of optimism.

The Awakening of the American Imagination.

I had written notes on the board and jotted down a few more on an index card tucked into my textbook. A new week on the horizon, a new unit. New hope. Maybe I'd survive my semester in hell, after all.

~ * ~

I woke with shreds of the dream still clinging to my conscious mind. I had returned to Huron Court with Misty and seen the pink Victorian in its original state, and on this second visit, Violet and Ginger were playing Frisbee in the yard.

Leaves rustled overhead, and the wind had a poignant sound reminiscent of a sigh. A delicious aroma of baking bread wafted through the open window.

Violet wore the same outfit. The same powder blue pedal pushers and white knit top. Her sapphire earrings glittered in the sunlight.

She said, "Where have you been, Jennet? I thought we were going to walk our dogs together."

"Where have you been?" That was what I wanted to ask. Instead I said, "I'm here now. Would you like to walk to the end of the road?"

Ginger pranced around her feet, barking, like any dog would at hearing the word 'walk'.

"Oh, I'd love to, but I can't today," she said. "I have to stay here."

"Do you have something in the oven?" I asked.

She answered, but her words blew away in the wind. She appeared to freeze, she and the collie, an eerie tableau. Then they lost color and faded away. Before my eyes, the house slowly fell apart until nothing remained but a skeletal structure the color of the gray sky.

Violet was gone, Ginger was gone, and I stood at the edge of the road with Misty, wondering why I was suddenly so frightened.

I willed myself to go back to sleep, but the memory of images fading stayed with me, along with a lingering sense of fear.

Was this dream trying to tell me something? If so, what?

Then I heard the by now familiar sound of whining on the first floor.

I couldn't sleep, not yet.

Twenty

The dogs were asleep in their usual bedtime places. Halley guarded the doorway to our bedroom. Downstairs, Star lay on the sofa, Candy and Gemmy near the fireplace, and Sky under the dining room table where she felt safe. I found Misty stretched out at the kitchen door with her toy goat.

Déjà vu again.

No one was whining. Misty woke and started barking, eager for the night to be over as perpetual puppies always are. I shushed her.

Could the whining have been part of the dream? Ginger crying as she faded into nothingness?

No. I remembered being awake when I heard it. Feelings, as of fear, could carry over from a dream, but that wasn't true of sounds.

In any event, nothing troubled my collie family at the moment. Vowing that the next time I heard whining, I would ignore it, I went back to bed. I had three more hours to sleep before getting up to fix Crane's breakfast.

Tomorrow —no today; it was already tomorrow —would be the last day of Spirit Week. Afterward, I was looking forward to telling Lucy about my latest experience at the pink Victorian and showing her the pictures in my cell phone. Not that she'd be likely to have relevant information, but perhaps the tea leaves would.

If I went right back to sleep, maybe the dream would continue, and I could ask Violet why she couldn't leave her yard...

It didn't, and I slept without dreaming until the alarm rang.

~ * ~

I had a dark green velvet jumper and a lacy white blouse that I usually wore around the holidays.

October is close enough, I thought, as I pinned an antique brooch sprinkled with faux emeralds to the collar. There! I was as dressed up as I was going to be on a school day.

I didn't expect the barrage of compliments that came my way beginning with Crane over breakfast and Leonora on the way to school.

What amazed me was the (pasted on?) smile of approval on Grimsley's face when we met in the hall.

"You look nice today, Mrs. Ferguson. "We should make the teachers dress up more often."

His words were so out of character for him that I let a moment pass before I remembered to thank him.

The next compliment came from Slade Johnston, of all people. "Lookin' good, Mrs. Ferguson," he said.

Were my enemies in league to unhinge me?

"Don't be silly, Jen," Leonora said at lunch when I voiced that sentiment. "You always look nice, but green is your color, and that brooch is spectacular."

"I found it at Green's House of Antiques last Christmas," I said.

She stared at me. "Did you color your hair?

"No, of course not."

"It seems to have more of an auburn cast. It looks nice."

"You, too? It's the lighting."

"That doesn't make sense," she said. "The lighting here is always the same."

"Then maybe my hair is changing color by itself. At least it isn't turning gray."

I unwrapped my turkey sandwich. I liked the jumper and blouse, felt that I looked my best in them. The outfit gave me confidence. I should wear green more often.

With shortened periods, the day sped by. As the photographers posed the Homecoming Royalty outside in front of the floats, Leonora and I headed for the Taurus and were soon on the freeway heading north.

"What are you going to do with your free hour?" I asked.

"Bake a cake," she said. "I invited Jake over to dinner tonight."

I dropped her off at her house and drove on to Dark Gables where Lucy was expecting me.

She was raking leaves, an unusual activity for her, and Sky was rolling in them. Still, I noticed, Lucy was wearing her signature black, a long broomstick skirt and floaty black blouse on which a trio of gold chains glittered.

"Isn't it a beautiful day?" she said. "I never saw a bluer sky.

I agreed. The air was warm with a refreshing breeze, not enough to relocate the raked leaves. That was Sky's job.

"Come in and tell me about the new development at the pink Victorian," she said, letting the rake fall on the leaf pile.

"It confirms that we're dealing with the supernatural," I said.

I handed her my cell phone. She scrolled through the six pictures in 'Camera Roll', a puzzled look on her face.

"Am I supposed to be seeing something special?"

"I thought I was taking pictures of the pink Victorian as it used to be," I said. "At least that's what I was seeing."

"And the camera gave you —reality, I guess you'd call it. I don't believe it's possible to take a clear picture of a ghost or a ghostly phenomenon. You just end up with some kind of light or distortion."

"Well, I tried."

"When you looked at your subject again, what did you see?"

I had to think. *Had* I looked back? No. Incredible as it seemed in retrospect, I'd looked to the road, led the dogs away from the house, walking as fast as I could.

"I was so spooked, I just got out of there. I guess I should have stayed, should have checked."

Easy to say now.

"Let's go inside," Lucy said. "Now that I know what happened, I feel a little shaky. I remember what I felt when I leaned against that post. I'll make some tea," she added.

We walked through the house, Sky leading the way and shedding leaves on the rugs. Dark Gables was a large house, but I couldn't have described the living and dining rooms if my life depended on it. Only the sun room was familiar. That was where Lucy wrote her books and entertained her infrequent guests.

I sat on the wicker sofa and patted the cushion for Sky to join me. I knew she was allowed on the furniture, as my dogs were. While I stroked her soft fur, I said, "You've had time to think about your experience there. Do you have any ideas about what's going on?"

"Only that you're getting brief glimpses of the past."

"Yes, but why?"

"We don't know yet. Maybe we never will. Maybe there's no reason. That section of Huron Court may just be a place that slips in and out of time and takes people with it. I'll say it again, Jennet. Stay away from there. You might get caught in the riptide, so to speak."

I imagined myself swept out of my current time, waiting for Crane to drive by in his cruiser, hoping he'd know I was there, even if he couldn't see me.

I would be like Violet, no more solid than the air. Except I wouldn't be laughing.

"I didn't hear laughter this time," I said, "but afterward, I felt so tired. I thought I couldn't make it home. That feeling passed as I left the house behind."

"Mmmm," Lucy said.

Which didn't help.

"Annica drove out to the house on her own. She felt depressed. She came back talking about the intransience of time."

"There's something there," Lucy said. "I know you saw lovely, happy things that first time. Autumn leaves falling and a girl playing with her collie, but I sense that place is evil. I think it would be a mistake for Brent to buy it." She filled the teakettle and opened the cupboard, no doubt looking for cookies to go with the tea. "Once he's made up his mind, Brent doesn't listen to me."

"I don't think it's the best location for an inn, and the cottage is so rundown it'll require a lot of work."

"That never stopped Brent," Lucy said. "Especially since he won't be the one doing all the work."

She filled a plate with shortbread cookies, and we waited for the teakettle to whistle. I mulled over the news that Brent was indeed going to purchase the pink Victorian. Would that be the end of the supernatural goings-on or just the beginning?

Time would tell.

Twenty-one

"The Mystery House is mine," Brent said. "I have the key right here in my pocket. Who's up for a tour?"

Crane spoke up while I was still processing the news. "I don't want Jennet wandering around that derelict shack. She's liable to get hurt."

"Won't happen, Sheriff. The stairs to the porch need replacing, but the floors inside are stable. The cottage is empty. There's no possible way Jennet can get hurt."

"Please don't forget I'm in the room," I said.

I was the one pouring coffee and serving slices of my hastily baked banana-nut bread. I hadn't expected company tonight until Brent called, inviting himself over.

"Annica wants to see the inside," Brent said. "Let's agree on a time when we're all free."

"How about Saturday?" I asked. "If Annica isn't working at Clovers."

"She gave me her schedule." Brent opened his wallet and consulted a slip of paper, apparently torn from Annica's ordering pad. Where Brent was concerned, Annica wasted no opportunity. "Good. She's off."

"I don't know." Crane slipped Candy a piece of banana bread and suddenly all the collies converged on him.

"That's why I always make two or three loaves at a time," I said.

Brent resettled himself on the rocker as Misty had jumped down from his lap to join the beggars.

"The girls will be safe with me, Sheriff," he said. "I wouldn't let anything happen to them."

"Well..."

Crane didn't give up his reservations easily.

"I'd love to see the inside," I said. "It might be helpful."

His frosty gray eyes were grave. "Jennet, promise me you'll be careful."

"I will. I always am."

I hadn't told Brent about my latest foray into the realm of the unknown. Nothing of the kind was likely to happen to me if I visited the house in the company of other people.

"I'm not scheduling any renovations until the spring," Brent said. "Inside, the house is in fair shape for having been vacant so long. It needs a thorough cleaning, and I'm going to have the walls repapered. The exterior is a disaster."

"Did you find out who the previous owners were?" I asked.

"A Mr. and Mrs. George Gardener, both deceased. They'd used the house as a summer place. A realtor snapped up the property hoping to sell to a developer, but that didn't happen. He was eager for me to take it off his hands."

"I'm glad you bought it," Crane said. "The fewer developers we allow in Foxglove Corners, the better."

I agreed. Unfortunately it wasn't up to us.

"Was Mrs. Gardener's first name Violet by chance?" I asked.

"No, Lily. Hmm. Another flower name."

Until this moment I'd forgotten my earlier intent to research the house and its past tenants. I'd do that as soon as possible, maybe after our tour. That tour, I reflected, might net something of interest even though Brent said the house was empty.

"I don't like it, but I guess I'm outnumbered," Crane said.

That was probably true, and I wished it wasn't. "I always consider your feelings, Crane."

"Yes. Then you do what you like."

"This is something I have to do," I said. "You know why."

"Why?" Brent asked. "Because of that ghost girl you saw?"

I paused to taste my own banana bread for the first time. Then I took a few sips of coffee, giving myself time to think. I found it difficult to articulate my feelings and hard to admit to two men who admired me that I was afraid.

Finally, I said, "I don't think Violet is a ghost. I don't know what she is, but I have to find out."

~ * ~

Saturday was another picture-perfect autumn day with an azure sky and a brisk breeze that sent still more leaves cascading to the ground. Brent parked his vintage Belvedere at the roadside, and I checked my shoulder bag to make sure I'd brought my cell phone. I might want to take more pictures.

What if my camera recorded the pink Victorian in all its glory?

Well, that wasn't likely to happen. It certainly would be difficult to explain to my friends.

Against a background of nature's splendor, the old Victorian was a shabby interloper. It appeared to list slightly to the right as if the next strong wind would blow it over. I looked again. No, perhaps it wasn't quite level, but it wasn't leaning either.

"Can you really save it?" I asked.

"Sure," Brent said. "A piece of siding reattached here and there, new stairs and windows, a fresh coat of paint, and I give you Ginger's House, open for business."

He remembered the name I'd suggested for the inn, rather than Violet's house.

Annica said, "But wasn't Ginger the dog?"

"It was Jennet's idea," Brent said.

Annica looked at me.

"I don't know why," I said. "It just came to me. It seemed right."

"Let's not sit here talking," Brent said.

Annica and I had dressed in jeans and turtleneck sweaters for plowing through the overgrown yard and exploring an unknown structure. Annica hadn't forgotten her earrings, though, a cluster of tiny copper stars that brought out the gold in her red hair.

Brent helped us ascend the rickety stairs, then unlocked the front door. A wave of chilly air engulfed us as we walked through the vestibule into a large room, most likely the living room. The house gave us a cold welcome. Faint light filtered in through the windows, and dust motes trembled in the dry air. Only our footfalls and the echoes of our voices broke the thick silence.

"Look at all the cobwebs. Ugh." Annica ran her hand through her hair.

"And stale air," I added. "It's to be expected. I wonder how long the house has been shut up."

"It has an easy flowing floor plan," Brent said, "but I plan to knock a few walls down."

I imagined how the rooms would look with furniture and fresh paint or wallpaper. Graceful mahogany period pieces and Tiffany lamps. Old time oil paintings on the walls. A bowl of gold chrysanthemums on lace-trimmed linen...

I had the oddest feeling that I'd been inside this house before —in a dream, of course, as I'd certainly never been here in real life.

Brent led us into a small kitchen with cupboards painted a garish lemon color, their surfaces peeling and dented. "This will be gutted. It'll be totally modern with all new appliances. The bathrooms will be done over, too."

"It needs some tender loving care —desperately," I said.

"It'll be a small rustic inn off the beaten path. We have six large bedrooms on the second floor, three on the third level, and an attic. That's not counting several smaller rooms.

"An attic." Annica shivered. "That's where the resident ghost hangs out."

"It may," Brent said. "That's the one area I didn't investigate. The realtor says it's empty except for some boxes."

"Boxes?" I said.

"Empty," he added. "Stored there after a move."

"Can we go up to the attic?" Annica asked.

"Everyone knows attics have the best secrets," I added.

"Hell, no. The inspector told me the floor's unfinished. You'd have to walk on boards. I promised the sheriff I'd take care of you girls."

Annica tossed her head, a move that set her copper stars in motion. "We can take care of ourselves."

"It's my house. I do the protecting."

She had no answer for that.

"I'd like to see the turret," I said.

I'd always loved turrets, from the outside, that is. From the inside, I had to admit they were just regular rooms, but they'd fascinated me from the time I'd seen my first one, in the exquisite white Queen Anne Victorian on Jonquil Lane.

Having gotten his way, Brent gave Annica a smug smile. To me, he said, "That'll be safe enough."

In the east turret room, I gravitated toward a window that faced the road. What a magnificent view! Everything was soft and green, except the sky, of course, and that was pale blue, filled with the requisite fleecy white clouds. The trees... I hadn't realized there were so many trees on the property. Their leaves were the palest green, not yet fully open...

What?

The leaves should be falling. They should be crimson and gold and brown. It was autumn, not spring; October, not May.

Slow down.

Outside, the dirt of decades streaked the window, and inside lay a thin veil of dust. Vision-distorting dust. There seemed to be a light mist in the air... I closed my eyes, kept them closed while I counted to ten silently and opened them...

The dirt and dust remained, but the mist was gone. It was October again. The leaves were turning and falling.

Thank God.

At a disturbance at the door, I turned around, came down on a loose floorboard, and almost lost my balance. I grabbed for the windowsill, felt my hand connect with a layer of grit.

"Jennet!"

Hearing the alarm in Brent's voice, I said quickly, "I'm all right, but my hand is dirty…"

He drew a large white handkerchief from the pocket of his plaid shirt. How odd for him to carry a hanky. Did men still do that?

"Here, take this," he said. "The water's shut off."

It came in handy, though. I wiped both hands. From now on I wouldn't touch anything.

"I'll wash it," I said.

"What happened?" he demanded.

"Just a little misstep. The board is loose. I'm all right."

"If you're sure," he said. "Let's go upstairs. You'll have to walk carefully. There's no railing."

As I moved forward, I became aware of something stuck to my shoe. In this empty house, I had stepped on something, some bit of debris. Not, I hoped, a bug.

I pulled away a bit of dark blue material well coated in dust. It had a fringed edge and a yellow dot in the center. It looked like a flower.

A violet.

Twenty-two

"What is it?" Annica asked.

"A little cloth violet," I said. "It feels like velvet. It's so soft but somehow fragile."

It seemed to shine in my hand like a blue jewel. A sapphire.

Annica touched it with her finger. "It looks so real, just like the wild violets that come up in the grass every spring." She turned to Brent. "You said the house was empty."

"I was talking about furniture and appliances," he said. "Who could see something so small?"

"Jennet could."

I held the violet in my palm, wondering why I hadn't noticed it when I had entered the east turret room. Probably because I'd been focused on the window. And speaking of the window and the view of a springtime world, I decided to keep that to myself. It would be difficult to explain, was probably not part of the strange goings on at the pink Victorian, and my friends would think I'd lost my hold on reality. Again.

Only Crane and Lucy would understand.

"I stepped on it," I said.

"Let me see." Brent held out his hand. "You didn't hurt it any. Like Annica says, it looks like a real flower. What are you going to do with it?"

That was a good question. "Take it with me, if it's okay with you."

"Be my guest."

I slipped the violet into my pocket.

"Violet," Annica said. "That's the name of your ghost girl, Jennet. Do you suppose there's a connection?"

"Maybe," I said. "I wonder if it was part of a hair ornament, or maybe a decoration on a dress."

Her hair ornament; a decoration on *her* dress.

If it had belonged to Violet, it was proof that she had once lived in the house. Well, I never doubted that. I'd seen her playing with Ginger in her yard. She must have lived here before the Gardeners bought the place.

Annica said, "I think it's a clue." Her eyes took on the bright gleam they always had when she found herself confronted with a mystery. "This means there's other stuff to find in the house. Let's look in all the rooms, in all the corners."

"I don't know, Annica," I said. "Remember the Gardener family also lived here. Surely one of them would have seen the violet at one time or another."

"They didn't stay here all year around. Didn't Brent say they bought the house for a summer place?"

"Still, someone would have seen it when they cleaned the floor. You'd think."

Unless it came from another dimension. Unless it had been left behind when the house changed from the pink Victorian in which Violet had lived to the falling apart structure we were now exploring.

"Let's look," Annica repeated.

"*You* can look," Brent said. "For myself, I'm thirsty. First thing I'm getting in here is a refrigerator. I'll stock it with beer."

"The air *is* dry." I swallowed. "I could use something to drink myself. Only I'd like a cup of tea."

"We'll stop for lunch when we're through here," he said. "My treat."

"Is that all you two think about?" Annica asked. "Who knows what else is just waiting for us to find?"

"When my housecleaning team is finished, there won't be anything to find," Brent said.

"Then we'd better look now."

While they discussed Annica's proposed search, I renewed my intention to keep the brief vision of an impossible spring to myself. After all, it wasn't part of the phenomenon. At least I didn't think it was. Because this could be explained as a combination of dirt-streaked windows, mist, and my imagination functioning in overdrive again.

It was strange about that mist, though, the way it came and went between one heartbeat and the next. That wasn't the nature of a mist. It didn't dissipate in an instant.

I glanced out the window. The world was normal again, the way it should be in October with crisp leaves blowing in the breeze, an azure blue sky and the sweet fields of late autumn poised on the brink of change.

I was alone in the turret room. Annica's voice reached me from the kitchen. It held a note of flirtation. She was trying to persuade Brent to let her look in the attic, which surprised me. Mystery aside, I didn't think she'd want to get cobwebs in her hair which looked freshly washed. Bent was refusing, citing dangerous boards and possible broken ankles.

"I won't sue you, if that happens," she countered.

Suddenly searching the house seemed overwhelming to me. Not pointless but a project for another day. I felt unaccountably tired. No, what I felt was drained and desperately in need of a nap.

Tired? Exhausted?

Ah. My fleeting glimpse of spring was part of the supernatural phenomenon, after all.

~ * ~

I recovered my energy during lunch at a lakeside restaurant Brent had discovered. The menu had a sea theme with Mermaid's Brew, which turned out to be an old-fashioned root beer float, and sandwiches heaped with tuna and salmon salad.

It hardly seemed Brent's kind of place, but he was in his own world, expanding on the improvements he planned for Ginger's House and asking for advice.

"You could set aside one of the smaller rooms on the first floor as a tea room," I said. "You can serve sandwiches like these and pastries."

"And knock out a wall and have a patio installed so people can eat outside in the summer," Annica added.

Brent nodded, his enthusiasm for his new enterprise growing. "I like that idea. You girls can help me decorate."

"Have all Victorian antiques," Annica said.

"I don't like all that clutter."

"Just a Victorian flavor, then. Pictures and doilies and fancy lamps."

"I guess my mounted deer head would be out of place."

Annica made a face. "I should say so."

I left them to their idea exchange. As my energy returned, I realized that curiosity had supplemented my latent fear.

I still couldn't fathom why I alone saw the pink Victorian in its former pristine state, but that didn't concern me at the moment. Aside from a passing feeling of exhaustion, the house had done me no harm. As always I wanted to see Violet and Ginger again and the gracious pink Victorian unravaged by time and weather.

I resolved to do the research I'd once planned. Not today but soon. Perhaps I'd discover that the phenomenon was one of the many mysteries of Foxglove Corners like the road said to lure travelers to the end of the world, at which point they fell off into nothingness, or, in other words, disappeared without a trace.

I didn't have the inclination or courage to travel on that road.

While I'd been woolgathering, Brent and Annica had finished their sandwiches. Annica was reading a dessert menu decorated with pictures of seashells. She was saying, "They have Seafoam Mint pie. I'll have to try that."

"From the picture it looks like plain old key lime pie," I said.

"That's good too."

Brent pointed to the day's featured dessert. "Those jumbo Sandbar Brownies look good. I'll order a couple. Jennet?"

"Mmm. The seafoam mint pie."

"Coffee anyone? Tea?"

The important matter of dessert settled, I reviewed my plan to research the house on Huron Court at the library one day next week. Brent wouldn't initiate his renovations until spring which gave me several months to unearth its secrets.

~ * ~

Sunday was another perfect fall day.

"How much longer can it last?" the weather forecaster mused. "Enjoy the warmth until the middle of the week. Then rain moves in…"

It turned out to be a singularly uneventful day. I sent Crane off to his shift with a hearty breakfast, walked the dogs and played with them, baked my own version of the seafoam mint pie, and cooked steaks for dinner.

When Crane came home, we talked about the violet.

"What did you make of it?" he asked.

"Of all the flowers in nature, why would I find a violet in the house unless it belonged to Violet?"

"You tell me."

"It may not mean anything, then again, it may be a clue."

"To what, exactly?"

I didn't answer immediately. I couldn't.

He held the violet in his large tanned hand where it seemed to shrink.

An illusion, surely.

"It's sure looks real," he said. "You have to touch it to know it's made of cloth."

"I think it came from the past and belonged to Violet. How it survived years of another family's tenancy is a mystery."

"And solving mysteries is what you do best," he said.

"Right now I don't think I can solve this one."

To do that, I'd have to step into the past again.

I didn't say that aloud.

Twenty-three

Coming down from a triumphant, festive weekend is always a bit traumatic. Stripped of green and gold streamers, the halls of Marston were drab and uninspiring. Positively spiritless.

It's your job to inspire, I told myself as I unlocked the classroom door. Listen to a bit of chatter about the Homecoming game —which our team had won —and the dance—by all accounts a fitting end to Spirit Week. Then on to inspiration.

My first hour class, consisting of sophomores, hadn't been as involved in Homecoming activities as the upper classmen. They settled down nicely with our next selection, a classic science-fiction story regrettably tame for kids who were used to Star Wars action.

As always, my fourth period American Lit class was boisterous and restless, reluctant to turn their attention to American literature. If they were quiet and attentive, I would suspect imminent treachery.

I had built my lesson plan around symbols in preparation for studying the works of Nathaniel Hawthorne. Showing the class a picture of the American flag, I asked what it symbolized. The answers came quickly.

"Patriotism."

"America."

"War," suggested Slade.

"Peace", countered Jasmine.

"You're stupid, Jaz," Slade said.

"No, you're stupid, Slaaaade."

It never ended.

"Let's stay on track," I said.

My first pictures were easy. I showed them a skull and crossbones. No argument there. They all agreed it symbolized death.

"A red heart?

"Valentine."

"Love."

I shuffled through the stack of symbols I'd clipped from magazines and pasted to large index cards, finding a white dove perched on a branch. "This one?" I asked.

"Earth," said Gerry who rarely said anything.

"That one's peace." Slade was participating in class today. I wondered why. How sad to suspect enthusiasm as a trick.

"A four-leaf clover?"

Alicia raised her hand, a rare occurrence in this class of shouters. "That's a symbol of good luck. Everybody knows that."

The class might be loud with a tendency to yell answers at the same time, but I sensed a level of involvement that was unusual. If only Grimsley would wander into this show of exuberance —before I ran out of cards. My next assignment would be low-key, a handout with a dozen words and blanks for symbols.

I held up the last card, a picture of a —violet? I stared at it.

When had I cut that out? And why? I couldn't remember.

"A flower?" Ellen asked.

"It *is* a flower," Janet said. "She wants to know what it symbolizes."

"Damned if I know."

I couldn't match that last answer with a name, but the voice was male. Still, I said, "Let's remember, classroom language, please."

"Okay," Ellen said. "A violet is a symbol of summer."

"Or spring," Janet added. "My mom has a book of flowers and their meanings. I can bring it in tomorrow."

"That would be helpful," I said automatically. "This one is a little tricky. Let's save it for tomorrow. Meanwhile, think about it."

As if they would.

I was still shaken. When had I cut out a picture of a dew-kissed purple violet? And why?

This was another occurrence I had better keep to myself. Even from Crane.

~ * ~

Leonora was more animated than usual at lunch. She wore a sparkly pendant set in silver. It shone on her black sweater like a tiny star. I hadn't seen it earlier as she'd been wearing her coat.

"It's a present from Jake," she said. "I have a feeling he's going to propose soon."

"Propose what? Marriage?"

"Of course. My next gift will be an engagement ring."

"Did he say so?"

"Really, Jen, not everything has to be in words. I have a feeling."

"I'd just hate for you to be disappointed," I said.

She touched the pendant. "I won't be."

Such faith.

I remembered I'd been unsure of Crane's intention, had gone so far as to ask him if he was seeing someone else. He wasn't. His proposal, when it came, was a surprise, taking place after a harrowing experience that might have cost me my life.

"My life is finally coming together," Leonora said.

And mine is coming apart, I thought.

Perhaps that was why my thoughts so often turned to the past.

~ * ~

That night I heard a sound of whining — and yes, I was awake. As I pushed back the covers, I remembered my resolve to ignore it. If I didn't, if I got up to investigate, I'd most likely find all the collies asleep. Possibly I'd disturb them and end up having to let them outside.

That decided, I pulled the blanket up to my neck and tried to go back to sleep, back to the half-forgotten dream of a golden meadow and unknown fruit waiting to be gathered.

The whining continued, the most soul-wrenching sound a dog could make, conveying need and loneliness and despair.

I told myself to ignore it. To remember the dream. Golden pears falling from trees, purple plums glistening with morning dew, a shower of sweet cherries all three in the same season.

Please, please, please...

The whining seemed close, almost as if it were on the second floor.

Please...

Surrendering to the inevitable, I reached for my small bedside flashlight and aimed it at the doorway. Halley lay asleep, a relaxed bundle of coal-black fur. Her white markings had a shimmer in the light. She was asleep but woke and wagged her tail as I drew near.

Wouldn't one dog respond to another's incessant crying? Halley had always had remarkable hearing. She knew when I took a piece of bread out of the wrapper and was sensitive to the moods of her sisters.

I glanced back at the bed. Crane lay quietly, not moving, unhearing. That was good. He had a long shift ahead of him and had to be alert, ready for any eventuality.

Please, please come...

Oh for heaven's sake! Enough of this whining would wake him up.

Taking the flashlight, I threw my robe over my shoulders and went downstairs, slowly adjusting to the cooler temperature of the house.

You'll never learn, I told myself, already knowing what I'd see.

The collies had changed places. Candy claimed the sofa, Star and Sky were sleeping side by side under the dining room table, and Gemmy lay alone by the fireplace.

Misty must be in the kitchen then.

She wasn't. Neither was her toy goat.

I walked through the downstairs rooms again, covering every yard before deciding that she had to be upstairs.

Since when did Misty separate herself from the pack at night?

I found her lying in the doorway next to Halley, both of them guarding the bedroom from nighttime intruders. Misty and her companion goat.

Misty gave a pathetic little whimper. It didn't sound like the frantic whine I'd heard earlier. This had more of a 'Notice me' tone.

"Do you have to go out?" I asked her.

Halley opened her eyes. Misty just looked at me.

I assumed that meant 'no'.

So, all was well. Only... Why hadn't I seen Misty when I'd left the bedroom moments ago?

I could think of only one reason. She hadn't been there at that time.

But I hadn't passed her on the stairs...

I didn't need another minor mystery in the middle of the night. I'd think about it tomorrow. Tomorrow the answer would be evident.

<h1 style="text-align:center">Twenty-four</h1>

No one had raked the leaves at the library. They lay in high artistic drifts where the winds had blown them.

The old white Victorian resembled an abandoned mansion of days gone by. Only the half dozen cars in the parking lot suggested that the beloved institution was still being used by the residents of Foxglove Corners.

No one had taken in the wicker chairs on the porch. Well, the weather was still warm. Occasionally during the day someone would check out a book and start reading it outside, in which case a chair came in handy.

This afternoon Blackberry, Miss Eidt's cat, sat on a fluffy pillow in the most comfortable chair. Pumpkins in various sizes lay in no particular order on the floor.

Ah, yes, Halloween was approaching, and Miss Eidt loved seasonal decorations. After all, the library had been the Eidt family home before she donated it to the town, along with hundreds of her own books. She had been known to throw elaborate Halloween parties. The unraked lawn was likely part of the décor.

Blackberry looked up as I climbed the steps to the porch. She held me with an inscrutable green-eyed stare. You could never tell what a cat was thinking. Never tell if it was welcoming you or warning you away.

"Hello, cat," I said.

Although I was one hundred percent a dog person, I owed Blackberry a debt. On the day Crane had asked me to marry him, Blackberry had saved my life. If she hadn't, I wouldn't have been able to enter the happiest phase of my life.

I had just been thinking about that day, adrift in the past again.

When I opened the door, my gaze fell immediately on the cardboard carousel crammed with Lucy's books. In the summer, we had been afraid that a certain fanatic, who wished to rid Foxglove Corner of evil fiction, had like-minded confederates who shared her obsession for destruction. That had proved to be a figment of that fanatic's imagination.

Best of all, Brent's gift to the library, a stone dinosaur, remained unmolested. I couldn't see it unless I went out to the backyard, but if it had come to harm, I would certainly have heard about it.

Miss Eidt's young assistant, Debbie, was taping cardboard cats and pumpkins to the front desk while Miss Eidt unwrapped a life-sized doll dressed in raggedy attire. The library was as quiet as a forgotten mausoleum. I almost hated to speak.

"Miss Eidt..."

"Hi, Jennet." As she held the doll up, bits of crumbly white packing fell on the desk, some of it adhering to her pastel blue suit. "How do you like my scarecrow? I ordered him from a catalog."

"He's —er —impressive."

"I think so. He's going to sit on the porch. It'll be a nice touch. Now then, what can I do for you today?"

"I'm looking for material on local ghosts and phenomena," I said. "Really local, as in Foxglove Corners. Do you have anything new?"

"Nothing new, but we have several books that might interest you. I'm sure you've already seen some of them. So, are you investigating a new apparition?"

I didn't know what to call whatever was happening on Huron Court. The Pink Victorian Changeover?

"Sort of," I said. "I'm interested in a certain house."

"In Foxglove Corners?"

"In and around. Near Sagramore Lake."

"That doesn't ring a bell. Well, you know your way around the stacks as well as I do."

I did, and a leisurely survey of the supernatural collection netted two books: *Haunted Houses of Foxglove Corners* and *The Secret Diary of a Ghost Hunter, Volume III, Lapeer County*.

I brought them up to the front desk. The scarecrow was gone, presumably at its destination.

"Good choices," Miss Eidt said. "Are you going to tell me what's going on?"

"One day," I said. "I don't know myself yet."

"Come back later in the week. Do you remember my doll house? The replica of the library?"

"I do. It's beautiful."

She hadn't brought it out of storage for years. I couldn't wait to see it again.

"I'm going to unpack the furniture and set it up as a haunted house," Miss Eidt said. "I'll have those fake cobwebs and ghost figures. Debbie's found some miniature Halloween decorations, the tiniest pumpkins imaginable and miniature black rats."

Ugh. "I can't wait to see it," I said.

"Good luck with the books. If you don't find what you're looking for, maybe I have clippings in the vertical file that'll help."

Our library was unique. Miss Eidt owned a computer and knew how to use it, but she held on to the old ways. Card catalogs, vertical files, tea and doughnuts in her private office. Somewhere I was certain to find information on Violet's house, if it existed.

And if it didn't, I'd try something else.

~ * ~

Later, with a ham dinner in the oven, I settled down in the rocker to read. Nowhere did I find a mention of a strange house in the Sagramore Lake area or an experience similar to mine. Nowhere was there a reference to a girl named Violet.

When I finished my own spirit book, there should be a market for it. Apparently I was the only one, besides Henry McCullough, who had seen the phantom Christmas tree. The snow collies of Lost Lake and the ghostly ice skater were my own, as was Rosalyn Everett who walked the snowy fields of River Rose clad only in a gown of bridal white.

For a moment I allowed myself to dream on. I'd easily find a publisher and soon have my own place in Miss Eidt's cardboard carousel and extra money in royalty checks, perhaps a sum equal to what I made as a teacher.

I was getting carried away. First I had to finish writing my book. The mystery in which I was involved at present might well be the most intriguing of them all. Only I couldn't see the end, couldn't even imagine how everything would work out.

Violets bloomed at its center, the velvet violet I'd found in the turret room and the paper one I'd clipped for my symbolism assignment.

I still didn't remember doing that, but I must have because I came across a page from *Michigan Countryside* advertising Wood Violet perfume, 'as subtle as the scent of spring'. One of the violets was missing from the illustration.

All right. I had been distracted. It wouldn't be the first time I'd whipped up an assignment with my mind in another place.

Tomorrow in American Lit, I had to talk about violets again. I'd see what Janet's flower book had to say. On the Internet I'd found that a blue violet, like the one in the picture, symbolized love and fidelity while a white one was a symbol of innocence. No one in my class would be likely to come up with that.

Sue Appleton's call interrupted my drifting thoughts.

"How's Star doing?" she asked without preamble.

"Fine. She gets along with everybody, especially Sky and Crane."

I detected something different in her voice, a hesitancy.

"I heard from Star's family," she said. "They've decided they miss her and want to know if I'd found a home for her yet."

"Well, you did. They can't have her back."

"That's what I told them. I said that before they break another dog's heart they'd better be sure of what they want to do."

This wasn't the first time the placement of a rescue had been challenged. In a previous case, a person other than the dog's legal owner had surrender him or her. I couldn't remember the collie's gender. The Rescue League had narrowly avoided a lawsuit.

"Don't worry," Sue said, "They'll never know who adopted Star."

I knew that, but I wondered how Star would feel if she were given the choice.

Remember *Lassie Come-Home* and countless other loyal collies in real life and fiction.

I hoped Star would choose us, but I'd never know.

Then I remembered the nighttime whining that I thought had been Star mourning for her lost home.

No. The whining had another origin.

"Don't worry," Sue said. "I just thought you'd like to know."

"Thanks. I sure hope they don't get another collie."

"I think they may. The kids want a puppy."

"Well, that's out of our hands."

I said goodbye and ended the call.

Puppies were wonderful, and so were older dogs; and so was the bond established between a dog and her owner. Not everyone understood or honored that.

Even though I wasn't worried about losing Star, I was suddenly depressed —for all dogs separated from their humans, no matter the reason. For every dog who cried in the night and waited for somebody to come.

I wondered again if I'd ever know the source of the mysterious whining.

<h1 style="text-align: center">Twenty-five</h1>

In Oakpoint rain fell all afternoon, turning the wooded field outside my classroom window into a quagmire. ('Quagmire' was one of my nineteenth century vocabulary words.) With the rain came a high wind and leaves flying through the air. A few of them landed on the glass and stuck there. Our glorious autumn color was on the way out.

Sitting at my desk during my sixth period conference hour, I wondered how muddy the roads of Foxglove Corners were. I wouldn't be able to take the dogs for a long walk, couldn't do much with my evening except cook and plan tomorrow's lessons.

Nathaniel Hawthorne. *Young Goodman Brown.* To my fourth hour class, that story would feel like a return to the Puritan age. I could almost hear the protests in the silent room. "You said we were through with this witch and devil junk."

Ah well, I couldn't very well skip Hawthorne.

"Mrs. Ferguson? You busy?"

I recognized the voice. Jasmine from American Lit stood in the doorway, a jeans jacket over a short blue floral dress. Usually when their class was over, I didn't see those students until the next day.

"No," I said. "Just unwinding."

"Can I talk to you for a minute?" she asked.

I closed the World Lit textbook I'd been idly leafing through. "Sure, Jasmine. What can I help you with?"

She came slowly into the room, glanced at a desk but apparently decided to stand. "It's about our stories," she said.

"Can you be more specific?"

"The ones we wrote last week about sleeping for twenty years then coming home. You know, the stories you thought you lost."

I waited, willing myself to stay calm. I'd almost forgotten the incident, had decided I wouldn't see that folder again. I'd also decided that I hadn't lost it.

"What about them?" I asked.

"Someone in our class made them disappear."

I'd suspected as much.

"And you know who did it?"

"Yeah. I saw him, but you can't let on that I told you."

"I won't," I promised. "Where are they now?"

"Gone. He threw them away."

"I see."

She looked behind her, but no one was there. Presumably she was the only student roaming the halls during sixth hour. Still, she came closer and lowered her voice.

"He doesn't know I saw him."

"Who took them?" I asked.

"It was Slade. He walked by your desk to use the pencil sharper and knocked them into the wastebasket. He did it deliberately. You were helping Janet with her spelling and didn't see him."

Slade Johnston.

"What are you going to do about it?" she demanded, forgetting to whisper.

"I'm not sure," I said.

But I was. Nothing. Every teacher's instinct I had advised to proceed with caution. I'd detected a curious dynamic between Slade and Jasmine. Conflict, yes, but something more. Could I trust this information?

Slade would deny any accusation of wrong doing, of course, and I didn't have any proof. It was his word against hers. No, that wasn't right. Jasmine didn't want to be identified as the informant, and I could hardly say I'd seen him knock my folder into the trash. Not at this late date.

I believed he was the guilty party, though. There had been the torn seating chart a few weeks ago, undeniably his work. I hadn't said anything to him on that occasion. I hadn't any proof then either and apparently no one had witnessed the destruction.

"I'll keep an eye on Slade," I promised. "The stories are long gone, and you all have grades based on the paragraphs you wrote."

"That isn't fair."

The eternal cry of injured youth. Her voice took on its characteristic whine.

"I worked hard on my story. Slade didn't even do one. How is that right?"

"It isn't," I said, "but in the circumstances, it's the best I can do."

"Okay, I guess. I just wanted you to know."

"I'm glad you told me," I said. "Thank you."

She looked over her shoulder again. "I gotta go."

Jasmine left and I was alone with the falling rain. How depressing to know that I couldn't trust a student.

You always knew that, I told myself. *And don't generalize. There are one or two rotten apples in every barrel.*

Slade was rotten to the core, if Jasmine's accusation was true.

I thought it might be. She didn't have to tell me what she'd seen. I couldn't see what she had to gain one way or the other.

Pencil sharpener, indeed. There was one in the classroom. Like the American flag, it was standard equipment, but the English Department rules required that all work handed in for a grade be written in ink. By rights, Slade shouldn't even bring a pencil to class.

~ * ~

"I don't believe it," Leonora said on the way home.

She was driving, more slowly than usual as the freeway was slippery in places. It was still raining, and as we drove further north, a mist crept over the lanes. It made me think of the mist that had enveloped the pink Victorian for the briefest of instances. That unnatural mist. This one was simply inconvenient.

She turned on the lights, and I said, "Why do you say that?"

"Slade and Jasmine went to the Homecoming Dance together. They were pretty lovey-dovey all evening."

"How do you know?"

"Adam and I were there. We were chaperones. Remember I told you."

"Mmm. That was only this past weekend. Why would she try to get her boyfriend in trouble?

"Who knows? Maybe he smiled at another girl. This is her revenge."

"What drama!" I said. "I was suspicious of him anyway."

"Watch your purse. Watch your gradebook. Watch everything and especially your class."

"With all that watching, when would we have time to teach?" I asked.

"We're miracle workers," Leonora said. "Didn't you know that? Grimsley thinks we are. You never told him about the missing stories, did you?" she added.

"Good heavens, no."

"Then I'd just leave it."

"I hope nothing else goes missing."

"We need one of those nanny cams."

"No. That's what you use when you're not there. I never leave that fourth hour alone in the room."

I remembered once, early in my career, I'd strolled into class after most of the students were in their seats only to find 'Witch's Room' scrawled on the board in yellow chalk. The letters were gigantic and stretched from one end of the board to the other.

Instead of reacting to the name calling as the perpetrator hoped I would, I'd calmly erased the words and ever afterward tried to be the first one in the room.

Some lessons, once learned, stay with you.

Twenty-six

I underestimated Annica's powers of persuasion. She had talked Brent into letting us explore the attic of the pink Victorian.

"I convinced him he couldn't take the word of a realtor that the boxes were empty. I'll bet the realtor never went up to the attic himself. It isn't easy, not like opening a door."

I'd stopped at Clovers for a take-out dinner, decided on hot turkey sandwiches and pumpkin pie, and took advantage of Annica's break to have a cup of coffee with her and bring her up to date on the 'Pink Illusion" mystery.

"I couldn't find any written material about a mysterious house on Huron Court," I said. "But I've had violets on my mind."

I told her about the violet that had insinuated itself into my symbols lesson.

"Violets for love and affection," she said. "That's sweet. But I thought they were for remembrance."

"That's rosemary."

"Oh! I should know that after all the times I've read *Hamlet*."

"My mother used to collect African violets," I said, jolted into remembrance. "She liked all colors but preferred the purple and white ones. I used to buy her new plants every Mother's Day."

"Violet is a pretty name." Annica refilled our coffee cups. "We didn't have a chance to explore the house thoroughly. Maybe this time we'll find something else."

"In the attic," I said with a smile.

Annica clicked her coffee cup against mine. "Here's to the attic."

"And discovery," I said.

~ * ~

We stood under the entrance to the attic, an unpainted square board in the ceiling that you pressed on to raise. Brent had brought a ladder from his barn.

"Stay close to me," he said. "Walk only on the boards. There's no floor. Use your flashlights. We won't have much light. Look first, then walk. Don't wander off, and whatever you do, don't trip."

That last order he directed to me. When had Brent begun to sound like Crane?

"Be prepared for dust and cobwebs, spiders, mice, bats..."

"Oh, no," Annica said. "Bats? Like in *Dracula*?"

I looked for the telltale teasing gleam in his eyes. It wasn't there. "Surely not bats," I said.

"There may be. Since, as Annica reminded me, no one has been in that attic in years, it's anyone's guess what we'll find."

"But how could they get in?"

"Through some opening in the roof or wall we haven't found yet. Do you still want to go up?"

"Yes," she said. "I'm telling myself there's no opening."

"Don't worry," I said. "If any creatures moved up here, we'd hear them. Bats don't like light."

I was hoping to find something, anything, even a small token like the velvet violet. Annica was sure the boxes contained treasures from yesteryear. We'd both be disappointed if the attic contained nothing but empty containers and dirt.

Brent went first, hoisting himself up, presumably standing on a stable board, and reached down to help Annica ascend. I was next. We all had our flashlights on.

The stale air was freezing, and Brent was right. Only the faintest light made its way into the vast area. The shadows of a mound of boxes loomed in a corner. It appeared that Brent's realtor was also right. The attic contained only the boxes, no cast-off furniture or household furnishings, the kind people usually consign to an unused part of a house.

Standing beside me, Annica coughed. "It's hard to breathe up here."

"It *is* an attic," Brent pointed out.

An attic, dim and silent. So much for the mice. Spiders, however... They were everywhere in the house, insidious, silent, unseen entities spinning their webs in darkness.

"No bats," Annica said in a whisper.

Even the whispers seemed to have echoes.

"There's no squirrel cage on the chimney," Brent said. "I aim to remedy that."

A faint fragrance floated on the dry air. It was faint but discernible.

As subtle as the first scent of spring?

A violet? But...

Violets don't really have a fragrance, not like lilacs or the daffodils I planted a few weeks ago.

Perfume then. Clinging to something inside one of the boxes? A box itself?

"Does anyone else smell something sweet?" I asked. "Like perfume."

"I'm wearing Joy," Annica said.

I knew that scent. It wasn't Joy.

Annica coughed again and in the faint light appeared to sway.

Brent glanced at her and apparently decided she was all right. He shone his flashlight on the boxes. "It's curtain time. Follow me. Annica, take my hand. Jennet, stop in your tracks. Wait for me to help you. I don't want to do anything to get the sheriff on my case."

"Oh, for heaven's sake," I said. "I don't need anyone to hold my hand."

I suspected Annica didn't either, but she was always quick to take advantage of an opportunity to be close to Brent.

I stepped carefully on the closest board and joined them, wishing for a banister to hold on to. And there was the first box waiting to be opened.

Don't be empty, I prayed.

"Do we really want to do this?" Brent asked.

"We've come this far," Annica said.

Her voice sounded strange, a strangeness not entirely accounted for by the almost empty attic. It seemed to come from far away — from the field of grass starred with purple violets into which my mind had wandered. In places it looked as if the grass had turned purple, so thick were the violets. But here was a clump of dark blue violets streaked with white, like the kind I used to buy for my mother.

The violet scent was stronger.

"Jennet!" Brent's raised voice called me back from my fleeting reverie.

"I'm all right," I said. "Let's do this."

He stood over a box that could better be described as a steamer trunk made of sturdy, dusty cardboard. He lifted the top with ease and coughed at the cloud of dust that drifted up from the lid.

Along with dust I breathed in a scent of violet. Maybe there was a perfectly natural explanation for it. Like... Somebody had tucked a sachet into the trunk before closing the top.

"Oh, my God," Annica whispered. "Look!"

The trunk-box was filled to the top, crammed with papers and photograph albums and scrapbooks, along with smaller boxes and framed pictures. Everything I'd hoped we'd find.

"Paydirt!" Brent said.

~ * ~

Annica and I were all for tearing into the abundance of riches immediately, unmindful of the dirt and cobwebs of decades. Brent, in charge of the expedition, prevailed.

"Patience," he said. "We have all day."

We didn't, really. I had to be home in time to cook dinner. Annica had to study for a test. Only Brent was a gentleman of leisure.

"Let's check out the other boxes right away," Annica said. "They may have stuff in them too."

"They're not going anywhere. We can come back. First things first."

He pushed the box over to the entrance —exit now —complaining how heavy it was for a container made of cardboard. It was the contents that made it heavy, of course, and whatever was inside probably hadn't belonged to the last family to live in the pink Victorian. If they had, they would have taken the boxes with them.

That meant I was about to find a tangible connection to Violet.

"We can only go through one box at a time, and we can't do it in the attic," Brent was saying.

He stood on the ladder's top rung. "Here's what we'll do. I'll stand on the ladder. You girls push it toward me. We'll get it down the landing, then find some light and see what we have."

It was taking forever. It seemed —a weird fancy —that the box didn't want to leave the attic, as if the old boards were exerting an unnatural force to keep it from moving.

Still, we pushed it to the exit. Brent reached for it, lost his grip, and it tumbled down the ladder on its own steam, landing with a crash on the floor below. Brent swore and helped us descend more gracefully, one by one.

"I thought I had it," he muttered. "It should have had handles."

"It looks like it did at one time. They're gone," I said.

He moved it into a small third-story room with a view of the acreage in back of the house. After the dimness of the attic, the light pouring through the two windows seemed brilliant. It was about twenty degrees warmer than the attic in the house proper.

"Now let's see what we have here," Brent said.

Angela took an album, Brent handed me a smaller box with the Sanders logo on top. Once it had contained two pounds of dark chocolate fruits and nuts. For himself, he lifted a large box illustrated with red and green Christmas trees.

My Sanders box retained a whiff of candy. Not the violet fragrance I'd smelled earlier. Strangely the sweet chocolate smell was not only present; it was overwhelming. Setting aside a sudden desire for chocolate anything, I opened it.

Inside were brittle yellow clippings unevenly cut from newspapers. As I read the heading of the top clipping, a chill settled over me:

Search Continues for Missing Girl.

<h1 style="text-align:center">Twenty-seven</h1>

Her name was Violet Randall. One May afternoon she had gone for a walk with her dog, presumably to the lake. No one in her family knew her destination for certain, but she loved the lake. Then on that walk she had disappeared.

The reporter described her clothing when last seen: powder blue pedal pushers, a white knit top and sapphire earrings. That was what Violet had been wearing when we'd met.

The dog was a year old sable and white collie named Ginger.

I rifled through the clippings, looking for a triumphant headline like *Missing Girl Found Alive*, but it didn't exist.

"We found her," I said and read the first article to my companions.

"Oh, my God," Annica said. "There's another weird road in Foxglove Corners."

She referred to that storied road on which the unwary traveler reached the end of the earth and fell off, never to be seen again.

"I doubt it," I said. "I've been up and down Huron Court and I'm still here."

"Did they ever find her?" Brent asked.

"Not according to the clippings in this box."

One of the earlier articles included a picture of Violet. She was the girl I had seen tossing a ball for Ginger. There wasn't the slightest doubt in my mind.

What does that tell you?

"Afterward, her family must have put all her things in boxes and stored them in the attic," Annica said. "How sad. This album is filled with pictures of a collie puppy."

"Ginger," I murmured.

"I have greeting cards, letters, and postcards, Brent said. "She saved everything."

He turned back to the trunk. "In the bottom are books, some clothes, and a music box. Here's what looks like a jewelry case." He opened it. "Yes, she had some nice jewelry, not a whole lot."

As he rummaged among Violet's possessions, a vision formed in my mind. Pale figures sweeping up the contents of a young girl's bedroom, one of the rooms in this house, and packing them away in boxes.

That indicated acceptance of Violet's death.

Annica's thoughts were similar to mine. "Somewhere on that walk, Violet met up with a killer. It's a ghost you saw that first time, Jennet."

"And it looks like the killer was never found," Brent added.

The winds, mild when we'd begun our adventure, were picking up. Not only were they stronger, they were increasingly vocal. It didn't take too much imagination to fancy them saying, "Nooooooooooooo."

"Not so fast," I said.

Their scenario sounded logical. A girl walking on an isolated rural road that should have been safe. Someone with evil intent whose path crossed hers. Foxglove Corners had acres of dark woods where a body might be buried and never found.

"I see two problems," I said. "What about the dog? Where was Ginger? You'd think Ginger would have protected her."

"Killed, too?" Brent suggested.

"Also I still don't think Violet and Ginger are ghosts," I said. "And I'm someone who has seen ghosts before."

Think? Somehow I knew she wasn't but couldn't explain it, not even to myself. But if Violet wasn't a ghost, what was she?

"This is a story without an end," Annica said. "I hate that kind."

"Or we haven't found the ending yet." Brent glanced at the rest of the items in the trunk. "There may be more clippings in another box."

"Jennet, you have to go back to the library and do more research," Annica said. "You'll be looking for a disappearance, or a murder rather than an unusual house. We have a last name, Randall. Can we bring down the rest of the boxes now?" she added.

Brent shook his head. "And take them where? My Belvedere can only hold so much. I say we leave everything here and make a date to come back. Bring sandwiches and drinks. Make a day of it."

"But will they be safe?" Annica asked.

"They've been here for decades. Who's going to bother them now? Besides, I had the locks changed. This house is as secure as any other."

"But no one lives here or anywhere near," Annica pointed out.

"On our next trip," he said. "We'll each take what we have right now and examine it more carefully. You girls bring the sandwiches. I'll supply the soft drinks."

Annica couldn't argue with him. He was the undisputed leader of our exploration. He had the car, he had the house keys, and after all, the pink Victorian was his.

"I think Jennet should bring Misty along the next time," she said. "From what Jennet says, Misty is aware of the ghosts."

They aren't ghosts.

"I have no objections," Brent said. "Misty is a good dog."

Sensing Brent was in a mellower mood, Annica said, "Couldn't we just take something else with us today?"

"On our next trip," he repeated.

~ * ~

So Brent had spoken. All we could do was go back to our lives and wait for the next day when we would all be free. That was next Saturday.

At home, while dinner cooked, I read the remaining articles. As might be anticipated, they grew shorter in length and appeared less frequently. New stories often merely reiterated past facts.

It seemed to me that the fragile old clippings retained the scent of violet.

I was happy to know that the police had searched the adjacent woods thoroughly but never found Violet's body.

Because it was some other place? Or because she hadn't been murdered and buried.

Murder will out. I believed that.

But not in every case. I believed that, too.

I couldn't wait to tell Crane about our discovery.

"Looks like you have a bona fide mystery to solve," he said.

I'd glossed over the condition of the attic floor, boards with dangerous gaps between them. But not about the scent of violet.

"I think you're right about a sachet in the trunk," he said. "Or maybe violet-scented soap. My Aunt Becky keeps bars of lavender soap in her linen closet. Did you look for something like that?"

"No, we were too wrapped up in our discovery."

"Look the next time you get together," he said. "Not everything has to be ghostly."

I agreed with him, but only to a point. How long would soap or a sachet retain its perfume? And how far could it reach? All the way to the first floor of the house?

And why did I think so often of violets?

For the first time ever, perhaps, I looked forward to going to school. Dealing with the myriads of problems a teacher encounters every day could bring the cascade of violets that disturbed my peace of mind to a halt.

~ * ~

Okay, you asked for it.

Fourth period American Literature was positively diabolical today. What else would you expect from the class from hell?

On entering the room, they were even noisier than usual, refusing to quiet down, some refusing to sit in their assigned seats until I'd raised my voice —all right, yelled—which told them I was on the verge of losing control.

They didn't like the day's lesson, obviously didn't like Hawthorne, and loathed *The Minister's Black Veil.*

"It's stupid," Slade informed us.

"I don't know what any of those words mean." Nancy's voice was a pathetic wail.

"Look them up, stupid." Slade again.

"That's what dictionaries are for," I said. "But you should know them. Check last week's vocabulary list."

They had written definitions for my list of unusual vocabulary words, accompanied by original sentences using them. *Visage: A look of horror distorted his pale visage.*

Pamela Lyndley asked, "Did they ever make a movie of this?"

If only they had. Had they? "Not to my knowledge."

"Good thing," Slade said. "Who'd go to see it?"

Pamela didn't like to let go of one of her rare ideas. "If there was one, you could show it to us. Will you look for it, Mrs. Ferguson?"

"Maybe. If you read the story first."

The class had been assigned a modest number of pages to read for homework. Anticipating apathy, but not outright rebellion, I'd created a short quiz covering the assigned work.

My announcement drove the angst up several notches.

"No fair!"

"You didn't tell us."

"We didn't finish reading the story yet."

"It's a surprise quiz," I said. "Expect a vocabulary word or two."

I turned around to pick up the quizzes. They weren't where I'd left them, on the left side of the desk, under the textbook.

Oh, no!

Quickly I scanned my desk. For once it was neat.

Each thing in its place is best.

I glanced at the wastebasket but didn't see them.

I could hardly rummage through the trash with every eye in the room trained on me. With the culprit —Slade? —watching me.

He'd never looked quite so innocent.

Sometimes a teacher has to improvise. "Let's make it an oral quiz," I said. "What does the minister's black veil symbolize? Anyone?"

I wasn't the slightest bit surprised to feel the first throbbing of a headache.

Twenty-eight

If there was a saving grace at Marston High School, it was Leonora. Being able to share experiences and confidences with her over hastily eaten sandwiches or on tedious commutes helped me view the most shattering of school traumas with a fresh perspective.

In the meantime stay vigilant.

If one of my students was determined to make trouble for me, there wasn't much I could do to counteract it, unless I could identify him or her. Dismal, but true.

The thought of what would disappear next was particularly worrisome. So far I'd had my seating chart shredded and a folder of student stories stolen. Neither had caused irreparable harm.

"My quizzes just disappeared," I said as I ate my sandwich, not really tasting it. "I always leave the materials I'll need for the day in that one corner of the desk."

"Somebody noticed that. You can't do anything in secret with an audience of thirty or so."

"After they left, I checked the wastebasket. My quizzes weren't there."

What was there was half a jelly doughnut loosely wrapped in a napkin and dripping strawberry on yesterday's absence list. Ugh. They weren't supposed to bring food into the classroom, but that doughnut had sailed right past me.

"Maybe your informant saw what happened," Leonora said.

"Jasmine? I wonder. I'm not going to ask her though. I promised I'd keep an eye on Slade Johnston, and obviously I didn't. If it was Slade."

"I hope you don't have two thieves in that class."

"It's possible. The copy-cat effect."

"A conspiracy?" Leonora murmured.

"I'm glad Grimsley didn't stop by today. That would have been the last straw. He's not the brightest principal we've ever had, but he'd know I was covering for something and want to know the details."

I spilled an Aleve tablet out of my pill box and swallowed it with tea that had grown lukewarm. Would I keep getting these headaches until the semester ended? What if the next groups were worse?

Positive. Think positive thoughts. The bad class is over for today. The sun is shining. Leonora brought homemade pineapple drop cookies for us to share.

"There's a pattern here," I said. "What's going to vanish next? A form I have to send to the office? Something personal?"

"You don't keep your purse on the desk, do you?" she asked.

"I did. Not anymore."

It went straight into the closet with my jacket, and I locked the closet before the first student arrived.

"All you can do is keep watching," she said. "Those materials you keep on the desk? You'd better keep them *in* the desk from now on or in the closet. Take them out as you need them."

"Good idea."

I glanced at the clock. How helpful to digestion was it to have to eat with an eye on the time? We had five minutes left. Just enough time to eat our cookies.

My first class, after lunch, was a section of World Literature. They were an agreeable group willing to learn, if not exuberant about it, and the selections, classics gathered from around the world, were appealing for all ages. The stories in their textbook weren't like the heavy work of the early American writers.

"Our survey of American literature is moving at a snail's pace," I said. "Sometimes I feel as if I'm trapped in the Puritan Age."

"How dramatic."

"The material doesn't help. When I was in high school, I loved *The Minister's Black Veil* and even *The Scarlet Letter*. Kids today don't care for Hawthorne's style or for the symbols."

"Symbolism is an integral part of the study of literature," Leonora said. "There are symbols all around us. They have to understand the concept."

"I know that."

Violets for affection and love. Pansies for thoughts.

"I was thinking," I said. "Maybe I should listen to the kind of music popular with kids today. The lyrics might have symbols in them."

"That's pretty drastic. I wouldn't do it. Just go with the flow. Sooner or later you'll find something the kids like."

"That's all I can do. Poe is our next writer. In World Lit, they loved *The Tell-Tale Heart.*

"Instead of brooding over what might happen in the future, why don't you concentrate on the pink Victorian?" Leonora said. "By the way, the next time you go, I'd like to tag along. Now that Brent owns the house, we won't be breaking the law."

"Sure. Let me know when you're free."

"Any Saturday but this one."

Leonora was seeing Jake Brown more frequently these days, but I felt certain she'd make time for a new mystery. Everyone in whom I'd confided was interested in Violet. What had happened to her? Where she was now, assuming, as I insisted, she wasn't a spirit? Would the unopened boxes in the attic yield an important clue?

The bell rang. I gathered wrappings and stuffed them into my brown bag, still crunching my cookie.

Our lunchroom conversation had planted violets in my mind again, purple and white petals with ruffled edges. The kind I used to buy for my mother.

~ * ~

On Saturday I leashed Misty and drove to Clovers to pick up Annica and the sandwiches. She'd made them herself, no doubt with Brent in mind.

"Ham and cheese on rye," she said. "Roast beef and a couple of turkey."

Brent would be impressed. His vintage Plymouth Belvedere was already parked in front of the pink Victorian when we arrived. The porch was now free of leaves, and the front door was open. I hoped the mosquitoes and their ilk had gone for the season.

In the empty living room I saw a cooler, a broom, and a jumbo package of Double A batteries.

Annica set the package of sandwiches on top of the cooler. Misty lunged toward it, a bright gleam of acquisition in her eyes.

"Uh oh, wrong choice." I moved it out of her reach.

A thumping sound came from the third floor.

"He went up to the attic without us," Annica said.

"That's all right. We've seen what's there. That room where we left the trunk was more comfortable anyway."

"What do you suppose we'll find?"

"More of Violet's possessions, I think. I can't understand why her family didn't take them when they moved."

"I'd like to know *why* they moved. If somebody in my family disappeared, I want to stay put and wait for her to come back."

Apparently Violet had never returned, unless it had escaped the notice of the press. I hadn't had a chance to go to the library all week. By the end of the school day, I had little energy to spare for research. Well, all in good time.

"I thought I heard someone down here." Brent's voice boomed out in the deep silence of the old house as he came down the stairs.

"Anyone could wander in," I said. "Why did you leave the door open?"

"To let some of that nice warm autumn air in."

It wouldn't circulate, though. It wouldn't travel up to the third floor.

Concentrate on filling your lungs with air, and you'll find you can't breathe.

I stopped thinking about breathing and immediately became aware of the scent of violets.

Did some violets have a fragrance? I wondered. Add that to the research list. On the other hand, they must. How else to account for violet perfume?

"I got all the boxes down from the attic," Brent said. "Hello, Misty. Are you going to help us today?"

Making sure the door was closed, I unleashed Misty and took a Nylabone out of my shoulder bag. That should keep her happy.

But it didn't. Whining, she began a thorough inspection of the living room.

"She senses a presence," Annica said.

"Maybe. Or she's just exploring a new place."

Since her arrival on our front porch one snowy Christmas Eve, Misty had never been inside another house.

Brent lifted the cooler, and Annica took her packages of sandwiches. And I? All I had brought was Misty.

The room in which we were going to work seemed to have shrunk. It was the boxes, of course, shoved against one wall. The trunk was just as we had left it, top up, treasures yet to be explored.

There were clothes. Pants and shorts and tops. A swimsuit and cardigans. A plain lavender cotton dress without sleeves and a pale blue dress with ruffles. Lingerie and pajamas.

Another box held Violet's winter wardrobe. Still another concealed a charming bedroom lamp. A little cream-colored Cupid leaned around a column wrapped with a blue-flowering vine. The lamp rested on a patchwork quilt whose predominant colors were blue and white.

Brent plugged the lamp in. Amazingly it worked. The light of a hundred-watt bulb flooded the room.

"She liked blue," Annica said.

"And collie figurines."

I held a sable and white collie, a Ginger lookalike.

"What are we going to do with all this stuff?" Brent asked.

"Donate the clothes?" Annica said. "Everything looks to be in good condition."

At that moment I remembered the sound of the wind on our previous visit. It had seemed to say, "Noooooooooo."

Ridiculous. There was no wind today, only a soft autumnal breeze.

"Why don't we take some of it, like the lamp and the figurine and the quilt and use it to decorate one of the rooms?" I said.

Annica nodded. "I like that idea."

"Violet's room," I said.

Twenty-nine

Engrossed in the contents of the attic boxes, I had forgotten Misty until I heard her barking. She hadn't followed us to the third story, preferring to lie on the uncarpeted floor and chew her new Nylabone.

"I'd better see what she's barking at," I said.

It could be the presence of a wild animal in the yard, deer maybe, or almost anything. But this was the pink Victorian. I'd brought her here for a reason.

"Wait up," Annica said and replaced the little picture she'd been perusing —an angel watching over a sleeping child —on top of its box.

Misty raced up the stairs, meeting us on the second floor landing. She nudged me and retraced her steps. She stood in the middle of the living room, pawing at the hardwood floor and whining frantically.

"She discovered a loose floorboard," Annica cried. "There's a body buried under the floor."

When I'd first met Annica she had been fond of spinning outrageous stories about the antiques she sold at Past Perfect. Rings with poison embedded in the setting, necklaces that had the power to meld to the throat of the wearer.

"No," I said. "I don't know what upset her, but there's no loose board." I turned to Misty. "What's wrong girl? You're scratching Brent's floor."

"And moving dust around. I think I'm going to sneeze…"

She didn't.

Misty refused to abandon her haunted place. She kept whining, kept pawing at the floor, trying to tear it up. As if the floor were dirt and she was digging a hole.

"Misty senses something," I said.

"The ghost?"

"Another dog?"

Ginger?

Ginger had most likely lived in the house; she must have been in every room on the ground floor at least.

Brent came down the staircase. "What's all the racket?"

"Misty found something," Annica said.

"An invisible something," I added.

"I thought some creature got in and was killing her," he said.

Thinking to distract her with her bone, I scanned the living room floor beneath the picture window which was where I'd last seen it. It wasn't there.

"Does anyone see Misty's bone?" I asked.

Misty looked at me, tilted her head. Licked her chops. And returned to her attack on the floorboards.

"I'll look for it," Annica said.

But she rejoined us a few minutes later. "I don't see it. What do you make of that?"

"I don't want to think."

One strange happening steps back, something equally disturbing comes forward. I didn't hear laughter today. Now Misty's bone had disappeared into a black hole.

"I'll take her outside," Annica said.

We had draped our jackets over the staircase post. I'd left Misty's leash there, too. With leash in hand I approached her and reached for her collar.

She whipped her head around, teeth a fraction of an inch from my hand, and uttered the angry sound of a dog warning her victim of imminent attack.

Startled, I backed away.

"Misty!"

She didn't show the slightest sign of remorse but gave the floor another swipe with her paw. Sharp nails raked the floor. They might as well have raked my heart.

"Misty! That's enough!" Brent's voice echoed in the cavernous space. "Here, Jennet, give the leash to me."

He grabbed Misty's collar with an authoritarian hand and attached the leash to it. She didn't even whimper.

Quickly I swallowed back the giant sized lump that had appeared in my throat. I wouldn't cry. Now about this. Only...

It was the first time one of my collies had ever shown a sign of anger toward me. She'd showed me her teeth, for heaven's sake. Misty, my little white collie puppy, whimpering in the cold of a snowy Christmas Eve.

I only thought I held back the tears. They were streaming down my face.

"Jennet," Annica said. "Don't. She didn't mean it. My puppy, Angel, growls at me when I try to take food away from her. Food she stole," she added. "So I learned. Don't try to take food from the mouth of a dog."

"And don't try to separate two dogs fighting," Brent said. "Unless you have the strength to pull their hind legs out straight. That forces them to sit."

"Or turn the hose on them," Annica added.

"How often are you going to be near a hose?" I asked.

"A pail of water, then."

"Which is conveniently close to the fighting dogs?"

We'd strayed far from the point.

"It wasn't food," I said. "It wasn't anything like that. I was just trying to put her leash on. I do that a dozen times a day. She loves it. It means she's going for a walk."

It didn't mean that today.

"It's the house," Annica said. "It's evil."

She sounded like Lucy. Violet and Ginger and autumn games in the yard of the pink Victorian aside, I was beginning to wonder if they were right.

~ * ~

Dogs don't remember their own transgressions, which is why it's futile to punish them after the fact. I'd never punished Misty. She had known nothing but kindness and gentleness from my hands ever since I brought her inside out of the cold and snow.

Dogs don't remember, but people do.

It would be a long time before I forgot the sound of Misty's anger, the wolfish glare in her eyes, her teeth so close to my hand.

Annica gave me a hug. "It's this house, Jennet. Not Misty. She didn't mean it. Misty loves you."

I dabbed at my eyes with the tissue she offered me. From where? I was scarcely aware of her. Brent had taken Misty outside, dragged her rather. She had always been a favorite of his.

Yes, but she was mine.

"My mom says any dog can turn on you. Even Lassie, I guess."

"With provocation. There was none here today."

I knelt down to run my hand over the section of the floor that had so captivated Misty's attention. There was no loose board. Under the carpet of dust, the hardwood floor was in perfect condition.

Therefore, no skeleton lay beneath the wood. I didn't think it did.

The front door opened. Brent and Misty burst in, accompanied by a rustling wave of leaves. Misty's ears were flat against her head; her tail was wagging, her eyes bright. She looked like a dog who has just come home after a brisk walk.

Brent left the leash on her. "She's coming upstairs with us."

Annica offered Misty a drink in the collapsible bowl I'd packed for her. It was lucky I'd thought to bring bottled water.

"She seems fine now, Jennet," Brent said. "I walked her a way down Huron Court."

"Misty." I touched her head. The touch turned into a caress. She leaned her head against my leg.

Repentant?

No, just affectionate. As always.

People remember. Dogs don't.

But I owed it to Misty to forget and forgive.

~ * ~

While Misty lay in the doorway watching us, Brent surveyed the aftermath of our exploration. We were going through the last box.

"We'll set aside the lamp, the quilt, and these collie figurines for one of the rooms," Brent said. "It'll be one of the smaller ones. Maybe we won't rent it. Just keep it as a kind of museum."

I couldn't resist examining Violet's books more closely. Like me she had been —was? —fond of books in a series. She had several of the earliest Judy Bolton's and a few Beverly Gray's. There were dog books, of course, many by Albert Payson Terhune, and childhood classics like *Little Women* and *Alice in Wonderland*.

And a small blue book whose gold letters spelled the word *Diary*.

Thirty

I opened the diary. Nearly every page was covered with entries neatly written in blue-green ink. The writer had indented and left ample margins on the right. It would be easy to read.

A new year, a new diary. I have so much to look forward to...

A light floral scent rose from the yellowing pages. As I leafed through the little book, a dried violet fell to the floor.

It was purple —thin, and fragile. Too old, I'd have thought, to retain the fresh springtime fragrance that wafted up from the floor.

"I found a diary," I announced.

"Violet's diary?" Annica asked.

"Her name is on the first page."

"Now maybe we'll have some answers," Brent said.

"Every mystery needs a diary or journals or letters, something written, to fill in the blanks, whether it's fiction or real life."

Which didn't always mean there was one. We were lucky.

"I wonder what she wrote about," Annica said.

"We'll have to read it."

"You read it, Jennet," Brent said. "You're the one who found it."

"I will, but it'll take a while."

I looked for Misty who hadn't stirred from the doorway, although she appeared to have lost interest in our activities. She lay on her side. Her eyes were closed.

My little snow-white Misty girl. Her angry outburst had slipped out of her mind.

But the reason for it still existed, in the middle of the living room. We'd have to give that section of the floor a wide berth on our way out of the house.

"What do you say we break for lunch?" Brent said. "I brought a plastic tablecloth and an empty trash bag. Sorry, but we'll have to sit on the floor."

"That's all right. We'll pretend it's a picnic."

"I'm famished." Annica retrieved the package from Clovers. "What kind of sandwich would you like, Brent? Turkey, beef, ham and cheese?"

"One of each if you brought enough."

"I brought enough for an army."

"I'd like turkey," I said.

Misty opened her eyes and padded toward Annica, her bright eyes gleaming. It's a rare dog who sleeps during the distribution of food.

Brent opened the cooler, and I reached for a can of ginger ale. "How quickly the mind turns to food after our momentous discovery."

"Sleuthing is hungry work," Annica said. "Look at it this way. We're prolonging the suspense."

"This may just be a young girl's diary," I reminded them. "It doesn't have to be an account of what happened to her. In fact, it probably isn't."

But I hoped it would be more. I couldn't wait to find out if Violet's entries would shed some light on her disappearance.

"This is tasty beef," Brent said. "The best I've ever had."

Annica cast me a conspiratorial look. "Glad you like it. I cooked it myself."

~ * ~

After lunch, as I slipped the diary in my shoulder bag, I saw the empty Nylabone packaging. About to throw it in the trash bag, I saw the word 'Edible' on the front.

So the bone hadn't fallen into the proverbial black hole. Misty had devoured it and in record time, but that was no mystery. I'd bought the wrong kind of Nylabone.

I held the package up. "We can stop looking. It's edible."

"I was thinking Ginger, the ghost dog, took it," Annica said.

I recalled an observation Crane had made. 'Not everything has a supernatural explanation.' Or words to that effect. It was easy to forget that in this house.

I glanced at my watch. As always the vision of my stove confronted me. The empty broiler and the chicken in the refrigerator. Lucky Nancy Drew. She didn't have to worry about feeding a hungry husband at the end of the day, but Judy Bolton did. So did Jennet Ferguson.

Annica was clearing away the remains of our lunch. She'd fed Misty a whole beef sandwich. Misty, naturally, shadowed Annica's every step, hoping for more.

"Are you positive you swept the attic clean, Brent?" Annica asked.

"Not literally, but all the boxes are in this room."

"You may have overlooked something."

"Could be. If I did, it'll stay there."

"Can't we go up to the attic again? Just to make sure?

"Maybe. Not today."

"I'll start reading the diary tonight and give you a report," I said.

Brent took hold of Misty's leash. "Just in case."

The vanishing Nylabone had been explained but not Misty's interest in the middle of the living room floor.

Win one, lose one, I thought.

~ * ~

I began reading Violet's diary after dinner, feeling a little guilty because I had met her and talked to her. I felt as if I were violating her privacy, which, of course, I was. But I also felt that the circumstances justified this intrusion.

After all, someone, presumably not Violet, had left the diary behind to molder in a box stored in an old attic.

Violet appeared to have been a typical teenager writing about a new shade of fingernail polish, learning to bake, a family trip to the Upper

Peninsula, and the wonder that was her new puppy, Ginger. Violet had had her birthday the month before the entries began.

Violet had told me that Ginger was a year old. That meant there was a good chance that whatever happened to her had taken place in the year covered by the diary.

I read on, learned about new paint in her bedroom, a color known as Lake Blue, about books she was reading, tricks she was teaching Ginger, a cake she had baked to surprise her mother. It had been a success, even the frosting.

When had Violet taken that fateful last walk?

I looked up to rest my eyes. I'd thought Violet's writing would be a breeze to read, but my eyes were growing tired. It might be the color of ink against the yellowing paper or Violet's tendency to scribble toward the end of an entry.

I was aware of the faintest scent of the dried violet that we'd left behind in the house.

Crane was looking at me.

"I don't like Misty snapping at you," he said. "I think you'd better find an obedience course for her."

Hearing her name, Misty raised her head and studied his face. Was something good coming? A treat? An unscheduled walk?

"She's never done anything like that before," I said. "It was something in the house."

I'd neglected to tell him how Misty's behavior had brought me to tears. I didn't intend to.

"That house," he said. "That's what I don't like. You and Brent and Annica are playing with fire."

"You may be right."

"What's the diary like?" he asked.

"So far unspectacular. It's just a record of Violet's everyday life. Cakes and vacations and her collie puppy."

"Fowler assured me he'd look out for you and Annica."

""He has," I said. "Nothing happened to us. Well, Misty... That wasn't Brent's fault."

"It's his house."

Brent had taken control of Misty's leash. I hadn't objected. I'd forgiven her and was trying to forget, and I didn't want it —whatever it was —to happen again. I'd had to tell Crane, of course, but never anticipated he'd suggest obedience school for Misty. As if I didn't have enough school in my life already.

Now Crane would think the pink Victorian was a haunted house intent on luring us into a trap.

Don't you already think that?

No, never. The pink Victorian cottage was the rundown place Brent planned to renovate and open as an inn.

That at times reverted to its former pristine state. But that was another matter.

Still, at times I had the disturbing notion that the old house didn't want to change. That it would do anything necessary to maintain the status quo.

"I'd better get back to my reading," I said. "I want to finish the diary tonight."

Brent and Annica would be anxious to know what I'd discovered.

"Okay, honey." Crane picked up the *Banner*.

Rubbing my eyes, I turned a page and read about a new dress for Easter, a vegetable garden, a pair of sapphire and diamond earrings, the stones having been taken from Violet's mother's dinner ring. About piano lessons, a string of rainy days, and...

Something really weird happened to me yesterday. I haven't told anyone yet, but I will as soon as I sort out the facts. The ones I remember, I mean.

At last!

Thirty-one

(From Violet's Diary)

This is what happened yesterday. At first I thought I was dreaming. I was alone in the house, sitting in the living room, mending a rip in my blue pants. It was raining. Ginger was fussing because she always goes for a walk at this time of day. I let my mind wander, and the needle slid into my finger. Blood dripped down on my dress. I thought I'd dab the stain with cold water, but first I got up to find a bandage and for some reason felt dizzy.

When the spell passed, I was in a strange place. The chair I was sitting on was gone. Everything was gone. I was in an empty room with bare walls that seemed familiar but somehow weren't. The rain had stopped, and the sun was out. In the light I could see dust on the floor and cobwebs dangling from the ceiling. How could I see dust on the floor? We had a rug.

I heard Ginger whining, but I couldn't see her. She must be in another part of the house.

Then I realized that this was my house! But everything was gone. All I could think of was Ginger. I had to find her. As soon as I found her everything would be back to normal.

I'd gotten blood on my dress. There was more on the floor. My finger throbbed, and my head felt light.

I looked out the window. The view was different and brighter. Tall weeds grew where the grass had been, right up to the porch. Where were the trees? The cherry tree and the apple tree I used to climb and the all the maple trees?

After that I can't remember what happened. It was all hazy, like being in a dream. Suddenly the room filled with furniture. The pictures were back on the wall, and there was a rug under my feet. My chair was there with the sewing basket on the floor beside it. The pants were on the floor. The lamp was on, and it was raining again. Five hours had gone by.

Did I dream it? I don't think so, not anymore.

~ * ~

"My God," I said.

Crane froze in the act of throwing Misty's goat for her, Misty having charmed her way back into his good graces.

"What's wrong, Jennet?"

"Listen," I said, and read him the entry.

"That sounds made-up," he said.

"Why would anybody write a fictitious story in a diary?"

"I don't know. Maybe she wanted to be a writer and the diary was her notebook. She sure had an imagination."

"I think it happened," I said.

"What happened?

"Exactly what Violet described. What she saw is the view from the house the way it looks today. Well, not quite. Brent had one of his men mow the weeds down. There were more trees when I first saw the pink Victorian, when it was whole and beautiful. As she says, an apple tree a cherry tree, and more than one maple."

"I don't often tell you what to do..." Crane said.

"Ha!"

"Ha? I'm a lenient husband."

"Not all the time."

"Stay away from that place. Even if you're with Fowler. I don't know why he wants to turn it into an inn. He's asking for trouble."

Prudently I changed the subject. "Do you know what I think?"

He waited. I could tell he was curious, in spite of what he said.

"Violet slipped into the future," I said. "She was at home and just like that —I snapped my fingers —she traveled forward in time. It's the Rip Van Winkle effect."

"Where's the magic brew?"

Sometimes Crane surprised me. Why didn't I realize he was familiar with Irving's story?

"And Violet didn't go to sleep," he added. "When the spell or whatever happened to her was over, she was right back where she started."

"Five hours later."

"Mmm. Right. She lost five hours. That's odd. If it's true."

"Ginger didn't go with her —wherever she went," I murmured. "She doesn't say where Ginger was when this happened, only that she was fussing about her missed walk. Later she hears her whining but doesn't know where she is."

"The girl had a great plot for a science-fiction story," Crane said.

"Since you think this experience was a figment of Violet's imagination, why do you want me to stay away from the house?" I asked.

"Just in case it really happened," he said. "We'd miss you."

"It isn't going to happen to me."

"How do you know?"

That was a good question. I didn't. I wasn't sure I believed a person could travel back and forward in time. Still, consider all the time travel books. Mark Twain's *A Connecticut Yankee in King Arthur's Court*, for example. We had an excerpt from that novel in our American Lit textbook. The idea had fascinated many writers. Could there possibly a grain of reality in it?

"I really have to finish reading the diary now," I said. "This may just have been the first of many weird occurrences."

At a whiny prompt from Misty, Crane threw her goat into the dining room. "Let's have hot chocolate first and talk more about it. Did you ever think Violet might have been crazy?"

"Never," I said.

"You only met her once."

"Something else is going on," I said. "Remember. I'm the one who saw the pink Victorian as it was in the past."

"That," he said, "is what worries me."

~ * ~

We drank our hot chocolate by firelight and talked about Violet's diary and every strange thing I had experienced at the house on Huron Court.

I loved this quiet time sitting in front of the fireplace with Crane and our dogs. On any other night I would want it to go on forever. Tonight, however, I was eager to read more of the diary.

Finally Crane took Candy, Gemmy, and Star out for their last walk of the day. Before they were out of the door, I was reading the diary again.

Gone were the everyday musings that had filled the early part of the diary. Violet wrote exclusively of her experience. She referred to it as a 'time slip'.

She didn't tell anybody what had happened to her. "Not until I understand it myself," she wrote. "Mom would only worry. Dad would say I imagined it."

She lived in fear of it happening again, of time running out of control and taking her with it. Of her beloved house growing old and faded and decrepit in a matter of hours, losing everything that made it a home.

It happened again, that summer. Violet was pulling weeds in the vegetable garden while Ginger lay nearby supervising her work, as a dog will.

Violet reached for a dandelion and...

(From Violet's Diary)

It wasn't there. Instead of the dandelion, I held a bunch of tall grass. I was kneeling on the ground surrounded by grasses and seedlings and a plant with large white flowers. Something was scratching my knee. Bees were buzzing around my hand, and the sun was hot on my head, so hot that it seemed to burn my hair.

'Wear a hat,' Mom always said. But it wasn't that hot when I left the house. Just pleasantly warm. Or else I wouldn't have been working outside.

I remember thinking that it was happening again. That I couldn't stop it. It was too late. And where was Ginger?"

She was running toward me. As she reached me, I saw the burrs and tiny green seeds clinging to her fur. We were in a field. The garden was gone. So was the scarecrow, the box, the trowel. Everything gone.

I could see the back of the house with its peeling paint and a gutter hanging by a thread. It didn't look the same. It was a whole different color.

I grabbed Ginger and held her so tightly that she squealed in protest. I remember thinking I couldn't let her go. If I did I would lose her forever. The sun burned on, and I felt too weak to walk up to the house. Anyway, it wasn't my house anymore.

Once again I sensed that I had drifted into a dream. When I woke up, when I was kneeling between the rows of cucumbers and tomatoes again, when I saw that the house was pink, I summoned the energy to walk all the way back up the sloping lawn to the back door.

This time I'd lost four hours. Mom was worried. She said, "I looked for you a little while ago but didn't see you."

I wanted to say, "Because I wasn't there."

Thirty-two

The third time was the worst. The season had changed. The leaves were turning, the flowers of summer fading, and the vegetables in the Randall garden were ready for harvest.

Violet had forced herself to think of the time slips as a product of her imagination when she thought of them at all. Then:

(From Violet's Diary)

Yesterday Ginger and I went for a walk on Huron Court. I can't remember exactly when I knew something was wrong. My head started aching all of a sudden. That never happens. I almost turned around but for some reason kept walking. We usually go down to the where the road forks, then turn and head back home. But yesterday the road seemed to go on and on.

I've gone that way hundreds of times with Ginger, but on this day it looked different. It was wilder. Long branches hung over the road, cutting off the sunlight. I wondered if I'd come to the fork in the road and turned around without being aware of it, but that couldn't be.

The canopy of leaves were thicker. The road grew darker. I walked on until Ginger lay down in the road and refused to take another step. She never did that before. I let her rest for a few minutes, then coaxed her up. All the time I kept thinking I'd better turn around.

When I did turn around, I found that I couldn't move forward. Something I couldn't see was in the way. Some barrier that wasn't there before. It was like what happens when you're dreaming of running away from the bad guy and there's an immovable force in your way.

I kept on walking. There seemed to be no end to the road. I had the oddest feeling that I was dreaming. None of this was real. The branches on either side were meeting each other across the road. It was so dark I could hardly make out Ginger's shape, although she was walking just ahead of me on the other end of the leash.

I held on tight to the leash. The road stretched out in front of me. It was narrow and slippery with fallen leaves that had gotten wet in a recent rainstorm. But it hadn't rained in days. Then I saw my house in the distance, glowing pink in the sunset. It was really my house. This time I had lost six hours.

But when had I turned around, and how had I walked through the barrier?

~ * ~

"Oh, no!"

The rest of the pages were blank. Violet hadn't written anymore.

There had to be another diary in one of the boxes, one we'd overlooked, a Part Two. A diary should cover all the months of the year. This entry —I'd call it the Endless Road —had been written in the fall.

We'd have to go back to the house.

I heard the sound of a door opening and paws on the kitchen floor and Crane's voice. "No, you don't, Candy. This is for Jennet."

He came into the living room. All the dogs were prancing around him.

"What happened, honey? Did something in the diary upset you?"

"It ends with another time slip," I said. "But there has to be more. It's only autumn."

"Yes," he said with a merry gleam in his eye. "I thought you knew that."

"Autumn in Violet's diary, I mean."

He dropped a small white package that smelled incredibly delicious in my lap. No wonder Candy was jumping up at his hand, which he'd been holding high above her.

"What do you have?" I asked.

"Fresh oatmeal raisin cookies from Camille. She met me in the lane."

They were still warm.

With a sigh I set the diary on the coffee table but held on to the bag. Camille's cookies were a welcome diversion. It was too late to call Brent tonight. I'd get in touch with him tomorrow. Surely when I told him about Violet's time slips he'd be amenable to letting us visit the pink Victorian, maybe even its attic.

We had to find another diary. It was essential that we know more of Violet's story.

I said, "I'll put the teakettle on, or would you rather have coffee?"

"Whatever you're having, honey."

"Tea, I think."

Yes, I had an agreeable husband. Most of the time.

~ * ~

That night I dreamed about the pink Victorian. It was hardly surprising. I'd thought of nothing but Violet's time-slips since reading her diary. Also I'd eaten one too many of Camille's cookies, but then food didn't create nightmares. A mind in turmoil did.

This dream... I lay awake trying to gather its strands before they dissolved in typical dream fashion.

Think... Remember...

Violet and Ginger were in the dream. A thick white mist hid the woods on either side of Huron Court from view. I couldn't see Violet and her collie, but I knew they were travelling the road with me. They were a little farther ahead.

What else?

The dream strands were slipping away from me, as impossible to hold as a dandelion that had grown in a garden years ago.

Time-slips.

I was so sure that Violet wasn't a ghost. Could she be lost in time? Neither in the past or in the future —my present —but stranded in some impossible zone between time?

The dream was gone. All I retained was the road and the mist and the knowledge that Violet and Ginger were sharing this strange walk with me, although I couldn't see them.

All this thinking wasn't conducive to going back to sleep, so I was awake when the whining began. As usual, Crane slept on.

I got out of bed quietly, took my flashlight, and tiptoed past Halley. Misty stood at the bottom of the staircase, one white paw on the first step. She was whining. My midnight whiner unmasked.

Halley, quick to wake at any disturbance in the environment, stood at my side.

"It's okay, Misty," I said. "Come up."

She needed no further invitation, a baby in desperate need of soothing.

I stroked her warm head. "Did you have a nightmare, too?"

Of whatever had happened in the middle of the living room floor in the white Victorian?

Or what lay beneath? Buried?

Misty whimpered.

Don't think about anything or anyone buried.

The house had a basement, presumably empty, but who knew for sure? Brent had never said anything about it.

All right. Another place to look.

Thirty-three

It isn't easy to step out of the ever enticing unknown and deal with mundane matters like packing lunches, navigating the freeway, and holding the attention of groups of teenagers, most of whom would rather be outside in the unseasonably warm weather than cooped up in a classroom.

Not at all easy, but necessary. Every hour spent trying to unravel the mysteries of the pink Victorian was balanced by one filled with everyday tasks: taking attendance, passing out graded papers, steering students toward classics, and explaining why a paperback romance wasn't acceptable for an American novel review assignment.

I was in the school library with my fourth period American Literature class. Theoretically my students, list in hand, were supposed to be choosing American novels for an independent reading assignment.

"Sorry, but Jane Eyre is an English novel."

"What's the difference?"

"The course is a survey of American literature. Maybe next year in English Literature..."

Or

"Yes, To Kill a Mockingbird is an American novel. A wonderful one. But you read that in World Literature."

I'd uttered variations of these sentences at least a dozen times today.

In spite of her old-fashioned name, Pricilla Barnes was no gentle Miss Eidt. Priscilla might have been an army sergeant, strict, efficient, and visibly disapproving of my rowdy juniors who had no concept of being silent in a library.

At the moment she was glaring at Slade Johnston and his buddy, Calvin Garren, who had made paper airplanes out of my reading list. One flew through the air. I intercepted it and set it on the table in front of the rebels.

"Did you boys find your novel yet?" I asked.

"I got one at home," Slade said.

"Bring it in tomorrow. I'll let you know if it's acceptable."

"It should be. It's *Jaws*."

I sighed. *Jaws* was a novel. Peter Benchley was American. I could insist that he choose a book from the reading list, *The Red Badge of Courage*, for example, but then he'd simply refused to do the assignment.

"How about you, Calvin?" I asked.

"Uh —not yet." He straightened the crumpled missile. "I'll get one now."

Priscilla said, "May I remind you people that you're in a library? Find your books. Check them out. And be quiet! If communication is necessary, whisper."

In the brief period of silence that followed, I said, "Would anyone like help finding a book?"

No one did.

"Okay," I said. "You have fifteen minutes left. I want everyone to have an American novel in class tomorrow. You can have some of the period to begin reading."

Now where did I leave my books?

Unguarded. On a table in the back of the library. I'd taken the precaution of locking my gradebook in the closet, but my shoulder bag was with the books.

There was no cause for alarm. I saw them neatly stacked with the day's mail on top of them. Where I'd left them. I hated being so suspicious.

Feeling as I had just dodged a bullet, I sat down and waited for the bell.

~ * ~

At lunch, Leonora said, "Did you ask Brent if I could go with you the next time you visit Violet's house?"

"I haven't had a chance, but I'm sure it'll be all right."

Leonora had been fascinated by the contents of the diary, but a little fearful as well.

"What if," she'd asked this morning on our way to school, "you step in the wrong place and go back to the past or, even worse, to the future?"

That was what Crane was afraid of. It unsettled me to think about time travel too. That was the stuff of science-fiction, of fantastic tales spun by some of my favorite authors. Fun to read about. Not so pleasant to live.

A weird thought made its way into my contemplation of my ham sandwich on which I'd failed to spread a layer of mustard.

I'd look in a mirror and see myself twenty years from now, about twenty pounds heavier, my dark brown hair streaked with gray, wrinkles, ugh. Maybe a scar of two obtained during one of my misadventures.

The Rip van Winkle effect.

Would Crane, still fair-haired and handsome, find me desirable?

Maybe time travel wasn't such a great idea.

"Then I'll have a grand adventure," I said. "I'll have something to write about in my spirit book."

"Better you than me. I like the year I'm living in and everything about it."

"I don't think that's going to happen," I said.

"You're being pretty *laissez-faire* about this," she said.

The vision of a plump, gray-haired Jennet slowly faded.

"Lucy did tell me the house was dangerous for me. And Crane wants me to stay away from it."

"But you like to live dangerously. Do you want to know what I think? Brent owns a great piece of property. Instead of renovating that old house, he should have it demolished and build a brand new one. They're doing that all over Oakpoint. Tearing down good brick ranches and erecting big houses that take up most of their modest-sized lots."

"Brent lives dangerously, too," I said. "I hope he doesn't do that."

Leonora opened another bag of her wonderful oatmeal cookies. "There's plenty of sugar in them and other good stuff. It'll get you through the rest of the day." She passed one to me. "But, seriously Jennet, what if that house is a time machine?"

"Let's come back to the real world," I said.

As if on cue, the bell rang.

~ * ~

Halfway through my conference hour when I was correcting quizzes, a messenger from the office rapped on the door. She handed me a slip of paper. Oh, no. From Grimsley's office.

The angry words leaped out at me. They might as well have had teeth:

Mrs. Ferguson: Do you plan on seeing me in my office today as directed? Report to me immediately.

As directed?

I frowned. When had he...?" Oh my God. The library. My books and purse left on a table while I roamed the fiction stacks. I'd made a stop at the office to pick up my mail.

Someone had seen the slip. Not me. It was probably underneath one of the envelopes. I hadn't had time to sort the mail then.

Or perhaps it had fallen from the stack? No, this was my enemy striking again. Same class, different location, new opportunity.

How could I explain this to Grimsley? Either way cast me in an unfavorable light.

Well, there was no time to waste wondering who had taken the message. I locked the classroom door and set out for the front office, rehearsing my apology on the way.

~ * ~

Grimsley looked particularly forbidding. His pasted-on smile must be in his desk drawer.

"I'm sorry," I said. "I got tied up…"

There was still a half hour until the bell to end the period rang. He didn't ask me to explain. "I got a call from Mrs. Garren. Her son is in your fourth hour class."

"Yes, Calvin."

"Mrs. Garren is upset because you're requiring your students to read *The Grapes of Wrath*. She finds its subject matter objectionable. Now I can't say I agree with her, but perhaps you should consider offering Calvin an alternative."

"They are required to read and review two American novel in the course," I said. "That's an English Department requirement. I give them a list of suggestions. *The Grapes of Wrath* isn't on it. The only selections they have to read are the ones in the textbook."

That was easy.

"Then there's no cause for concern?"

"None."

"You might want to call her," he said. "She threatened to take her story to the newspapers."

For heaven's sake. And that didn't clue you in?

"I'll do that."

"Tomorrow after noon. She works in the morning."

I rose. "If that's all…"

"That's all, Mrs. Ferguson, but in the future please respond promptly to messages from me. It might have been an emergency in your family."

Crane, I thought. *His job. He might have been hurt…*

Whoever stole that message had struck too close to home.

Should I apologize again? It wouldn't hurt.

"I'm sorry," I said.

He nodded.

Another bullet dodged.

Thirty-four

Brent was on our doorstep a half hour after I called him, just in time for dinner. As I had expected, he was eager to search for a second diary —in the attic, in the basement, wherever our search led us.

"It may be in the same box where we found the first one," I pointed out. "Just out of sight."

"If it exists, we'll find it."

I made the mistake of telling him about Leonora's idea to demolish Violet's house and build a new one.

"I didn't buy that old Victorian to tear it down," he said. "A place with history will make an excellent inn."

"A dark history," I added.

"It all sounds dangerous to me," Crane said. "I don't like Jennet being involved. I hope you know what you're doing, Fowler."

"I'm dreaming of a whole bunch of inns, all of them haunted."

Had he abandoned his favorite pastimes of hunting the fox and allowing himself to be pursued by beautiful women? Probably not. He hadn't mentioned either one lately. On the other hand, Brent seemed to have time for everything.

"You have to remember," I said, "no one ever said the house was haunted."

"What would you call what's going on there then?" he asked.

"An anomaly."

"That's another name for ghost."

"Not true," I countered. "Anyway, dinner's ready. Who's hungry?"

Candy raised her head.

"The humans' dinner," I said.

The collies had already eaten, last night's leftovers topping their kibble.

"What are we having tonight?" Brent asked.

Good grief. He sounded as if he lived with us. What would he do if I said beans and franks?

"A nice pork roast with potatoes and homemade applesauce."

"Perfect. Sheriff, do you know how lucky you are to have Jennet?"

"I sure do. She's multi-talented and pretty, too."

Usually I'd demure, but my ego needed healing after the episode at school.

If someone was out to get me at Marston, I had two stalwart champions in Foxglove Corners. A pity I couldn't take them to school with me.

~ * ~

So here we were in the pink Victorian on another windy Saturday afternoon —Leonora, Annica, Brent, and I. By mutual agreement we had left Misty at home.

"It looks promising," Leonora said brightly but without her usually bubbling enthusiasm. "You'll need to have a lot of work done, though."

"That's okay. Imagine it with a fresh coat of pink paint... Watch your step."

He held out his hand to assist Leonora up the crumbling step. "I'll have new stairs built out here with a railing. There'll be a whole renovated interior with Victorian furnishings."

We gathered in the living room where Brent had left the cooler. We hadn't brought food today. Brent was going to take us out for a late lunch.

"It's freezing in here," Annica said. "Colder than last time."

There was no violet fragrance in the air. Not yet anyway. But the wind had picked up. From inside, it sounded like a howling.

Surely that was natural in this part of the state on a fall day?

"Be careful where you walk," Brent said. "There's something odd about the middle of the room. Misty nearly went bananas trying to get at something."

"She snapped at me," I added.

Annica knew that, having been in the room at the time, but Leonora was shocked. "Your baby, Misty? She's so sweet."

"Ordinarily. This house brought out her wild side."

"The main action is upstairs," Brent was saying. "All the boxes from the attic are in one of the rooms."

In Violet's bedroom.

How on earth could I know that? I kept the thought to myself.

It has the nicest view and it's kind of private. I can imagine I'm in my own ivory tower.

I must have read that in the diary.

With a jingle of her silver bell earrings, Annica said, "Don't forget the basement and the attic. We have to find that other diary."

But what if we didn't? Perhaps Violet had never purchased a new book, never written another entry. What if one day she'd lost more than a few hours?

Then we'd never know what happened.

"The way to the basement is through the kitchen," Brent said, distributing flashlights and leading the way. "The kitchen is going to be gutted. You won't recognized it when we're through."

"That's a good idea," Leonora said. "It looks so dated."

Annica ran her hand over a dusty speckled counter. It was a shade known as robin's egg blue. "I like the kitchen, but I can see where it won't do if this is going to be an inn."

Brent opened a door and turned on a light. The lower level blinked into view. The illumination was inadequate, a sixty watt bulb at most. The air that blasted us was chilled and uninviting.

"I have to replace the light bulbs," he said. "Not that we're going to spend much time down here. There's no railing but these steps are okay to walk on."

He preceded us down the stairs. I walked carefully, wishing for a railing on at least one side.

The basement proved to be a disappointment. It was a cavernous space with an old furnace and ancient laundry tubs but no washer or dryer. An old workbench occupied one corner. Its surface was paint-spattered and scarred —distressed, they would call it today. I couldn't see any tools lying about, not even a hammer, but the bench had several drawers.

On an impulse, I opened them. They were empty, lined with brittle yellowing shelf paper. Obviously no one had worked at the bench for years.

Above it a handmade lazy Susan, of sorts, gathered dust on the ceiling. Screwed to the cracking wood circle were jars filled with nails, buttons, shower curtain rings, paper clips, everything that accumulates in a household that doesn't have a proper place for each item.

"Well," Brent said, sweeping the expanse with his flashlight. "There's nothing here to find. They must have just used the attic for storage. Who's going up with me?"

"I will," I said.

"Me, too." That was Annica.

"And me," Leonora said.

We climbed back to the kitchen where it was still cool but some degrees warmer than the basement.

"I'm not expecting to find anything else up there," Brent said.

Nor was I. He had removed all the boxes. If anything had fallen out in transit, it had landed in one of those ever-present black holes.

"It has to be in the box where Jennet found the other diary," Annica said.

In Violet's room.

The voice was like an echo. Not quite an echo. A fly-by thought.

The attic was another disappointment. Brent stood in the middle of the floor, balancing on two boards, and turned his flashlight on all four corners. Clearly the attic was empty.

"It's with the other stuff," Annica said.

I thought so, too. Three disappointments would be too many.

~ * ~

In the end, we found not one but two diaries. One of them had never been written in. The other was filled with writing in the same blue-green ink I'd seen before. Violet's choice of color.

They were wrapped in a pretty floral scarf at the bottom of the trunk-box with a pile of pastel cardigans on top.

Almost as if the writer had wished to hide them from prying eyes. But then why was the first diary lying loose?

I hoped the one I held in my hand wouldn't be an earlier version, covering months before the first time slip had occurred. Well, there was only one way to know.

"I knew we'd find something," Annica said.

"Now we're getting somewhere," Brent added.

"I'll read it tonight and let you know what happened."

Suddenly a scream erupted from the lower level of the house. A scream and a dog barking.

"What the hell?" Brent said.

"Did you close the front door?" I asked.

"Yeah."

"And locked it?"

"You girls stay here. I'm going to see what's going on downstairs."

<h1 style="text-align:center">Thirty-five</h1>

Naturally none of us listened to Brent. We waited on the landing, standing close together as if to protect one another from an unknown threat.

"What is it?" I called down to him.

"See for yourselves," he said.

We joined him in the living room where he was looking through one of the windows.

There was no dog in the room, no human. Only Brent, apparently mesmerized by the scenery.

"I don't see anything," Annica said.

"That's the problem."

I thought I detected a whiff of violet scent. Or was my imagination working overtime again?

"There's nobody here," Brent said. "The door was closed."

"Well..." Annica leaned against the banister. "We heard something. Do you think it was the ghosts?"

"Or the wind?" Leonora asked.

The wind was louder than usual, and from somewhere in the house came a sound of scratching. A branch brushing against the window. Probably.

"The wind doesn't scream and bark," I said. "Although it does howl."

"Then what did we hear?" Leonora asked. "We all heard it, right?"

"I just told you," Annica said. "The ghosts. You wanted a haunted house, Brent. You got your wish."

With a surreptitious glance at the middle of the floor, Brent walked away from the window. "There has to be a rational explanation. Like someone was inside the house. She had a dog. Something surprised her or scared her, and she left before I could get down the stairs. I was hoping to see her running away."

"Something like what?" Leonora asked. "There's nothing here."

He didn't answer, only shrugged his shoulders.

"What do you think happened then?"

"The wind?" she said faintly.

Brent's theory sounded rational. But who would enter a strange house and bring a dog with her? And how could she have gotten away so quickly? Brent had charged down the stairs before the echoes had died away.

I noticed we were assuming the intruder was a female. Well, of course, it had been a woman who had screamed. Or a girl.

"I'm going to have nightmares about this place tonight," Leonora said. "It's a virtual house of horrors."

"Are you sorry you came?" I asked.

"Not a bit. I like to be in the loop."

"It's spooky here," Annica said. "At least we have one another."

She directed an admiring glance at Brent which he failed to see.

"We have what we came for." Brent started up the stairs. "I'll get the diaries, and we can blow this popsicle stand. All these shenanigans are making me hungry. How about lunch at a steakhouse?"

"I'm game," Annica said.

I was, too, in a sense, but part of me wanted to stay in the pink Victorian and investigate the sounds.

"Maybe she's still here, hiding in another room or in the basement," I said. "Shouldn't you look?"

"You're right."

He swept through the house like a wildfire. We waited. I half hoped he didn't find anyone.

"Nothing," he said. "My guess is she went out the door and is long gone."

I hoped Brent was right about an intruder entering the house and immediately exiting for some reason, even though it didn't seem likely. How many pedestrians came this way? And who would let herself into someone else's house? Especially with a vintage Plymouth Belvedere parked in front.

Who but Violet and her collie, Ginger?

The mysteries kept on coming, and there was no solution in sight.

If we'd heard Violet and Ginger, then I wasn't the only one to experience the strangeness in Violet's house. That was a comfort. Still I didn't believe my friends shared my sometime connection with the other world. At least they had never given an indication of it.

It was easier to believe that the intruder was a regular person, the scream a reaction to some natural cause.

For perhaps the hundredth time, I asked myself what was going on in the house on Huron Court. And how did it affect me?

Because it did. That I knew.

~ * ~

After a cheeseburger-and-fries lunch, I wasn't hungry for dinner, but Crane had to eat. I took a steak out of the freezer for him, walked and watered the dogs, then sat down for what I hoped would be an uninterrupted reading session.

The first few pages recorded everyday events that took place after her third time slip when Violet had lost six hours.

Then I came upon a paragraph that shocked me so thoroughly I let the little book fall out of my hands. With growing unease, I read the entry, then read it again, scarcely believing my eyes.

(From Violet's Diary)

I was playing ball with Ginger today when something unexpected happened. I met a young woman walking with three of the most beautiful collies I've ever seen. One was black, one silvery blue and the other mostly white with a black and tan face. We talked for a while. She lives nearby on Jonquil Lane, although I don't recall a road by that name. Beyond Sagramore Lake, it's mostly undeveloped land.

We're going to meet one day soon and walk our dogs together. I'm looking forward to it. It'll be nice to have a companion.

In the next entry she wrote about a shopping trip to Detroit to buy fall clothes and look for a winter coat.

Until now, I'd assumed that Violet had been the time traveler. It now appeared that *I* was the one who had wandered out of the twenty-first century with my collies.

Because I had to be the woman with the three collies. Who else would assemble a tri, a merle, and a white collie for a woodland walk on a fall afternoon? There could be no mistake, even though I wholeheartedly wished there were.

The diary was old. How old I couldn't tell. No wonder Violet claimed she hadn't seen any other collies in the area. There weren't any.

As a development, the houses on Jonquil Lane hadn't existed in Violet's time. The only house on the lane was Camille's yellow Victorian, which was truly old.

I didn't want to accept the truth of what I had read. There had to be another explanation.

Violet was a ghost who, in life, had had second sight?

Fantastic. Not so fantastic as experiencing a time-slip of my own.

Think, I told myself. *Remember that day. The leaves were falling. It was warm. Misty knew something was wrong. She was looking for Ginger's ball...*

Every moment of that encounter with Violet came back to me. Every item of clothing she wore, even the blue stones sparkling in her earrings. Every word we said. Misty searching for a ball that was lost in time.

Scenes from all the time travel movies I'd ever seen played in my mind. *Somewhere in Time*, filmed right here in Michigan, *Back to the Future...*

This wasn't the kind of adventure I was accustomed to it. This didn't happen to a high school English teacher who, in all other ways, led a normal life.

I was too disturbed to read on. Maybe tomorrow. Maybe after I'd discussed Violet's revelation with Crane. In any event, the diary had fallen to the floor... I picked it up, set it on the coffee table.

Lucy and Annica were right. The house on Huron Court was evil for me. And yet, whatever happened hadn't occurred inside the house but in the yard in front of it.

Lucy... I had to talk to Lucy again.

Misty nudged my knee, her eyes bright with an inquiry I couldn't understand. Did she want to play? Where was her toy goat?

Oh, well. Crane would be home soon. It was time to put his steak in the broiler and make a salad.

But I felt suddenly nauseous, not wanting to be around food just yet. That brief, chilling entry had zapped me out of my comfort zone and left me hanging.

It was an unpleasant, unsettling place to be.

Thirty-six

"What do you think?" I asked Crane later that day after we'd had our dinner.

"What I've always thought," he said. "Fowler is in over his head this time. He's taking you girls along with him. I don't like it."

I had told him about the scream and the barking in the pink Victorian and of Brent's theory, unsupported by the sight of a person on the premises.

"Then there's this," I said. "Violet wrote about our meeting in her diary —a long time ago. There's only one way to interpret that."

"She imagined it. Or she was writing science-fiction again."

"I don't think so. We were with her in her yard, the three collies I had with me that day."

"That can't be," he said.

He didn't sound convinced.

"Sure it can. It would explain a lot."

"It could be a coincidence," he said. "Say she was lonely. She wanted company and made up your visit."

"And conveniently added a tricolor, a blue merle and a white collie?"

"You said it. It's a coincidence."

"Most people have never seen a blue, a tri, and a white," I said. "Certainly not together. At a dog show maybe."

"Coincidence," he repeated.

"Here," I said. "You can read the entry for yourself. Then tell me if you still think it didn't happen."

I reached for the diary and opened it only to find it was the wrong one, the diary in which Violet had never written.

Where was the other one?

I looked under the *Banner* which he'd thrown down on the coffee table when he'd come in. Surely it was there, only covered.

"What's wrong?" Crane asked.

"It isn't here."

"I didn't move anything," he said.

"It has to be here!"

What would my friends say when I told them I'd lost the diary before I finished reading it? Wait! I didn't lose the diary. I didn't take it out of the house.

I knew that. Still, my heart began to pound. I was aware of an odd feeling descending over me. A combination of panic and a squeezing in the general area of my throat.

I had to find the diary. It contained proof that I had traveled back in time, and possibly so much more. I had just begun to read it.

I'd held the proof that all the strangeness associated with the pink Victorian had really happened and had let it slip out of my hand. Literally.

But then I'd retrieved it and put it on the coffee table where it would be safe.

Except for...

Misty was looking at me, curious, her tail wagging slowly.

Not in the least repentant. She never was.

Her beloved toy goat had disappeared once and mysteriously reappeared one day.

"Misty," I said. "What did you do?"

She continued her scrutiny. Her tail wagged harder.

I found it in the dining room, under the table. Chewed!

Dear God! Misty had chewed Violet's diary, and hadn't stopped with nibbling on a corner. The entire book was shredded. Cover and inside pages lay in a wide pool of soggy paper. Anyone could tell it was beyond repair. If I'd caught her playing with her earlier, I could have salvaged some of it, maybe the all-important page.

I couldn't believe it, couldn't believe that tears were streaming down my face. I wiped them away impatiently. Tears wouldn't bring the diary back. Would anything?

As I swept up the remnants of the diary, I tried to tell myself this damage could be reversed. Somehow. The situation could be salvaged. All the while I knew it was irreversible.

"Bad dog," Crane said in his most intimidating voice. "Bad Misty."

It's futile to scold a dog after the deed has been done. I truly believed Misty didn't think she'd done anything wrong and by now had forgotten about it. Perhaps Violet's scent still lingered on the diary, and Misty knew that scent.

"You're sure about what you read, honey?" Crane asked.

I bit my tongue before I could snap at it him. "Positive. You *do* believe me, don't you?

"If you say so," he said. "But I still don't think it's a true account of what happened. I don't see how it could be."

"It's like I wasn't supposed to know about that day," I said.

"That's attaching way too much significance to it. Misty is still a puppy in many ways. She always was a chewer."

"But to take something off a table... She never did that."

"She never wanted anything badly enough. Maybe it's for the best."

"How can you say that?"

"Because you're upset. You don't need this aggravation. You have enough to deal with at school. I'm going to have a talk with Fowler. From now on, that house is off limits for you."

"I saw Violet and Ginger in the front yard, not in the house," I reminded him.

"The whole area is off-limits," he said. "Every square inch of Huron Court."

Ordinarily I would have challenged his return to his authoritarian ways. Tonight I didn't have the energy. I felt as if I'd come close to understanding what was going on, only to have the proof of it snatched away from me.

Misty was a bad dog, I thought. *The naughtiest one of the pack. Worse than Candy.*

This was her second transgression, and both were connected with Violet's house.

As soon as I formed the thought, I was ashamed of myself for blaming Misty. She was a lively, inquisitive collie, in so many ways still a puppy. Furthermore, she and I had been together when we'd met Violet and Ginger. My companion in time.

I should build on that fact.

~ * ~

Lucy, dressed in her traditional black garb, poured boiling water over the tea leaves in my cup. I gave them a stir and watched them settle at the bottom. The tea was too hot to drink. The vanilla cookies were just right.

"I don't know what to tell you, Jennet," she said.

The large gold charms on her bracelet jingled as if to say they didn't know either.

"I've never seen anything like it, but I agree with Crane. Stay away from that house. I told you that before."

"I know," I said. "I couldn't stand not knowing."

"Brent told me what happened on Saturday. A girl screaming and a dog barking in an empty room. That doesn't sound good to me."

"It's one of the most tantalizing mysteries I've ever come across," I said. "I thought the diary would answer some questions. Then Misty chewed it to pieces."

"Dogs," she said. "But we have to forgive them. I think Crane is right about something else. You can't believe everything you read in a diary, except I agree that most people wouldn't write about something that never happened."

"That was our only proof," I said. "The only written record Violet left behind."

"As I understand it, you made a thorough search of the house, even the attic and the basement, and didn't find anything else."

"That's true."

"Then there's no need for any of you to return to the house. Curiosity isn't a good enough reason to court danger. Brent isn't starting his renovations until the spring. He's going to have to do a lot of planning, lining up contractors, making decisions, in the meantime. If he intends to turn Violet's house into an inn."

"I wish he wouldn't," I said.

"I tried to tell him it wasn't a good idea, but he wants a chain of what he calls haunted houses."

"I wish he'd concentrate on his stables," I said. "The Spirit Lamp Inn is doing well. He doesn't have to work for a living."

"This is a challenge for him," Lucy reminded me. "I'll admit I'd like to see that old Victorian spruced up. The way it was when you saw it the first time."

"It *was* beautiful," I said. "The paint was the softest shade of pink, and it had a stained glass window…"

I came to a stop. When had I seen a stained glass window? I had one in my own house between the two gables, and I'd always loved them, but…

I'd never seen a stained glass window in the pink Victorian. I was certain of it and equally certain that once there had been one.

Or had I seen it in my dream?

"What's the matter, Jennet?" Lucy asked.

I told her, adding that I'd just remembered that detail.

"The whole affair is out of this world," she said. "I wish I could help you, but at the moment I can't think of any way to do it. Let's see what the tea leaves have to say."

Thirty-seven

If the tea leaves had any secret knowledge about Violet or the pink Victorian, they kept it to themselves.

Lucy studied the leaves' formations for what seemed like five minutes. It couldn't have been that long. I kept petting Sky, who had jumped up on the wicker sofa to sit beside me, and waited.

Finally Lucy said, "I see turmoil, but it isn't connected to this time slip business. It looks like it's in your home."

My home?

I didn't want to hear that.

"Or in your classroom."

"That's more likely."

I told her about the missing seating chart, the quizzes that had vanished, and the important message from Grimsley that had gone astray.

"One of my students is watching every move I make," I said. "I try to be careful, but things disappear. Grimsley wasn't pleased when I didn't come to his office as soon as I was free."

"That's too bad. You always seem to rub him the wrong way."

"Except one time when I was laid up. He signed a Get Well card for me. I think he'd be happy if I resigned."

"Then this danger I see may originate at your school. You must be extra careful, Jennet. I read about a teacher in another state whose students were planning to kill her."

"Oh my gosh!"

"This was an elementary school," she said. "It wasn't the whole class, just four vindictive little thugs. Everyone thought they were just mischief makers."

Like Slade Johnston, wanting to choose his own seat, or his buddy, Calvin, lying to his mother about being forced to read a novel she considered immoral. Or someone else who was smart enough not to show his true colors.

"What happened?" I asked. "Did they kill the teacher?"

"No. One of the kids got scared and alerted the principal."

"I thought it was only someone wanting to make my life difficult," I said. "I'm sure I've never done anything to make kids want to murder me."

"You're a teacher, an authority figure."

"And I'm teaching stories they hate."

"Well, beware. I'm not saying anything like that is going to happen to you, but it could. As for this house of Brent's, everyone wants you to stay away from it. Except Brent. His idea of owning a string of haunted inns is becoming an obsession. But I had a long talk with him and pointed out there's no reason for any of you to darken its door again."

Beware. Darken its doors.

Spoken like a horror story writer. I had to smile.

A bit confused by the fortune, I fed Sky a cookie and nibbled on one myself.

"I may do that. It would make Crane happy if for once I did what he told me to."

"Making your husband happy is important. This includes not going anywhere near Huron Court. Just in case."

"Crane mentioned that."

"If you never know what happened to Violet or whether you actually did go back in time for a few minutes —perish the thought —it wouldn't be the end of the world."

"No, but I'd hate to leave a mystery unsolved."

Sky nudged my hand as a collie will. She was looking at the almost empty plate of cookies.

Still so hungry.

Lucy handed her the plate, which was paper, and Sky gobbled up the last cookie and licked every crumb.

Hungry and industrious. With food, all dogs were industrious.

Suddenly I had an idea. There was a place where I could continue my search for Violet, and Crane couldn't possibly object.

~ * ~

I was able to visit the library the next day after school. Crane was bringing a pizza home for dinner, giving me a few free hours. All I had to do was make a salad and dessert.

The Foxglove Corners Public Library wore its Halloween decorations proudly. The pumpkins had multiplied. Only a few of them glared at the visitors with carved faces. Others rested on beds of straw as if they were growing there. Miss Eidt's scarecrow had commandeered Blackberry's favorite wicker chair, but she didn't seem to mind. She lay in a bed of hay of her own with an orange checkered ribbon around her neck, looking like part of the décor.

Involved in my real life fright time, I had forgotten that Halloween was this Saturday. A pity Crane and Lucy had joined forces to place the pink Victorian off limits.

Or maybe not. Well, Violet's house didn't have to wait for a special night to terrify its visitors.

Miss Eidt had cleared a section of the main desk and set up her haunted dollhouse. It was every bit as marvelous as I remembered and was especially enticing with cobwebs, black cats, rats, and ghostly figures, all in miniature. In the kitchen a tiny witch stirred a cauldron with a black spoon.

I dropped my books into the return slot and stopped to peruse the Halloween-themed books in the cardboard carousel. Lucy was well represented, along with a selection of classic horror novels. *Dracula*, *Frankenstein*, and *The Castle of Otranto* kept company with books by Stephen King and other contemporary writers.

I couldn't linger, though. I planned to look for additional books on local ghosts, then ask Miss Eidt if I could search through her vertical file for possible newspaper clippings on the disappearance of Violet Randall. She kept this well-loved relic from another age in her office. I suspected I was the only one ever to use it.

Back in the supernatural section, a new book caught my attention mainly because of its size and bright red color: *Ghosts in My Neighborhood*. As I reached for it, a nearby voice startled me, almost making me drop it.

"That's a good book. I just returned it yesterday."

The speaker was a slender woman all in gray: Maxi skirt paired with a turtleneck sweater, worn under a jacket. Her hair, unfashionably long for a woman of her years was silver.

"Are they true stories?" I asked, then was sorry I had. Of course they were true, or the book would be shelved with the fiction, probably in the carousel because of its subject matter.

"So the author claims," the woman said. "I have my doubts. I haven't made up my mind whether I'm a believer or not yet. How about you?"

"I keep an open mind," I said.

As if I'd confide in a stranger.

"A ghost haunted this very library," the woman said. "When she was alive, she disappeared —probably from where we're standing right now."

"Really?"

I knew the story of the ghost, Jerilyn Mayhew. There had been a logical explanation for the lady's so-called disappearance, but I couldn't recall what it was at the moment.

She was before my time.

"Well..." I had the book firmly in my hands. "I'd better check this out."

Obviously the woman wanted to prolong our conversation, even though we had to keep our voices low. She extended her hand.

"My name is Edwina Endicott," she said. "I'm an amateur ghost hunter."

"Have you caught any ghosts?" I asked as we shook hands.

"I've seen my share."

This contradicted her earlier statement about not having made up her mind about her belief in the spirit world.

"You're Jennet Greenway, aren't you?" she said. "I saw your picture in the *Banner* once. Oh, it was a long time ago. But I never forget a face, or a picture."

I hadn't planned to introduce myself but couldn't be rude. Anyway I had to correct her.

"I'm Jennet Ferguson," I said.

She nodded. "Yes, the Deputy Sheriff's wife."

How much did Edwina Endicott know about me?

This encounter had turned weird. I felt as if I had been backed into a corner, as if something I didn't want was being forced on me.

An offer of friendship from a woman who might be lonely? A woman with whom I might have something in common?

In a minute she would tell me that she had a pet collie who looked just like Lassie.

"Hasn't Miss Eidt done a marvelous job of decorating the library for the holiday?" Edwina asked. "I just love that darling little dollhouse."

"It looks quite seasonal," I said. "I see Miss Eidt over there. If you'll excuse me. It was nice chatting with you."

"Likewise. I'll see you around the library. It's my favorite place to hang out."

With a half-smile, I made my escape.

Hang-out? Hanged man? Halloween?

I waved to Miss Eidt as I approached the main desk. Leaving Edwina Endicott behind really felt like an escape.

Thirty-eight

I sat at a table in Miss Eidt's office, sifting through old newspaper clippings. They reflected three decades of crime in and around Foxglove Corners. So far I hadn't found anything relevant, and I was running out of material.

I knew that I lived in a peaceful part of the state, but every now and then somebody stepped out of line. Or vanished into the thin air.

When I finally found a story about Violet Randall's disappearance, clipped from the *Banner*, it was the one I'd seen among the papers stored in the attic. There weren't any others.

I paused to finish the tea Miss Eidt had made for me.

From the lack of evidence to the contrary I surmised that the Randall case had never been solved. That didn't surprise me. It had become a cold case with no one interested in finding Violet or bringing her killer to justice. If she had been killed.

"Where is she now?" I said aloud.

"Did you say something, Jennet?"

Miss Eidt had turned the main desk over to Debbie and was taking a break, without any doughnuts or cake in sight, a most unusual occurrence. As Annica often did, she had chosen her dress to blend in with the décor. It was black with a sparkly half-moon pin at the bodice.

"I was just wondering what happened to a young girl who vanished in the Sagramore Lake area about twenty years ago," I said. "Her name was Violet Randall. Apparently she was never found."

"She's probably dead. Someone will stumble over her bones one day."

"I hope not."

"Is this research for your new mystery?" she asked.

I hadn't told Miss Eidt about Violet, Ginger, or the strange happenings at the pink Victorian. It was just as well. Miss Eidt was overly impressionable. When confronted with the unknown, she tended to go to pieces. Those of us who cared about her tried to shield her from distressful happenings whenever possible.

Besides, too many people already knew about Violet.

"Are you having any luck?" Miss Eidt asked.

"None. That is, there's nothing new here, and this is the end of the line for me."

"Line?"

"The last place I had to look."

With a sigh, I stacked the files neatly on top of the cabinet.

"I met the strangest woman back in the supernatural section," I said. "Edwina Endicott. She calls herself a ghost hunter."

"Edwina. She's more than a little strange. She's practically delusional. If you talked to her for any length of time you'll know what I mean."

"She isn't a ghost hunter then?"

"I have no idea. She reads all the books we have on the subject, some of them more than once."

"She knew me," I said. "She saw my picture in the paper. She knows I'm married to Crane."

"You're a celebrity."

"Hardly."

"The only stories about me are in the Hometown Activities column," she said. "You're on the front page."

I didn't want to continue the conversation for fear I'd say something appalling —that I'd taken an instant dislike to Edwina, for example, that I sensed I couldn't trust her. I couldn't explain that feeling. It wasn't my nature to judge people on a first meeting.

Well, I didn't have to explain or understand my feeling. It simply was. Chances were I'd never run into Edwina Endicott again, although we were both frequent visitors to the library.

As were countless other people in Foxglove Corners.

"I'd better go," I said. "I always like to be home before Crane, and it'll be dark soon."

Miss Eidt collected our cups and rinsed them in the office's little sink. "It's that time of year."

Literally and perhaps metaphorically as well.

~ * ~

The next morning was dark. An overcast sky and scattered raindrops cast an eerie pall over the classroom.

In fourth period American Literature, we were still studying Hawthorne, *Dr. Heidegger's Experiment*, a strange little tale that I had thought would hold my students' attention.

I was wrong.

"When are we going to get off this old-fashioned stuff?" Calvin demanded.

Like Calvin, I couldn't wait to move forward in our survey. Of course, I didn't say that. "Soon. In the meantime, the story goes nicely with the season."

Most the faces in front of me looked blank.

"Halloween," I said. "It's this Saturday."

They were unimpressed. This wasn't elementary school or Miss Eidt's library. Paper leaves still adorned the bulletin board, not yet ready to give way to a border of snowflakes.

From the back of the room came a prolonged "Boooooooooooooooooo."

Molly Kelly gave a little scream, strictly for show.

"It's the witches!" Jasmine said. "Run for your lives!"

I wished I'd let Hawthorne stand on his own merits without the seasonal buildup.

"Now that everyone understands the story…" I began.

Molly raised her hand. "I don't, Mrs. Ferguson. "It doesn't make no sense."

"Any sense," I said.

Perhaps they all felt that way, but she was the only one to speak up.

In this class? No, if they were acting true to form, all thirty-three voices would be raised in protest.

What was going on?

Hastily I reviewed the story for them, sidestepping the points I wanted to make in the essay topics I'd written on the board.

Was this story too sophisticated for a boisterous group of juniors? Better suited to a college class?

I didn't think so. Apparently neither did the learned professors who had gathered the selections for the textbook.

"You may have the rest of the period to write your essays," I said. "Choose one of the topics on the board, and remember to support your idea."

I turned around, intending to survey my work. The board was empty, a wide expanse of black without so much as a mark on it. Only a whitish residue where a surreptitious soul had erased my essay topics remained. My questions had gone the way of the quizzes a few weeks ago.

But pushing a stack of papers off the teacher's desk was less ambitious than erasing questions on a board. When had that happened? When I'd stepped into the hall to monitor the behavior of the passers-by, in accordance with Grimsley's instructions?

I had to think quickly. Unfortunately, I'd created my essay topics out of whole cloth and didn't have a written copy.

"I don't see any questions," said Slade, the ever-helpful.

"Trick or treat!" Jasmine said, setting everyone into a fit of giggling.

"I'll soon remedy that," I said.

Darn. To do that I'd have to turn away from the class, which was never a good idea. It might lead to heaven only knew what further catastrophe.

A paper airplane crashed into my back and fell to the floor, followed by a cry of *Trick or Treat. The teacher's beat.*

Oh, for the days when a teacher could whirl around and say, "All right, class. You're to write, "I will behave in English class" two hundred times.

I wrote the questions as quickly as I could, recreating them as I went along, and turned around.

Leave the airplane on the floor. Ignore it. Let them think they've won. Well, they have. This time.

I stole a glance at the clock. Fifteen minutes of hell remained.

"That's too much work," Sandra wailed. "We can't finish it today."

"Then make sure you copy the questions. They won't be on the board tomorrow. Complete the assignment for homework."

Homework! I'd said the hated word.

Grimsley chose that moment to stroll by, sent his artificial smile into the room, and walked on.

Thank heavens for that.

At this point I was beginning to detest Hawthorne, his entire body of work, and the austere scholars who sat in their quiet offices and compiled selections for textbooks but didn't have to teach them.

~ * ~

"Another bad day with the juniors?" Leonora asked.

"Is there any other kind? Someone erased my assignment from the board when I wasn't looking."

"Well, you have to look. All the time."

"When you're acting as hall monitor? I don't have eyes in back of my head."

"Grimsley thinks we do."

We had decided to buy lunch in the cafeteria after perusing the week's menu. The cooks were offering spaghetti and meatballs today, and their meatballs were almost as good as those at Clovers.

"Alas," Leonora said. "The prisoners are in control of the jail."

"Not funny. I managed to redo the assignment."

As I told Leonora about my hour in hell, it sounded almost humorous —to a point. There is nothing funny about a teacher whose class is running amok.

I recalled Lucy's story about the elementary school teacher whose students had concocted a plan to murder her. To be sure, it had failed, but still... Maybe it was time I stopped thinking of Calvin, Slade, and their buddies as just kids. In another year they would be graduating. Horrible thought. They'd be ready to wreak havoc on an unsuspecting world.

Maybe not. The world and a high school classroom were different places.

In that moment, as I broke off a piece of pineapple upside down cake, I felt the beginnings of a headache.

Thirty-nine

When I was safe at home, far from Marston High School and everlasting aggravation, I had time to reflect on the nature of the tricks played on me at school. If you could call them tricks. A trick was soaping a window. The incidents in my classroom had involved theft, leading to extra work for me, and one awkward, unpleasant encounter with the principal.

I couldn't stop thinking about the teacher whose students had planned her murder. The kids in that case were children. Mine were young adults. This didn't make them more or less dangerous, except perhaps older students had access to more innovative methods of destruction.

Horrible thought. But I couldn't believe one of my students was capable of murder. Surely I hadn't done anything to deserve killing. I only tried to help them appreciate literature.

All I could do was not to let my guard down, as Leonora advised, and in the words of Lucy, to beware.

What was the worst they could do?

Give me a headache. It hadn't gone away yet.

I slid the beef casserole into the oven and took my tea in to the living room where Star and Misty were engaged in a mock battle over a colorful plush parrot. When nudged with a tooth, it said, "Polly want a cracker!"

Clever toy.

Star abandoned the game to lean against me for petting. How quickly she had adjusted to our home. Collies were so much easier to deal with than teenagers.

I had hoped for a quiet evening with Crane, but knew that wasn't to be when I spied Brent's vintage yellow Plymouth pulling up behind my car. The dogs converged in a tail-wagging pack at the door to greet him.

Rarely one to visit without bringing a gift, Brent shoved a bouquet of lavender roses into my hands. I thanked him and filled a vase with water. They had a sweet fragrance, kind of like violets.

"Did you learn anything from the diary?" he asked without preamble.

"Something upsetting. Then Misty ate it."

"She did what?"

"She chewed it. You've heard of dogs who eat homework? Misty eats antique diaries."

I might as well tell him everything. "I hadn't finished reading it when it became unreadable."

"Well, easy come, easy go, I guess. What was so upsetting?"

"Violet wrote about meeting me."

"What?"

"The first time I saw her," I said.

"In her old diary? Before the house fell apart?"

"Yes. Draw your own conclusions."

"You were in another time when you two met," he said. "Her time. I don't think that's possible."

"Neither does Crane, but Violet describes the collies I had with me that day. One tri, one blue merle, and one white. It must have happened."

"So you were there, at the beginning?"

He appeared to accept it.

"I guess so. I don't remember anything different about that day. I was definitely in my own time when I left home with the dogs. The lake looked the same as always. I often take the dogs in a different direction for variety. I don't remember why I chose Huron Court over another road. It was just there.

I came to a fork in the road and after a while I heard laughter around the next curve. Misty knew something unusual lay ahead. My psychic collie," I added.

"Then we saw Violet playing ball with Ginger. At no time was I aware of crossing a time line."

There. I'd summed up the events of that day. It was good to keep reminding myself of exactly what had happened. After so many days had passed, the edges tended to blur and take on a hazy dream-like quality.

"So, several years ago Violet wrote about that meeting," Brent said.

"Yes. I can't argue with that."

"I don't intend to," he said.

"I only wish you could have read that entry."

"I believe you, Jennet," he said. "But I have to think about this long and hard."

~ * ~

About fifteen minutes later, Crane came home. "Who's been bringing my wife roses?" he demanded, noticing the bouquet.

"Who else?" Brent said. "They can brighten up your dinner table."

Crane locked his gun in the cabinet. "Can't you find a girl of your own, Fowler?"

"I have plenty of girls, Sheriff. Too many, in fact."

"You're welcome to stay for dinner," I said. "It's only beef casserole."

"It it's anything like your roast..."

"It's the rest of the roast with potatoes, onions and gravy."

"Sounds good."

"It's my mother's recipe," I said.

"Did you tell Jennet what we decided?" Crane asked.

What was this? I leaned forward.

"Not yet. Jennet, we're all staying away from the house for the time being. Whatever's happening there can happen without us."

Obviously he had talked to Crane.

"We have no reason to go back," I said. "But don't you want to donate Violet's clothes and books to a charity and decide what to keep for the room?"

"All that can wait till spring."

"If you think that's best," I said.

"Knowing you, I didn't expect you to give in so easily."

"Well, it *is* your house."

Apparently he felt the need to defend his decision. "If something bad happened to one of you girls there, I'm responsible."

"Yes, you can't take any chances."

Happy to let the subject die a natural death, Brent said, "What did you make for dessert?"

"Holland Rusk. And honesty compels me to admit that Camille made it. It was too ambitious for me on a school night."

"What are we waiting for?" he said. "Let's eat."

The men were content to drop the subject of the pink Victorian, but as I set the table and served dinner, it was still on my mind. Unlike my past forays into the great unknown, frequenting the pink Victorian was dangerous for me or evil or —whatever.

Or perhaps it was the idea that I had traveled in time, albeit briefly. That I might get lost in the past or future which was what I believed had happened to Violet.

If that happened, how would I find Crane again? Would my precious collies be dead?

In any event, my last link to Violet's mystery was gone, shredded by sharp collie teeth. To be sure, this was not unanticipated in a houseful of collies, but I wondered if it might be Fate at work. I wasn't supposed to delve into this particularly mystery.

No one was.

~ * ~

I left the lane and walked to my house crunching down the fallen leaves. There were so many of them. Fall had come to an end. A thick fog had developed, obscuring my house from view. Strangely, the stained glass window between the twin gables shone through floating cottony wisps.

Why weren't the dogs barking?

As I drew closer, the fog dissipated all at once, bringing the house into sharp focus.

My house?

The green paint had faded to a depressing gray. The porch posts leaned backward, and the bay window was boarded over. High fields of weeds grew where my summer flowers had glowed in sunlight.

And there I froze, several yards from the porch steps, not daring to go any farther. Because this wasn't the home I shared with Crane and my collies.

It was a ruin.

Like the pink Victorian.

Which meant...

Dear God. My fears had become reality. I'd time slipped into the future and come home to a house that was mine no longer.

Where was my husband? Where was my life?

~ * ~

Some people are blessed with the ability to forget their dreams, and some are cursed with the ability to remember. The next morning, as I prepared French toast for our breakfast, I found myself reliving every detail of the dream that had wrenched me into wakefulness in the middle of the night.

It had been horrible. Perhaps a combination of a lingering headache and a rich dessert. Perhaps Fate meddling in my life again. Who knew what planted a dream's seeds and caused it to grow?

Whatever the cause, it had seemed real, and that was what had terrified me in the hours before dawn, and still did.

I brought the syrup to the table and sat closer to Crane than I usually did. Candy sank down at my feet, her nose pointing to the steaming plate of French toast.

Dressed for the day in his uniform with his badge which seemed brighter than usual this morning, Crane had never looked more handsome or more desirable.

He must have noticed my scrutiny because he looked up, a piece of French toast speared on his fork, and smiled. There was a knowing gleam in his gray eyes.

Cherish the moment. Who knows how many more we have?

"I love you, Crane," I said. "So very much."

Forty

Halloween was Saturday, and nobody I knew had plans to mark the occasion. On my first Halloween in Foxglove Corners, I had hosted a memorable party with a magnificent witch cake and a grand finale in which a killer was unmasked. One year Miss Eidt had thrown an equally elaborate party in the library, complete with a fog machine.

Like Miss Eidt, Mary Jeanne, Clovers' owner, was fond of decorating. She was celebrating Halloween all week. A few cut-out witches and black cats added to the restaurant's autumn décor created a festive atmosphere.

As I observed Annica serving her customers in her glamorous witch costume, I wished I were having another party. It was too late now, although... Why was it too late? If I kept it simple... I could order pastries and cookies from Clovers and make sandwiches. Or perhaps Miss Eidt could be persuaded to put together a gathering on a smaller scale. We could ask Lucy to read passages from some of her scariest books.

The ideas kept coming. Lucy could do that at my house. It would be less imposing than another library event.

We couldn't let October pass without some sort of event. Now that the pink Victorian was off limits and Violet's mystery was destined to remain unsolved, I craved a little out-of-this-world excitement.

Annica turned her waitressing duties over to Marcie and sat down with a cup of hot chocolate topped with whipped cream.

"For energy," she explained.

I was having tea and a devil's food cupcake. Just one as I didn't want to spoil my appetite for the take-out turkey dinner Annica had wrapped for me.

"Taking care of a puppy and going to school is wearing me out," Annica said. "In contrast, working here at Clovers is relaxation."

"You should bring Angel over to my house for a playdate with the big collies," I said.

"She'd love that. When?"

"When you're free. Some weekend."

"How about this weekend?"

"It's a date."

Like most puppies, Angel was an energetic ball of white and gold fluff, still at the biting stage. I was looking forward to seeing how she would interact with my dogs. With Misty, for example, who still considered herself a puppy.

I told Annica about my impulsive decision to have a Halloween party.

"Who would you invite?" she asked.

"You, Brent, Lucy, Leonora, her friend, Jake Brown, Miss Eidt and Debbie, Camille and Gilbert... If Jake can't come, maybe Coach Barrett from school. I can hardly believe Crane has the day off."

"That'll be a pretty small party," she said. "It's too-last minute. Where are people going to get costumes?"

"Costumes can be optional. At Miss Eidt's party I dressed as a witch."

"We can be witch sisters," Annica said. "There should be three of us, though. Like in *Macbeth*. Maybe Leonora would be the third sister."

"Let's do it," I said. "I'll order the food today. I thought we could have Mary Jeanne's pastries and cookies. What else?"

"Hot dogs?" she said. "Mary Jeanne is decorating cookies for Halloween. They're simple, just ghosts and pumpkins. They'll be in the dessert carousel tomorrow."

"Well, ask her to set aside about three dozen for me. I'll bet Camille will offer to bring something."

While we'd been talking, my cupcake had vanished. How can you enjoy a luscious chocolatey treat if you don't remember eating it? I stared at the empty plate.

"I'll get you another one,"Annica said, "and more tea. This is exciting. It almost makes up for that wicked Misty chewing Violet's diary to pieces. Hey, I have an idea. You could tell everybody about what went on at the house, about how you met Violet and Ginger..."

"No," I said quickly.

"But it would be a perfect tale for Halloween, Jennet, and it's all true."

"I just can't do that," I said. "It's my own experience. It's private."

I had admitted this only to myself. In spite of Crane's order and Brent's edict, I didn't feel that it was over yet.

~ * ~

A few elementary teachers were having mini Halloween parties in their classrooms on Friday. This was one of the advantages of teaching younger kids.

A few days before Halloween, in honor of the day, I wound up our study of Hawthorne in my fourth period class without a quiz or writing assignment and showed them a trio of short films based on Edgar Allen Poe's lesser-known tales. In spite of their clamoring to eat candy while they watched the movie, I had to invoke the school's 'no food or drink in the classroom' rule.

But I ignored the occasional pieces of candy corn that found their way out of a box and into a few mouths. And fortunately Grimsley didn't make an appearance in our hall.

Then, my afternoon classes, hearing of Fourth Hour's treat, demanded that they see the movie, too. Translation, I had a rare easy day.

After school I stopped at the library to invite Miss Eidt and Debbie to the party.

"It'll be a small gathering," I said. "You'll know most of the people."

"It sounds like fun," Miss Eidt said. "What activities are you planning?"

I couldn't believe I hadn't thought about what my guests were going to do, other than mingle and talk to one another.

"Cards?" I said.

"Playing cards or reading them?"

"Playing, I guess."

Reading cards was not among Lucy's talents, but maybe she could read tea leaves.

Sure. For Crane, Brent, Jake, and Coach Barrett.

Think again, Jennet.

"I'll ask Lucy to do a few scary readings," I said.

"I'll bring my ghostly sounds CD. It's the one I played at my party."

"We're all set then."

Miss Eidt had a gentleman waiting to consult with her, so I moved on to the cardboard carousel where I found a new Gothic novel in the tradition of Victoria Holt. Then, holding on to my prize, I headed for the Supernatural Section.

An unfortunate decision. Edwina Endicott stood in the faint light that filtered through a window reading a thin volume with a garish cover. Holding that bright book, Edwina looked like an overgrown wren in her brown and gray outfit.

Darn. I wished I hadn't turned so definitely into the aisle. It was too late to retreat.

"Jennet Greenway!" she said. "We meet again."

"In our favorite place," I said, "and it's Jennet Ferguson."

"I just discovered this amazing book." She held it up so I could see the title: *Ghosts and Other Oddities Among Us.* "A few of the stories take place in our neck of the woods."

Double darn. Just what I'd been hoping to find.

"What a treasure," I said.

"Yes. The one I'm reading takes place not far from my home."

"Where do you live?" I asked.

"Near Sagramore Lake. It used to be a summer place, but I had it renovated. Now I have heat and central air and a magnificent view. Anyway, about the book. I could have written this story myself."

Curiosity overcame my natural dislike for this woman.

"What's it about?" I asked.

"A pair of ghosts, a girl and her dog. They've been seen walking on Huron Court, but only in the fall of the year. Isn't that strange?"

I tried to keep my interest low key.

"Why do you say you could have written that story?"

Edwina lowered her voice. "Because I saw them once. The girl had the loveliest long reddish hair. I guess you'd call it chestnut. She was dressed in blue and white, like an angel, and she was walking her dog, a beautiful collie. It looked just like Lassie."

My heart began pounding. "When was this?" I managed to ask.

"Just last year. I always wondered if anyone else had seen them. It says here that there have been numerous sightings. Numerous! Isn't that exciting?"

"It certainly is."

"The person who wrote this didn't ask *me*," she said. "I wish I'd see them again. I walk every day, for my health, you know. I always make sure I have my camera with me. The next time I see them, I'll take a picture."

I felt unaccountably weak, almost lightheaded. I pictured myself fainting right here in the Supernatural Section of the library. That would never do.

"I have to go," I murmured.

"But you haven't looked for a book yet," Edwina said.

"No."

I needed to be alone, not only to regain my equilibrium but to think about this new unexpected development. Somebody else had seen Violet and Ginger. Edwina and other people as well.

Had she also seen an elegant pink Victorian house that glowed in the light?

I should have asked her.

Again it was too late. I couldn't possibly go back now.

But maybe I'd see her again.

Forty-one

On the way home, I stopped at Dark Gables to invite Lucy to the party.

"I thought maybe you could read an excerpt from one of your books," I said.

"I'll do better than that. I'll write an original short story, just for your party."

"Can you do that, in just a few days?"

"Easily. I keep a notebook of ideas. Most of them are just snippets, too short to use in a full-length book but perfect for a short story."

"That would be great," I said. "Now let me tell you the latest."

She listened without comment to the account of my encounter with Edwina Endicott and pounced on a detail that had slipped my mind.

"Didn't Miss Eidt tell you this lady was delusional? You'll have to take her story with a grain of salt."

"But she couldn't know about a girl and her dog walking on Huron Court unless she'd seen them."

"That's true.

I had never seen Violet walking Ginger on the road. Only playing in the front yard. And I'd communicated with her. Perhaps my experience wasn't unique.

"I need to read that book, *Ghosts and Other Oddities Among Us*," I said, "but apparently Edwina checked it out."

"She won't keep it forever," Lucy said. "In the meantime, let's see what the tea leaves say."

My cup was ready for reading, my wish was made, and my hope was that this time Lucy would find something helpful in my fortune.

She peered into the cup, turned it, held it up to the lamplight. The charms on her bracelet clanged together in the silent house.

"That can't be good," I said at last.

"Unfortunately it's the same as before. There's trouble uncomfortably close to your home."

It seemed that the cup hadn't heard about my misadventures in the pink Victorian or didn't care to reveal any future happenings.

But I was forgetting that from now on the house was off limits to us. As Bent had said, "Whatever happens there can happen without us."

Where did the trouble originate then?

"That's all I see today," she said. "But your wish will be granted."

I had to be satisfied with that.

~ * ~

Leonora offered to bake another witch cake for the party and agreed to put together a witch costume from bits and pieces of her wardrobe. Camille was baking cupcakes. She declared that she and Gilbert were too old to dress up.

"I should have consulted with you before making all these plans," I told Crane that evening. "I just got carried away."

"That's all right," he said. "You're in charge of our social calendar."

"I am? That's news to me."

With our schedules and a houseful of collies, we hardly had a social life.

"It'll be nice to see everyone," he said.

And what could be safer than a party in our own home? I knew what he was thinking. I didn't remind him of my first Halloween party, before our wedding, when I had matched wits with a killer.

"Will you dress the collies in costumes?" he asked with a teasing smile, knowing I deplored cute outfits on animals.

"I'll tie orange ribbons around their necks," I said, remembering how striking Blackberry had looked with her orange checked neckwear.

"I bought six loaves of bread and pounds of lunch meat," I added. "Tomorrow I'm going to make sandwiches."

~ * ~

It never failed. Pleasant hours at home were balanced with horrible ones at school, thanks to my fourth period American Lit students who repaid me for letting them watch the Poe movies with the most appalling behavior imaginable.

To add to the misery, I had another headache. I should have taken a sick day but trusted medication to work its magic.

Wrong again.

The weather had turned on us. After a string of glorious autumn days, the temperature plummeted, and a drizzling rain fell. The classrooms at Marston were never adequately heated, in my opinion. At any rate, I was cold. A glimpse of gray sky through the window and branches almost stripped of leaves added to the air of gloom that hung over the school.

I longed for a hot drink. For lunch I could pour a cup of coffee in the teachers' lounge and empty the tea in my thermos down the drain. The thought of coffee cheered me somewhat.

The class wouldn't be quiet. They didn't like the lesson, Poe's theory for writing short stories, and rebelled in a hundred ways.

Slade Johnston was at his worst, firing sarcastic comments into the group. They set his friends into peals of laughter and put a smug smile on his face.

Above the general melee I heard an ominous cracking.

"Hey look!" Slade announced. "Cheap furniture."

He held the back of a desk up as if it were a trophy. It had been none too stable to begin with, but not in danger of breaking without help.

"Take it to the custodian," I said into the uproar, hastily scribbling a hall pass.

Smirking, he dragged the broken desk to the front of the class. The scratching on the tiles resembled fingernails on a blackboard. The pain behind my eye rose a notch.

I made a gallant attempt to resurrect my lesson.

"Who can tell me what three elements Poe believed every short story should have?"

Apparently no one. Even though they were listed on the board.

The noise continued. The minutes limped on. The door opened, and Grimsley walked in. He had left his artificial smile behind.

He scanned the room with cold eyes and strode to an empty desk by the window.

Ignore me, he might have said. *But know that I'm watching every move you make, hearing every word you say. I'm so glad I'm not one of your students.*

His presence made no difference in the students' demeanor. They were fearless. Shameless.

Somehow I made it through the long minutes. My head was pounding, and my throat was dry. I was aware of every word I uttered. It was as if I were hearing them from a distance. Boring, more boring, most boring.

I'm glad I'm not one of my students, too, I thought.

Slade returned, a can of root beer in hand.

"Mission accomplished." He took a long drink and plopped into an empty seat in the first row. This comment brought on another spate of laughter.

Grimsley remained impassive, or seemed to. He hadn't brought his notebook with him. He probably didn't need to record the goings on in my class to remember them.

My composure began to crack.

Finally the bell rang. Still noisy, the class exited the room. The principal held out his hand to detain Slade who tossed the empty can in the wastebasket.

"Just a moment, young man," he said. "I want a word with you. In the hall."

It was over. I didn't need a tea leaf reader to tell me that this second visitation hadn't gone well.

~ * ~

"I might just as well hand in my resignation before he fires me," I told Leonora ten minutes later.

The coffee had warmed me, but I'd lost my appetite for lunch.

"Don't be silly," Leonora said. "He can't just fire you. It isn't that easy to fire a tenured teacher. Besides, he's seen the group of miscreants you're dealing with. I'm sure he thinks you're doing your best."

"I wish I thought so."

"Let's talk about something else. I'm going to be a blue witch for the party. I have a tall pointed blue hat with signs of the zodiac. We used it in a play a few years back. Then I'll paint my fingernails blue and use a lot of blue eyeshadow. I may dye a blue streak in my hair. I'm not sure yet."

Blue, I thought. *A color favored by Violet.*

"You'll be a glamorous witch," I said.

"I'll bake the cake tonight. I wish I could remember how I decorated the witch cake at your last party."

"You used lots of green icing," I said. "I should have a picture of it."

I took a bite of my sandwich. Corned beef on rye. I was making a dozen sandwiches like this for the party.

"I'm looking forward to Halloween night," I said. "I just hope I get rid of this headache by tomorrow."

The bell rang. I stared at my half eaten sandwich. No time to finish now, but I drank the rest of my coffee in two quick gulps.

Sometimes I enjoyed my career. Sometimes I wish I'd never chosen it. This was not a time of enjoyment. My sister, Julia, had the right idea, pursuing her studies in England.

But tomorrow would bring a pleasant reprieve from the madness. I was even looking forward to cleaning house and making sandwiches.

Forty-two

Crane had carved a giant pumpkin and placed it in the wicker rocker on our porch —to greet our guests or scare them away with its diabolical leer. Meanwhile I put the finishing touches on the house. I'd laid the Halloween decorations on with a light touch. Artificial cobwebs here, bouquets of orange flowers there. After all, this wasn't to be a grand affair, merely a gathering of our closest friends and family.

Everything was perfect, even the rumble of thunder in the distance that provided free atmosphere.

The dogs looked gorgeous in their orange ribbons, but for some reason Misty had rebelled at wearing anything but her collar. That was all right. I had six Halloween collies underfoot. Raven had elected to join us in the house.

Leonora and Annica were the first to arrive. My witch sisters, Leonora all in blue as she'd planned, and Annica in traditional black almost unrecognizable in her green wig. She brought a black bowl —a cauldron —filled with candy corn.

Leonora carried a cake covered with plastic wrap. Underneath lay her splendid witch cake, with green frosting-hair to match Annica's wig.

"Where do you want the cake?" she asked.

"On the credenza where it'll be safe. Put it on the cake stand."

"It won't fit," she said.

"Well... Put it next to the cake stand. There's a large plate in the top drawer."

"Jake's on duty tonight," Leonora said, "but Adam's coming."

That was good. Leonora would have an admirer at the party, and Annica and Lucy would have Brent.

"Is that your witch costume?" Leonora asked. "It looks like your black maxi dress."

It was. Without the oatmeal open-front cardigan I usually wore with it. I hadn't had time to assemble a proper costume, only to throw a crystal pendant over my neck and paint my nails black.

I felt a brush of warm fur against my leg. Sky didn't like storms. Before long, she would seek refuge under the dining room table. I was surprised she wasn't already there.

"Well, I think you look nice," Annica said. "It's a perfect night for trick or treat."

"There won't be any tricks. Just treats."

Unless Mother Nature decided to throw a tornado our way. But if the weather forecasters were to be believed, the rain would start after midnight.

Crane came downstairs in jeans and a crisp blue shirt. Like Misty he had rebelled against wearing a costume. No matter. He would be the handsomest man at the party.

I heard a crash in the kitchen, followed by barking.

Dogs and parties, I thought. *Uh oh. Dogs and party food.*

"You greet our guests," I told him. "I'll see what the dogs are up to in the kitchen."

Misty followed me, the only collie not wearing a ribbon. That was okay. With her mostly white coat, I'd tell people she was a ghost.

~ * ~

In the kitchen one collie looked guilty and one looked smug.

"Candy!"

She must have moved the plate of sandwiches to the edge of the counter with her paw. A dab of mustard branded her the thief.

217

Counting sandwiches, I saw that there were ten corned beef on rye rather than an even dozen.

Gemmy, who knew Candy's maneuver was forbidden, was barking to alert me, I supposed.

"Bad, bad girl," I said to Candy. "You'd better not get sick."

It was too late for the sandwiches. I carried the tray into the dining room, amazed how many people had arrived in the few minutes I'd been in the kitchen. Brent and Lucy, Miss Eidt and Debbie, and Sue Appleton.

The doorbell rang, and Camille and Gilbert came in with Coach Adam Barrett from Marston. He had been at my first party, the one to which I had inadvertently invited a killer.

I trusted history wouldn't repeat itself.

Then Adam said, "It's foggy out. Visibility near zero. I almost hit a deer."

Déjà vu. There was a thick fog on the night of that other party.

Leonora gasped. Colliding with leaping deer was a frequent occurrence in Foxglove Corners, especially at dawn or dusk. Still, when it happened, it was a shock.

"Thank God you weren't hurt," Leonora said.

"I swerved. I know you're not supposed to do that. I just panicked. I'm not used to this country living."

"Well, have a seat," I said. "There's cider and soft drinks and beer, and Crane can find something stronger if you'd like."

Thunder crashed too near the house for comfort. Would this be one of the myriad times the forecasters were wrong?

~ * ~

Brent's voice was a match for loudest thunderclap. He had elected to come dressed as the Huntsman—which meant in the clothes similar to those he wore every day. A green plaid shirt and green pants set off his dark red hair. A hunter in hunter's green.

"Hey, Jennet," he said, eying the credenza which I'd turned into a buffet table. "This party needs livening up. Where's the music?"

"I brought a ghostly sounds CD," Miss Eidt piped up. "There's wind and howling and..."

"Oh, about that…" I thought of Sky safe under the table and of the thunder that wasn't in the forecast. "Maybe we'd better have music instead. Spooky music."

The Sorcerer's Apprentice and *Danse Macabre* were the only selections that came to mind. I had both CD's.

"Crane?" I said.

"I'm on it, honey."

My little party couldn't compare to the lavish affairs Brent hosted, but I was happy with my efforts. The buffet was crammed with good food and drink, people were mixing and talking, and we had Lucy's short story to look forward to.

Pastime with good company, I love and shall until I die…

We had that.

The first notes of *Danse Macabre* drifted through the room. From somewhere in the house, one of the collies howled. Except in the kitchen, candlelight replaced electric light bulbs, and the flames danced with abandon in the fireplace.

Welcome, Halloween, I thought.

~ * ~

At some point, the evening took on a somber, unsettling tone. Perhaps it was the rain. Yes, the forecasters were wrong. Perhaps it was the thought of the pink Victorian that insinuated its way into my thoughts, even when I was talking about something else entirely. Perhaps it was the music.

And perhaps I was the only one to feel —different.

In any event, I had to do something to turn the situation around.

"Everyone," I said. "Lucy Hazen has written a short story just for us —just for tonight. Whenever you're ready, Lucy…"

"Would you hand me my tote, Jennet?" she asked.

I found it tucked behind the rocker and handed it to her. She drew out several pages stapled together and put on her reading glasses.

"If you people think you're brave enough…"

"Everyone, find a chair," I said, and Lucy began reading.

The tale Lucy spun was about obsession or phobia. Both, it appeared. Her heroine, Catherine, was terrified of spiders. All kinds, all sizes.

Every time she saw a cobweb, she tried, always without success, to find the spider that had woven it. Nothing cataclysmic happened in the story, except for Catherine's mind. Her sanity kept unraveling. Soon she was seeing spiders everywhere, inside her house and out.

She set poison out for them and tried a deterrent suggested by a salesman —window cleaner. For every spider she destroyed, a hundred came to take its place. Then one day she saw a giant spider the size of a cat.

The story ended with Catherine in an institution, still terrified every time a spider crossed her path.

Lucy ended her tale with a heartfelt "Happy Halloween" and accepted the enthusiastic applause as her due.

I regretted the faux cobwebs I'd sprinkled around the house.

If I'd hoped to dispel the aura of disquiet that had descended on the party, I hadn't succeeded. Indeed, I found myself scanning the white living room walls for a wisp of cobweb or a nasty multi-legged bug.

Brent brought Lucy a glass of cider. "Nice going, Lucy. You've scared the women."

"The men, too," Gilbert added.

"Well, it is Fright Night," Lucy countered.

"Would anyone like anything to eat or drink?" I asked. "There's plenty more in the kitchen."

Candy brushed up against me, wagging her tail, the pilfered sandwiches forgotten.

"Okay," I told her. "Biscuits for the dogs."

While my guests took me up on my offer to rush the buffet, I spilled out biscuits for the collies who had suddenly appeared from all corners of the house.

Candy, Gemmy, Halley, Star... Even Sky, lured from her sanctuary, and Raven, our outside girl, all sporting their pretty orange ribbons.

I handed each one a bone and... Something was wrong. I had a biscuit in my hand.

One of the dogs was missing.

"Misty," I called.

All I heard were the strident notes of *Danse Macabre*.

Forty-three

Misty was nowhere in the house.

Don't panic, yet. She must be. Look again.

I glanced at my guests. Everyone was engaged in lively conversation. Everyone appeared to have enough to eat and drink. The dogs were in collie heaven, outdoing themselves to look cute and begging for handouts.

Every dog except Misty.

Arming myself with a beef and cheese sandwich, I slipped away from the party and climbed the stairs. A light burned in our bedroom. I searched there first, then looked in all the other rooms, even the ones with closed doors. I looked again. There was no sign of Misty, no sign of the toy goat from which she was rarely parted.

"Is something the matter, Jennet?"

Annica paused at the head of the staircase. Her wig glowed an eerie green in the dim hall light.

"I can't find Misty," I said.

It isn't time to panic yet.

Besides the sandwich, I still held a bone in my hand. For the dog who hadn't dashed to my side as soon as I'd opened the Lassie tin.

"She has to be here," Annica said. "Did you look everywhere?"

"Everywhere. Twice."

"I'll look again. Just to make sure."

"She always comes when I call her," I said.

Always came?

This night was different. I'd felt the difference even before Lucy had read her ghastly little story.

"She won't be there," I said.

But Annica was already at the other end of the hall, opening doors, turning on lights, calling Misty's name and saying, 'Treat'.

Misty was still a puppy at heart. I remembered the night I'd found her on the porch, a bundle of white fur whimpering in the snow and cold. The Snow Queen's collie.

"She isn't here," Annica said. "Let's check downstairs. Maybe something spooked her. All the candles, so many people, that creepy music. It could be anything. I'll bet she's hiding."

"Sky is the one to hide under tables," I said.

We paused in the vestibule. I glanced at the front door. It wasn't locked. In fact, it was slightly ajar. Misty couldn't have... No. Ajar isn't the same as open.

Star came up to me, ears flattened against the side of her head.

"Don't you think she looks worried?" I asked.

"She's picking up on your emotions."

"What are you two whispering about?" Brent demanded. He had a sandwich in one hand, a glass of cider in the other.

"We're looking for Misty," I said.

"I just saw her."

"When?"

He took a swig of cider. "That may have been when I came in."

Over an hour ago.

"Misty!" he shouted.

People stopped their conversations to look at him. For Brent, that wasn't unusual.

Candy bounded up to him, eyeing his sandwich with shameless longing. He gave her a rough pat on the head. "Is your name Misty?"

Crane joined us.

"What did Misty do now?"

"She disappeared," I said.

"Naah." Brent dropped the rest of his sandwich into Candy's waiting mouth. "She's around somewhere. I'll find her for you."

Crane put his arm around me.

"Nobody disappears from inside a house," he said. "No dog either."

He was forgetting that we were in Foxglove Corners where such occurrences were not unheard of.

"Then where is she?" I said.

~ * ~

Nowhere inside, nor outside, sheltering from the rain in Raven's doghouse.

The party had wound down, dwindled down to Annica and Brent. On departing, my guests promised to look for a white collie on their way home.

It didn't make sense. Unlike Candy and Raven, Misty had never wandered away from home. As for the idea that the party had spooked her, I couldn't believe that. Misty had a stable personality. She was a brave dog.

She had known something was off at the pink Victorian before I did. Suddenly I remembered something that had slipped out of my mind. Her feverish scratching at the floor of Ginger's house, the way she'd snapped at me when I tried to attach the leash to her collar.

Misty was my partner in the strange, sad affair. My psychic collie.

"I don't know what to do," I said.

Crane said, "You and Annica stay here, Jennet. Brent and I will drive around and look for her."

Brent jingled the keys of his vintage Plymouth. ""We'll find her for you," he said.

"You don't know that."

It was still raining. Surely any dog would look for shelter, if not in her own home, then elsewhere. In the woods?

"We'll find her," Brent repeated.

I wasn't so sure.

"You keep the home fires burning," Crane said.

As they left, the other dogs crowded around me. It was late, past their bedtime, but they were alert and restless. They knew something had broken in their secure world. If only one of them had seen Misty slip through the door, possibly when one of the guests had come in. A collie as white as a Halloween ghost.

But even if that had happened, she couldn't tell me.

Heartsick, I went through the rooms blowing out candles, turning on the light in the bay window for Crane and Brent, if he returned, and for my Misty Come-Home.

~ * ~

The lamp burned all night, but Misty didn't come home. I saw her in my dreams, a luminous white collie slipping forever out of sight as I traveled on a strange road.

Then it was Sunday morning. Thank God I didn't have to go to school.

I looked through the kitchen window at a clean-washed vista. All but the most tenuous of the leaves were down. Against a pale blue sky, the trees stretched upward like dark arms raised in supplication.

I fixed breakfast for Crane and toast for myself. Cracked wheat, dry. I didn't want that.

It was a new month. November.

And here was Candy begging for a piece of my toast, nudging me to make sure I noticed her.

"Don't you know that one of us is gone?"

I longed to ask her that, even though she couldn't answer. Well, no matter what life throws at you, hunger goes on.

"I'll be all over Foxglove Corners today," Crane said. "It'll be bright out. Easy to see a white collie. Not like last night."

He pulled me into his arms for a long goodbye kiss and left. I was alone with my fears and plans to call shelters and make 'Lost Dog' posters. All morning I fielded phone calls from Leonora and Lucy and Sue, all of whom promised to look for Misty.

Lucy said, "You'll find her, Jennet. I can almost see your reunion. It'll be soon. In the meantime, try not to worry. Although..." She paused.

"Although?"

"It may not be the happy reunion you hope for. I'm not sure why. The vision is a bit murky."

~ * ~

Somebody was pounding on the front door. I glanced through the bay window but couldn't see a car.

Being alone in a country house, ordinarily I wouldn't open the door to a possible stranger.

On the other hand, it might be Camille who had only to cross the lane. It might be about Misty.

With Halley and Star at my side, I opened the door. It was Jennifer, my young friend from Sagramore Lake Road looking cheerful in a bright yellow raincoat.

To her delight, the collies crowded around her, each one demanding attention.

"Did I wake you up?" she asked.

"No, I've been awake for hours. Come in."

"Did you lose Misty?"

My heart began to pound. "She ran away from home last night."

"I saw her."

"Where?"

"On my street. Molly and I were coming home from a party. We saw a white collie in the road. I didn't think it could be Misty, but we shouted to her and she turned around. We chased her, but she got away."

"Not to the beach, I hope, envisioning hungry waves and a dog's body.

"No, down Huron Court. It was raining so hard..."

Jennifer kept talking, but my mind focused on two words over and over and over again.

Huron Court.

Forty-four

I made Jennifer a cup of cocoa and one for myself and asked her to tell me about her sighting of Misty again.

The only new fact to emerge was the time. The girls had seen Misty on Huron Court around nine o'clock. By nine, all of my guests had arrived. Someone must not have closed the door tightly, allowing Misty to steal out into the night. Like a ghost.

The phrase kept repeating in my mind. Like a ghost.

I kept asking myself why she'd left the house. I remembered the last time I'd been aware of her. I'd been trying to tie the orange ribbon around her neck. She'd objected and backed away, tail wagging, eyes bright, as if to say, "No, mom. I'm not wearing another collar." After that... I'd been busy greeting guests, setting out sandwiches and pastries, pouring cider. The dogs were there, all around, begging for party food. I could still hear the strains of *Danse Macabre* in my mind.

"Molly and I will help you look for her," Jennifer said.

"I'd appreciate that. Let me give you some biscuits for her."

I reached for a small plastic bag and filled it from the Lassie tin.

"I could give her some of Ginger's treats," Jennifer said.

"There's no need. She loves these."

And she'd be hungry.

"We'll go right away," Jennifer said. "As soon as Molly gets home from church."

I was anxious to start my own search. However...

I took a sip of cocoa. It tasted better than my rushed, makeshift breakfast.

Because you have a clue. That makes the difference.

It was a clue with a major drawback, however. I had promised Crane and Brent that I wouldn't go near Huron Court. Well, to be specific, that I wouldn't go near the pink Victorian.

Had I said anything about the road?

The road leads to the pink Victorian. It leads to danger. Lucy said so. Annica said so. Influenced by Lucy, Brent also said so. And Crane? He had more or less forbidden me to go. Not exactly. He'd assumed that I'd listen to him and comply with his edict.

I'd planned to oblige my husband in this instance because, in truth, I didn't want to return to Huron Court.

All that changed when Misty disappeared. Surely Crane would understand...

Surely he won't.

"Keep the home fires burning," he'd said last night.

Just like a man. Let the men go to war, keep the home fires burning for their return.

This was the twenty-first century, and I was Jennet Greenway Ferguson who had opened her heart and home to a little white collie. I wanted to give her the happiest and most secure life possible and save her from harm.

A wicked thought reared its head. Would Misty vanish from my world as mysteriously as she'd entered it that Christmas Eve night?

No. She hadn't come to me through any twist of fate. Her owner didn't want her. I was a known member of the Collie Rescue League. Fate had nothing to do with it.

I had to find Misty.

I'd stay in the car the whole time. I wouldn't get out —unless, of course, I found her. I wouldn't even look at the pink Victorian.

My inner voice, intent on thwarting my resolve, had a suggestion. Call Crane on his cell phone and ask him to drive up and down Huron Court. Presumably he'd be safe.

He might have something else to take care of. A speeder. A criminal. His duty to the county was all-important.

I'd better do it myself.

"Thanks for the cocoa, Jennet," Molly said. "You have a pretty house. I hope someday I can have a whole pack of collies. Mom says one is enough, but I do all the work."

Say something. Don't let Jennifer know you haven't been listening to her prattle.

"When you're grown and have a house of your own, you can do what you like," I said. "And Jennifer, I'll look on Huron Court. Why don't you and Molly scour the beach and the other roads?"

Okay. I'd said it aloud. Now I had to do it.

Didn't I?

~ * ~

As soon as Jennifer left, I set out on the short drive to Huron Court. Not without misgivings. But how could I do anything else?

As for letting Crane know, I had an unaccountable sense that time was running out. Every minute counted if I hoped to find Misty and bring her home.

The nature of the calamity that threatened her eluded me. Was I afraid some woodland predator would pounce on her? Or that someone would assume she was theirs for the taking, one of the many stray dogs who roamed the woods of Foxglove Corners?

That could have happened already, but I kept Lucy's words in the front of my mind. We would be reunited.

For the first time since I'd realized Misty was gone, I had hope.

The day was clear, the sun bright in a sky strewn with puffy white clouds. It was a day made for optimism.

Huron Court lay ahead, quite different from the autumn-bright country trail I'd walked with my collies so short a time ago. The trees had shed their leaves, making the surface slippery. They threw their shadows onto the road. Stray rays of sunlight revealed pools of standing water. In places, it looked as if a pond had migrated from the woods.

I slowed the Taurus to a crawl and swallowed a lump in my throat, thinking of Misty.

It wasn't far now. I could see the curve in the road, could see...

Not much. Strange how the day seemed to have darkened, the trees along the edge of the woods to have moved closer together.

What had happened to the sun?

I frowned, turned on my lights. In my path, gauze-like wisps reached toward the car, grasping white tentacles enveloping the way ahead in mist.

How could a mist possibly develop that quickly?

I steered through a large pool of water, skidded on a slippery leaf mass, and...

There was a break in the environment. A huge body leaped out of the fog and into my path...

in a heartbeat...

I slammed on the brake. The car skidded again and careened into the woods, down...

Down...

And all the light went out of the world.

~ * ~

I opened my eyes slowly, painfully. I lay on the hard, damp ground on a nest of fallen branches, one of which was digging into my back.

Memory returned slowly, in sharp-edged fragments. The sudden cessation of bright sunlight. The mist. The leaping animal. It must be a deer. Everyone in Foxglove Corners, in any rural or semi-rural area, for that matter, knew enough to watch for deer crossing the road. Adam Barrett had had a narrow escape just last night.

Like Adam, I'd reacted without thinking, slammed on the brake, sent the car flying through space into the woods.

The car? My Taurus?

I didn't see it. The simple act of moving my head set it pounding. Or perhaps it had been pounding all along, and I'd just become aware of it.

My purse was in the car, and in my purse I carried a small bottle of painkillers for just such an emergency, when I was away from home at the onset of a headache.

But the car was nowhere in sight.

With my cell phone on the front seat.

You've done it this time, Jennet, I told myself. *Get up. Look for the car. The impact must have hurled me out of it, deposited me in the woods.*

Unfortunately, this couldn't have happened in a worst place. Few people traveled on Huron Court. With no inhabited houses or restaurants or stores on the road, no one had need to come this way. But all was not lost. I could walk back to Jonquil Lane. I'd done it before. To be sure, it was a long way, and my body was aching, along with my head, but if I didn't find the car, what choice did I have?

Not find the car? That wasn't possible. Where could it be? It couldn't have gone airborne.

But if it had landed anywhere near me, it would have left its mark on the environment. It might have taken out a few trees, crushed down low-growing vegetation.

I didn't see any sign of an upheaval. And the deer? What had happened to the deer? Had I killed it or had it escaped?

Deer are most active at dawn and dusk. Surely it was long after dawn.

I forced myself to my knees, then made myself stand. I felt all of the aches one would expect after being hurled out of a car, but nothing appeared to be broken.

I took a few tentative steps, up a slope toward the road's edge and into the mist. I had no idea how long I'd been unconscious, but visibility was as near zero as possible. I couldn't see beyond five feet. Wet waves of fog slapped at my face, and I was cold. I'd only worn a light jacket.

I remembered the curve in the road. I'd seen it before the deer leaped into my path.

And beyond the curve was the pink Victorian, the house I wasn't supposed to go near.

That was all right. I was going back toward Sagramore Lake Road, back home. Without my car. Without Misty.

Feeling defeated and bereft, I turned around and headed back the way I'd come in a car, trudging along on wet, slick ground, hoping I'd meet another vehicle, although I knew that was unlikely to happen.

Forty-five

My first steps were a bit wobbly, but as I made my way over saturated earth, I felt my strength returning.

I walked toward the lake, watching for some sign of a break in the forest where a car had crashed through, kept watching until I knew I'd gone farther than any accident could have thrown me.

So, where was my car?

Had someone came along, seen an unattended vehicle, and driven it away?

Through the pounding in my head, I could think of no other answer.

Except that people disappeared in Foxglove Corners. Cars didn't. The possibility of someone driving by was unlikely.

I could almost smell the lake, smell the freshness of water filled with new rain, and see the smooth expanse of sandy beach.

The mist was thinner, and the road beneath my feet had a slight upward slope that I didn't remember. The woods were thinner as well, black and gaunt without their vibrant fall color.

Huron Court was a lonely, godforsaken road. Why would anyone build a house in this wilderness unless they were heartily sick of living near neighbors?

I veered towards the road's edge to avoid a wide puddle of leaf-strewn water and saw that more water lay in my path, all the way to the curve in the road.

All the way to the curve?

I came to a stop.

No, that couldn't be. I had turned away from the curve and the pink Victorian. Toward Lake Sagramore and home.

Hadn't I?

Suddenly I wasn't sure. But I knew I shouldn't be seeing the curve.

Maybe I had more than a headache. Could I have suffered a concussion in the crash? It was possible. It would account for the pounding in my head. Had I unwittingly turned in the wrong direction?

I grasped at that explanation. Any explanation that presented itself for walking the wrong way would do.

But I'd know if I had a concussion, wouldn't I? I'd be confused.

And not know right from left?

Stop. Don't take another step. Think this through.

I had been walking a long time on slippery, inhospitable terrain. In a car, I could cover the same territory in a matter of minutes. Automatically I glanced at my wrist. I'd forgotten to put my watch on this morning. Still, I knew that I'd been walking at least a half hour by the ache in my legs.

Time enough to reach Sagramore Lake.

My thoughts spun around in ever-widening circles.

Forget how long you were walking. That doesn't matter. Just turn around and walk in the opposite direction. Whatever you do, don't walk past the curve in the road because if you do, you'll come to the pink Victorian.

I was never more anxious to be on the way home. For a moment, I'd forgotten my reason for coming this way. I'd forgotten my runaway Misty and Jennifer's early morning visit to tell me that she and Molly had seen her last night and chased her down Huron Court.

Yes, I must have a concussion. I wasn't ordinarily so confused.

Then turn. Walk the correct way. To Sagramore Lake.

I did and soon smelled the lake water and something else. A smokiness? Someone was burning leaves. Well, that was a familiar smell.

I'd be home soon. I could take pills for my headache, report my car missing, and see if the girls had found Misty.

Everything would be all right, although Crane would be infuriated that I'd ventured onto Huron Court again, and he'd have to know because my car was gone.

Deal with him later.

I walked on, dodging puddles, slipping on wet leaves. In the distance I could see the curve, although I knew it was impossible.

~ * ~

All right. What was going on? Something was, and it wasn't my choosing the wrong direction. I had turned around, headed toward the lake, walked long enough to have been within sight of it. I knew that. But instead of seeing the lake, I was seeing the curve where a curve shouldn't be.

The last of the mist had dissipated, but instead of a sunlit vista, the day had grown dim and mellow, almost like twilight, but not quite. I couldn't see the sun. Strange. How often that word came to my mind since the first time I had taken my dogs walking on Huron Court.

Should I turn around and try to go back to the lake yet once again?

I remembered that old movie, *Groundhog Day*, in which a man relives the same day over and over again. I was travelling the same road over and over again, first in one direction, then the other. I could walk up to a point. Then, without being aware of turning, I was going in the opposite direction.

Violet had written something similar in her diary. She'd referred to a barrier.

Violet's experience, her time slip, had ended.

Yours will, too.

In the meantime, what should I do? Just keep walking?

Okay. I'd try it once again.

I turned, heading toward Lake Sagramore. The ache in my legs intensified, and my shoes were damp from treading on the saturated leaves. Still I searched the woods for my car, even while knowing I wouldn't see it.

Maybe this time…

The curve swam in a weird light, seemed to beckon to me.

If traveling Huron Court in perpetuity was my destiny, I could either accept it or…

What?

~ * ~

Somewhere a dog was barking. Somewhere ahead. Beyond the curve in the road, beyond which lay the pink Victorian.

I recognized that bark.

Without consciously making a decision, I walked around the curve.

Misty bounded out of the woods. Her white coat was splattered with mud and covered with burrs, but her tail was wagging. She launched herself at me, yelping and circling me, leaping at me. I almost fell backward into the leaves. At the last moment, I grabbed onto her ruff and held.

"Misty, baby," I murmured.

My eyes were wet, my head pounding. I should be happy. I was happy, but I was also afraid. In spite of my resolve, I'd passed the curve in the road to meet Misty. That meant that Violet's accursed house was ahead, almost hidden from view by the folds of mist that seemed to swim by.

The dilapidated shack or the beautiful pink-glowing Victorian?

I walked on with Misty prancing along at my side like a little white reindeer. I wished I had Misty's leash. I'd never walked her without the leash, but I'd left it in the car, filled with hope that I'd find her.

Of course, I could turn around and try to reach Sagramore Lake yet once again. But it appeared that nothing I did made any difference. Right or left, I was doomed to retrace my steps infinitely.

Like a ghost.

I felt the way a ghost must feel. Sick and cold. So very cold.

A dog was barking. Another dog.

Misty froze. I thought for a moment my heart had stopped. Then it resumed its beat. Too fast. It shouldn't beat so fast.

"Ginger," I said.

It had to be Ginger.

Blending with the barking of the other dog, I heard a sound of laughter, clear and melodious drifting out of the mist.

Forty-six

Violet's laughter, at times so far away, so ghostly, had a real-life sound, as real as the dogs' frenetic barking.

"Ginger, fetch!" she cried.

The blue ball landed in the road and rolled toward the edge of the woods. Its tiny bell tinkled faintly. The sable and white collie leaped after it, but Misty was quicker. She caught it in her mouth and cast Ginger a triumph look.

Obligingly Ginger backed away, tail wagging. Misty let the ball fall from her mouth. The two dogs engaged in an age-old canine ritual of sniffing and play bowing.

"Look, Ginger," Violet said, "It's your collie friend come to visit."

I came closer, crossing over grass to the winding walkway. Violet stood in the shadow of the porch where I'd seen her the first time. Either she wore the same blue pedal pushers I'd seen before or she owned multiple pairs. The white top might have been different. I didn't remember the square neckline trimmed in lace, but she wore her sapphire earrings, blue stones winking in flyaway strands of chestnut hair.

237

She was no illusion. What, then, was she? Not a ghost. A spirit couldn't possibly look so alive, wouldn't have such a glowing, rosy complexion, such bright eyes.

Behind her the pink Victorian had a rosy glow of its own in the mellow light. There were the twin turrets, the graceful gables, and the white gingerbread trim I remembered from the last time I'd seen the house, when it was whole and elegant. More trees grew in the yard, and it was tastefully landscaped. It was years away from the sad ruin it would become.

I was in Violet's time.

In the past.

The ball forgotten, both dogs pranced in zany circles around me, then dashed up to the porch where, side by side, they drank noisily from a pail of water.

"Hello, Jennet," Violet said. "Where are your other dogs? And why isn't the white collie on a leash?"

I didn't know what to say. Countless times I'd rehearsed the questions I wanted to ask Violet when we met again, but my mind froze, unable to choose one.

Why not simply answer *her* question?

"We forgot the leash today. The other dogs are at home."

"I see she's been running in the woods. She's all over muddy. It must be hard keeping a white collie clean."

"Usually I don't let her run free," I said. "She doesn't like to get dirty. Misty is proud of her coat."

"She should be. She's gorgeous and so rare. I've never seen a white collie before."

That's right, I told myself. *Natural conversation, to begin with. Later? Play it by ear.*

My questions could wait. Like —I remembered one —What is the year?

How could I possibly ask that? She'd think I was crazy.

It appeared that our first meeting must have happened recently.

But in my time, weeks had gone by. In Violet's world, it was later in the season, a whole month later.

Wasn't it?

Suddenly I wasn't sure of anything. I looked around, saw a few leaves drifting through the air, felt a crunching at my feet as I moved.

No. It wasn't. With a start I realized that most of the leaves were back on the trees. They were colorful hues of crimson, gold, and russet. It was October again. I'd wandered back into the fields of autumn, all unaware.

A bizarre image formed in my mind. Leaves flying up from the ground, reattaching themselves to branches. Making time flow backward.

When had that happened? Not when I started my never-ending walk to the lake, or I'd have noticed the color in the trees.

"Wait up, and I'll get Ginger's leash," Violet said. "We can take that walk."

Which was something I couldn't do. For a brief time, stunned with the reality of encountering Violet and Ginger again, I'd forgotten the pounding in my head. I was newly aware of it, together with a light headedness that began to steal over me. I wanted nothing more than to go home where I'd be safe.

Could I do that? Was my house even there, one of the last two houses on Jonquil Lane? Camille's yellow Victorian was a genuine vintage dwelling. Mine had been built about a decade ago, in Victorian style. In Violet's time it wouldn't have existed.

But I could never know for certain, because whenever I tried to walk toward Sagramore Lake, I found myself traveling in the opposite direction.

If, by some twist in time, I was able to reach the lane, would Camille be there? We wouldn't have met yet.

That way of thinking was counter-productive. I didn't know the current year and didn't know when Camille had moved to Foxglove Corners.

Maybe that was for the best. Did I want to see a wilderness where my green Victorian farm house should be?

And Crane? My collies? My life? All reduced to an undeveloped wilderness on a lane that hadn't been planted with daffodil and jonquil bulbs yet. That hadn't even been christened.

Where was Crane now? What was he doing this minute? Would we ever find each other again?

I felt a sudden chill, as if a cold wind had begun to wind clammy tentacles around me. I was lost in time and apparently there was no easy way home.

Violet waited for my answer, a puzzled look on her face.

"Didn't you want to keep walking?" she asked.

"I... I don't think I can go any farther today. I have a headache. I just went out for some fresh air and found myself on Huron Court."

That was true, to a point, but I could hear myself babbling. Did Violet think I'd changed my mind and was making an excuse not to walk with her?

"Oh, that's too bad," she said. "Can I get you something? A drink of water? Maybe a soft drink? I'm sort of thirsty myself."

So was I. "That'd be nice," I said.

"Come on in then."

"I'd better leave Misty outside. Her paws are muddy."

"She won't hurt anything. My mom's not a fan of dogs in the house, but she's gone for the day."

So we followed Violet into the pink Victorian, the two collies and I, just as I remembered this was the last place on earth I should be entering.

~ * ~

I really felt lightheaded. Violet ushered me into a spacious living room that I'd last seen empty and draped in cobwebs. The sofa and chairs were burgundy. The fabric looked like crushed velvet. Cream-colored drapes kept the afternoon light at bay, and the rug had a jet black background splashed with pink and yellow cabbage roses.

Against one wall stood a mahogany piano with sheet music open on the rack. I had a fleeting view of paintings on off-white walls, mostly forest scenes, of vases, and framed photographs on every surface.

"I'll just get this out of your way."

She took a lavender cardigan from the armrest of the sofa. It had violet appliques running down the left side. As she passed close to me, her perfume wafted through the air. It was the scent of violets I associated with the future version of the house.

"Do you play the piano?" I asked.

She nodded. "I'm studying music at the Institute of Musical Arts. Someday I'm going to teach." She waved a hand at the sofa. "Have a seat. I'll get us some something to drink. Is strawberry okay?"

"It'll be fine."

Ginger followed her out of the room, and Misty lay down elegantly in the middle of the room with her paws crossed in a ladylike position she seldom adopted.

Left alone, I glanced around the room, hoping to see a newspaper with the day's date on it, but everything was as neat as if a maid had just swept through the house. I only saw sheet music stacked on the piano and books in a low bookcase under a window.

I heard the clinking of ice cubes hitting glass, and presently Violet returned with two tall tumblers on a wooden tray.

My eyes began to water. I had no idea why unless I was allergic to something in the room. I pulled a handkerchief out of my jacket pocket and dabbed at them.

She set the tray on a mahogany coffee table.

I had thought of a fairly innocuous question. "I suppose you usually walk on Huron Court."

"Sure, and all over. I try to cover at least a mile a day."

"Did you ever notice anything odd about the road?"

"Odd in what way?" she asked.

That was difficult to describe. Apparently she hadn't experienced her first time slip yet.

"Did you ever lose track of time when you were walking?"

"I'm not sure what you mean. Sometimes we stay out longer than I planned, especially if the day is nice and warm."

That wasn't what I meant, but I couldn't find the words to express what I needed to know. I assumed that the phenomenon hadn't always been... What? In effect?

"Our dogs get along well, don't they?" she said.

"Very well."

They were lying close to each other in the middle of the living room, heads almost touching. It was as if they'd been raised together.

Violet took a swig of her drink. "That's good. Strawberry's my favorite flavor."

I'd taken a sip from my glass and found it too sweet. What I needed was a cup of soothing black tea in my own house and pills for my headache.

I had to find the way home. I couldn't stay in this house with Violet indefinitely, trapped in the past.

"I hope you feel better the next time you come this way," Violet said. "But I'm glad you came today. Otherwise, it's funny, but I would think Fate doesn't intend for us to walk together."

If she only knew.

"I'd better be going," I said. I rose, stood for a moment until I was sure I could walk.

"Will you be all right?" she asked.

"I think so."

I had to be. Violet couldn't help me. If this encounter had occurred at another time, after she'd had her first frightening experience on Huron Court, for example, I might have been able to glean some helpful information on dealing with the intricacies of the unstable timeline.

As it was, I was on my own. I had to find my way back to my own time, to home.

Or not.

At least now I knew why I couldn't find my car.

Forty-seven

I hadn't taken a dozen steps before the mist reformed, throwing a thick white veil over the road.

Misty trotted along at my side. She showed no sign of wanting to be parted from me. Still, I wished I had her leash. Every now and then, I touched her head, to make sure she was still with me.

If she dashed away into the mist, leaving me alone, what would I do?

Keep walking.

I must have read hundreds of Gothic novels in which the heroine finds herself stranded in a desolate landscape without a soul in sight. The English moors, the wilds of Scotland, a sinister forest in Germany. She would have her reticule and perhaps a few coins.

Eventually a carriage or a man on horseback would emerge from the mists and transport her to a mysterious mansion where, after a series of traditional Gothic tribulations, she would find her happily-ever-after.

That wouldn't happen to me. It occurred to me that I had never seen another person on this road. Nor a car with the exception of Brent's vintage Belvedere.

Like the Annabella or Araminta of those old Gothics, I had nothing. My purse and money were in a car separated from me by unknown years, along with the keys to a house that hadn't been built yet.

All I had was a faithful white collie and a pounding headache that wouldn't quit. There would be no knight in shining armor coming out of the mists to rescue me. I hadn't met Crane yet.

You can do this, I told myself. *Be brave.*

I hadn't had to face the world alone for a long time, and never in circumstances such as these.

Eventually the invisible turnaround sent me back toward the pink Victorian again. From inside wafted the poignant strains of a Stephen Foster melody. Violet was playing the piano. I knew the lyrics:

Ah the voice of bygone days
Will come back again,
Whispering to the weary hearted
Many a soothing strain...

Tears streamed down my face, blending with drops of moisture that broke off from the mist and pelted me like raindrops.

"Misty," I whispered. "What are we going to do?"

Turn around again. Keep walking. Go around and around in a circle that never ends.

An idea dropped into my mind with an almost audible thud in the silent, mist-enshrouded world.

Why not just walk past the pink Victorian and keep walking. Maybe the phenomenon existed only on the stretch of road that led from Sagramore Lake to Violet's house.

It was worth trying.

~ * ~

For a while I thought I'd found the answer.

I walked on, Misty at my heel, and wasn't thrust back to the pink Victorian. The mist dissipated slightly, leaving the landscape swathed in a pale, eerie light. Not daylight, not twilight, not night.

I tried to create a map of the area in my mind. Start with Sagramore Lake. Enter Huron Court. Come to the fork in the road, choose the road not taken. The pink Victorian was the only house in this direction. And what lay beyond it?

A crossroad. I thought I remembered Brent mentioning it. A cemetery, Violet had said.

Okay. When I came to that crossroad, I would turn right. With luck, I would find a road that led to Sagramore Lake.

I still didn't want to see a vast undeveloped tract where my house should be, but it didn't matter, because if I followed the route my mind gave me, if I didn't find myself unwilling turned around again, I would have broken the time circle.

Maybe this was the way out.

The problem was that I didn't find the crossroad. The road beyond Violet's house seemed to go on forever. I couldn't see the woods on either side of me clearly because the mist that had seemed to dissolve had formed once again. I couldn't tell if the trees still held their October leaves or if I had found my way back to my own season.

I was growing tired, and my headache hadn't eased a bit. I needed water. So did Misty. Occasionally I heard her lapping water from a puddle on the road. I hoped I wouldn't have to resort to that, but we couldn't keep moving infinitely in this strangely-lit world. On and on and on into forever.

The light-headed feeling returned. If only I could conjure a bench at the roadside, set out for weary travelers. Weary-hearted travelers. I'd have to sit on the ground and rest for a while alone on this godforsaken road, my only companion Misty.

I felt my strength and resolve draining away.

My life is winding down, I thought. *At its end all I have is a little white collie. Somehow it's fitting because I've loved collies all my life.*

And the mist overtook me.

~ * ~

I heard music. The Stephen Foster song, "The Voice of Bygone Days." Violet was playing the piano. Someone was singing the words. A fresh woodland scent wafted through the air. And a voice from bygone days said my name.

"Jennet."

I opened my eyes to confusion. I lay on a cloud, wrapped in folds of white mist. Crane's face seemed to float above me, his gray eyes weary.

"Jennet," he said again.

I wasn't alone with Misty, then. Crane had come to escort me into the other world.

Had he died, too?

"Forever," we'd said at our wedding.

But forever had ended.

He drifted away with the music, with the scent of violet, with the mist.

I was wrong again. So often wrong. I was alone, after all.

~ * ~

A long black nose lay on the cloud. No, the cloud was a bed. I was lying in a narrow bed. Instinctively I reached out to touch the nose.

Halley. My first collie. My heart dog.

Encouraged by my touch, she jumped up on the bed.

"You're in a hospital, honey," Crane said. "There was an accident. I thought... We all thought we'd lost you."

"No," I said. "There was an accident, but I wasn't hurt."

He looked at me.

"I was just lost," I said, "in a terrible place."

I remembered it then, remembered it all and all at once.

"Where's Misty?" I asked.

"She came home the day after Halloween," Crane said. "She's all right. I got permission to bring the dogs in one at a time. This is Halley's second visit."

Seven collies, I thought. Halley had come twice. How long had I been in the hospital? No, not in the hospital. In the past?

My mind was suddenly unable of calculating the days.

And Misty? How could she be in two places at the same time? How could I, for that matter.

"I haven't been here all this time," I said.

"You have, Jennet. Mac found your car, but we couldn't find you. Talk about a mystery."

"But you did. You must have."

"Yes, miles from the car. You've been in a coma."

"No," I said. "That isn't what happened. I went back in time. I saw Violet again. She invited me into her house. Misty went too. I can describe how the living room was furnished. She gave me a soft drink..."

I tried to sit up, tried to include every remembered detail.

"Don't worry about it now," he said. "They brought your lunch."

I saw the tray. A sandwich. Coffee. A cookie.

Just like school.

School! "My classes," I said.

"You've had a sub. Leonora says your bad class is giving her hell."

"When can I get out of here?" I asked. "When can I go back to school?"

"Soon. We'll ask the doctor."

"When I left Violet's house, I tried walking back home, but every time I reached a certain point, something turned me around. I just couldn't reach Sagramore Lake."

I brought my account to an end. Crane was listening to me, but I could tell he didn't believe me. We had lived two different versions of reality.

"You've always had nightmares, honey," he said.

I knew where I'd been, knew about my endless walk on Huron Court, and I had a witness —albeit one who couldn't speak. Had Crane said Misty had been home? All the time we'd been together?

It wasn't possible.

Did it matter that Crane didn't believe me?

He'd covered my hand with his own, and I felt secure. His badge gleamed in the sunlight that poured through the hospital window with its dreary view of bare treetops. My handsome earthbound husband who had accepted ghosts and supernatural manifestations since he'd met me.

Did it matter whether or not he believed that I'd been lost in the past?

Yes, it did.

Forty-eight

I was home, wandering through rooms I thought I'd never see again, with two days' grace before returning to Marston High School. Misty followed me wherever I went, and Star was never far behind her.

At the moment, the two collies lay at my feet as I sat in the bay window, drinking a cup of tea and trying to make sense of what I insisted on calling my time trip. No matter that evidence pointed to my being in a coma.

Everything was the same, and yet it wasn't. I had stopped talking about my encounter with Violet and Ginger in the past. I knew Crane didn't believe me, although undoubtedly he wanted to. That knowledge drove a slight wedge between us. I couldn't understand it. He had suggested time travel as a possible explanation himself when we were talking after my first experience.

In the past I could always tell him anything and could count on his sympathy and input.

All right. Let him have it his way. I'd been in a coma the past week, and Misty had been home. I didn't want to argue with him. It was enough that I knew where I'd been.

It was all so confusing, though. How could Misty and I be in two places at once?

I couldn't explain it, after a while I didn't even try. The anomaly set my head spinning. Not that it ached. Perhaps because I wasn't fighting with teenagers every day, my headaches had gone away.

After I came home, I learned something new. When Mac found my car, he'd also found a dead doe and a prodigious amount of blood. I felt bad about killing one of those beautiful creatures. If ever I met a deer on the road again, I'd try to stay calm and not slam on the brakes.

I drank more of my tea, remembering how I had longed for tea in the pink Victorian.

I was attempting to keep every detail of my experience fresh in my mind, needing to prove to myself that yes, it had really happened.

Violet's lavender sweater. She'd invited me to sit on the burgundy sofa, first removing her cardigan from the armrest. The appliques on one side of the sweater matched the velvet violet I'd found in the house when I'd visited it with Brent and Annica. I still had the decoration but, of course, not the sweater.

Violet's perfume. The scent of violets lingered in the house even while its structure weakened with years of neglect.

Ginger's ball. What would have happened to it? We'd left it outside the house where Misty had dropped it. Made of rubber, by now it would have long since deteriorated.

The Stephen Foster song. The Voice of Bygone Days. The strains, complete with lyrics, kept running through my head.

And sometimes in dreams I heard a sound of laughter. Violet playing and laughing with Ginger.

If only Crane believed me.

Instead, he brought take-out dinners home and convinced me in every way possible of his love.

I wanted to be believed.

Leonora was my first visitor. She had hastily written two weeks' worth of lesson plans for my substitute. I had an experienced sub, but apparently she couldn't control my rogue fourth hour class any more than I could. Leonora brought back unsettling reports from Marston. Impossibly loud classes, students storming out of the room, a shower of disciplinary referrals, a grim Principal Grimsley.

"Your kids will be happy to see you," she said. "They keep asking me when you're going to be back in school."

That was good to know. If I could believe it.

Camille almost drowned me in containers of food. Stews, homemade chicken soup with noodles, stuffed cabbages, and even a pot roast in a slow cooker. Reminding me I'd lost a few pounds while in the hospital, she also brought blueberry muffins, oatmeal cookies, and a devil's food cake.

"So you won't have to cook or bake," she said. "I was so worried about you, Jennet. You're a part of my life. You're my niece, the daughter I never had. If I had lost you..." She patted my hand. "But it's all right. You came back to us."

"A long time ago you told me about how you ran away from your abusive husband, Richard, and came to Foxglove Corners. How you saw your house and knew it was where you were meant to be. But I don't know when you settled down here."

"Twenty-five years ago," she said. "The exact date escapes me. But why would you want to know that?"

I couldn't be sure, but I thought I'd traveled more than twenty-five years into the past.

If I hadn't found my way back to my own time, I would indeed have found a wilderness where a green Victorian farmhouse would one day be, and the yellow Victorian would belong to a stranger or be vacant.

"Just curious," I said. "It's good to be home."

"As they say, 'There's no place like home.'"

I hadn't told Camille about my time slip, hadn't told anybody except Crane. Why bother? They'd look at me as if the coma had robbed me of my senses. Lucy wouldn't, but she didn't know yet. She was going to visit me tomorrow. I was eager to share my experience with her.

Brent, appearing that evening with a bouquet of orange roses, cajoled me into telling him the story. Unlike Crane, he believed me.

"I don't understand how you could be in the hospital and taking tea with Violet in the past at the same time," he said.

"It was a strawberry soft drink."

"Whatever. What's that quote from Shakespeare about strange things in heaven?"

"It's from *Hamlet. There are more things in heaven and earth, Horatio, than are dreamt of in your philosophy.*"

"That's the one." He gave me a mischievous wink. "I couldn't remember exactly how it went. Now, Jennet, I have a surprise for you. There's another diary. I found it in the attic."

Another diary! Another chapter to the story. Perhaps I'd finally learned what happened to Violet.

"You said you weren't going to the house anymore."

"That was for your benefit and the sheriff's. I didn't think you'd believe me."

"I did. He did, too."

"It's my property after all. Do you think I'd wait till spring to check on it?"

"No, I guess not."

"So I took another little trip up to the attic. It was easier to look around without having to watch out for you girls all the time. The diary had fallen between the boards. It was right where the trunk was."

"Well, where is it?"

"I'll bring it tonight when I come back for dinner."

"Why didn't you bring it with you today?"

"I wanted to make sure it's okay with the sheriff. He doesn't want you dwelling on —er —on the past."

"For heaven's sake!"

It was time I shrugged off Crane's dictatorial tendencies before they took hold again. Time I reclaimed my life.

"I'm not cooking yet, you know," I said.

"That's okay. Camille's food is good, too."

"I want to go back to the pink Victorian," I said.

For once Brent was at a loss for words. Finally he said, "I don't think that's a good idea, Jennet."

"You did, and nothing happened."

"Those floors… They may need to be replaced. You can't risk another fall. You're still recovering from the accident. I'm a man," he added.

"I'll risk it," I said.

"The sheriff will never allow it."

Continuing this conversation was pointless. I'd rest for two more days, then go back to school. When Crane saw that I was indeed fully recovered, I could do as I pleased.

But, *Why do you want to go back to the house*? I asked myself.

I wasn't sure. To see if Violet's perfume still drifted through the empty rooms? To find and capture any vibes still floating around? To overcome a half-dormant fear of stepping across the threshold of Violet's house again? To see if the house had once had a stained glass window?

To see if Misty still reacted violently to the middle of the living room floor?

All those times she had whined in the night... Was she remembering our time in the past and confused and frightened by it?

Misty in the present must remember lying in that same spot with Ginger in the past. Here was proof that we had been in Violet's time, but no rational person would believe it.

I decided I didn't have to have a reason. And if I did, I didn't have to share it with Brent.

"We're having warmed up stuffed cabbages for dinner tonight," I said.

He smiled. "Good. My favorite."

Forty-nine

Brent returned the next evening with Lucy and Annica. He'd already told them the story of my time trip. As he'd promised, he brought Violet's new-found diary. He must have obtained Crane's permission.

"Keep it away from Jaws," he said as Misty jumped up on him.

I set it on the mantel, out of the reach of the most determined collie. Was it possible that Violet had recorded our second meeting? If so I would have irrefutable proof of my visit to the past.

"I found something else." He pulled a plastic bag out of his pocket. "It may be just a rag, but maybe it isn't. Go ahead. Take it out."

I did. Brent's find was a yellowing cotton square coated with the dust of years. In one corner, an embroidered basket spilled out a spray of purple lilac stems.

"Oh, no," I whispered.

The embroidery seemed to blur, a blend of purple and green.

"What is it, honey?" Crane asked.

"My handkerchief," I said.

It was warm from being in Brent's pocket. I stared at it, drawing obvious conclusions.

"How can you tell?" Annica asked. "One hanky looks like another."

"My mother gave it to me one year for my birthday. There were a dozen in all. They were decorated with different flowers."

"So you lost it in the attic," Annica said. "Big deal."

It *was* a big deal.

"Hold on," I said. "Everyone. Wait a minute."

I hurried to the front closet where I found the jacket I'd been wearing when I left the house to search for Misty. The hanky had been in the pocket. I always carried a handkerchief or tissue.

It wasn't there.

A memory came back to me, a flash of comprehension. When I'd been with Violet in the pink Victorian, my eyes had begun to water. I'd wiped them with this hanky. In the past.

I told them what must have happened. "Violet found it after I left. She must have kept it, meaning to return it to me, but we never saw each other again."

"And it was stored in the attic with Violet's possessions," Lucy said. "After she disappeared."

They believed me. Even Crane.

He said, "I don't know how it could be, honey, but if you say so…"

"You once suggested that I'd gone back in time," I reminded him.

"Yes, but I was just throwing it out there. I never thought that's what happened."

"I love the idea that we have this proof, but doesn't one blue flower look like another?" Annica asked, betraying her ignorance of botany. "You could have dropped it when we moved the trunk."

"Annica," Lucy said. "You can't deny the truth."

I still held the hanky, still wondered.

If I were right —and I didn't doubt it —this hanky had been in Brent's attic for years.

Before my mother had given it to me.

I only knew I was going to wash it by hand, iron it, and keep it forever, with the other eleven handkerchiefs.

"I don't understand," I said. "But I know."

"Now that's settled, let's see what's in the diary," Lucy said.

"There isn't much," Brent said. "Most of it is just blank pages. It's like Violet lost interest in keeping a diary."

"Or she wasn't able to," I added. "Okay, if everyone's ready."

I retrieved the diary from the mantel, opened it, and began reading.

~ * ~

(From Violet's Diary)

Yesterday, out of the blue, while I was taking Ginger for a walk on Huron Court, I had a premonition. Something bad is going to happen to me. I don't know when or how, but I feel certain that my life is coming to an end. It will be soon.

I wished I'd never been cursed with this ability to know future happenings ahead of time. Or if I have to have this so-called talent, why can't my visions be detailed enough so that I can have a chance to change them? I guess some things can't be changed.

Knowing what I do, I've lost my interest in living. Why plan for a future I'm never going to have?

~ * ~

I thought it happened to me yesterday. When we came home from our second walk, I saw a strange car in front of the house, and the house looked different, like it had grown old in an hour. The door was open. I went in and saw that all the furniture, everything, was gone. I screamed, scared Ginger, and at that moment everything came back, just the way I'd left it. Nothing happened the rest of the day, so I guess I still have some time.

~ * ~

"Oh, my God," Annica said. "That scream. We all heard it. This means that we're in touch with the supernatural, too."

Crane and Brent looked shocked.

"The Rip Van Winkle effect," I said. "Violet experienced it, too."

"What happened then?" Crane asked.

"Let's see...

~ * ~

I made Mom promise to take care of Ginger for as long as she lives. She told me not to be so morbid, that I was going to outlive Ginger and possibly her and Dad. "That's what usually happens," she said. "Children bury their parents, not the other way around."

I made her promise something else. If I should die first, I want to be buried in the little cemetery farther down the road. It's called Old Resurrection Cemetery, and it's the most peaceful place on earth. There's a little statue of a lamb on a child's grave. It has a basket in its mouth which is where you can put flowers, but it's usually empty. Maybe the child's parents died years ago.

If I have to die, that's where I want to spend eternity.

~ * ~

I looked up from the page to find Lucy and Annica in tears. Crane and Brent, being men, weren't crying, but they looked somber.

For myself, I was relieved at the thought of Violet lying peacefully in Old Resurrection Cemetery. I had been imagining her caught in the time curse of Huron Court, traversing the road endlessly, and without end being turned around in the other direction.

We would have to look for a cemetery beyond Huron Court as soon as possible.

"That is so sad." Lucy wiped her eyes with a handkerchief of her own. "But, Jennet, it explains something. Violet mentioned her ability to foresee future events. You've seen ghosts. Maybe that's why you two were caught in that time warp whereas the rest of us could come and go and nothing ever happened."

"That's an interesting theory, Lucy." I said. "But what about you? You have the same ability Violet had."

"I don't know the answer to that, Jennet. I sensed an aura of evil around that house. I knew somehow that the evil was meant for you. If I'd been hurled back into time, I couldn't have coped with it as well as you did."

"I don't think I coped very well," I said.

"So what else does Violet say?" Annica wanted to know.

I skimmed the remaining entries. There were about a dozen of them, but all were variations of the same theme. Violet's foreboding grew stronger. It took over her whole life. She sank into a deep depression. Then she stopped writing in the diary.

I summarized the rest of Violet's story for my audience.

"I think she stopped writing when her foreboding came true."

"But how will we ever know what happened to her?" Annica demanded.

"We *do* know. She disappeared. If she was ever found, or if her body was ever found, I couldn't find any indication of that in my research."

"Didn't that woman at the library tell you she saw her ghost walking with a collie on Huron Court?" Brent asked. "Doesn't that mean Violet is a ghost?"

"You mean Edwina Endicott. Miss Eidt didn't think she was reliable."

"But she *could* be a ghost."

"Or a time traveler," I said. "I know how we can find out, though. Let's check out the tombstones in Old Resurrection Cemetery."

Fifty

Before we could do that, I had to go back to school. I was amazed to discover that I was looking forward to it. Being November, the weather was cold. The forecast was for snow flurries. It was Leonora's turn to drive. I didn't feel like dealing with snow and my first day back at the same time. Besides, I'd have to buy another car.

I put on a long sleeved red wool dress with a turtleneck and added one of the pendants Crane had given me, for luck. Shortly after he set out for his shift, leaving me with a resounding kiss, Leonora arrived.

Let the day begin. The new day.

It felt strange to be walking the halls of Marston High School again, almost as if the school had changed during my medical leave. It was certainly quieter. Principal Grimsley made a point of welcoming me back.

"I couldn't have taken another week with that sub," he said.

"That's a difficult group. I'm not sure anyone could tame them.

Even you, I wanted to add. But I didn't.

My first two classes were visibly relieved to have me back at the helm.

Then came my fourth period American Literature class. They were as rowdy as ever. Chatty Jasmine, sarcastic Slade Johnston, his buddy, Calvin, who muttered, "Oh, no, she's back. Run for cover."

Early this morning before my first class, I'd written background notes for the next unit on the board. Mindful of my last experience, I kept my eyes on my work and took the added precaution of hiding the erasers.

I hadn't read all of the sub's report yet, but the class was still studying Poe. They had spent an entire week reading *The Fall of the House of Usher*. No wonder they were in rebellion. I'd have to change that. We'd take a long leap into Bret Harte. I simply couldn't deal with the macabre at the moment.

Even before I'd taken attendance, I was bombarded by questions.

"Where were you?"

"Did you take a vacation?"

"Did you catch that flu?"

And variations thereof.

I might have known I'd have to explain my absence.

"I had an accident when a deer leaped in front of my car," I said. "Here's a lesson for you. When you see those Deer Crossing signs, take them seriously. Now, please copy the notes on your board. Then we'll have something different. A genuine western short story. How many of you like westerns?"

"Not me!"

"Lame," shouted Slade.

"*The Outcasts of Poker Flat* is a genuine western story," I said. "It has a real rough, tough hero."

You're trying too hard, I told myself.

"Can't you find a story with a space hero?" Sandra asked. "Like Harrison Ford?"

I resisted the urge to smile. "I can look. Slowly but surely we're making our way through the century. The stories will be easier to understand. We'll even have a play."

I was looking forward to *Our Town* even with the heart-wrenching scene in which Emily returns to earth after her death. A play would give the class a chance to participate in class in a different way. Maybe they could enact a short scene in class.

Dream on.

While they copied the notes, I glanced at the window. All the color had gone from the wooded area adjacent to the classroom. The sky was an unappetizing stainless steel color, and a few flurries drifted through the air. Depressing, but so much better than a mist-enveloped country road that twisted through time.

Grimsley's face appeared in the door for a moment, then he moved on. His smile looked pasted-on as usual, even though I suspected that, in this instance it was genuine. Thank heavens he was out of earshot when Calvin said, "I'd rather have the sub than you."

Sandra piped up, "You're crazy, Cal. She's way better than the sub."

At one point, I looked at them, at those who were working, at others who were up to no good, and I realized something. They were just kids. Had I actually thought one of them planned to murder me? Maybe I'd needed that break from teaching, even though it had been a harrowing time.

During my conference hour, I sat at my desk, drinking a cup of coffee and relaxing. Physically I was ready to return to school. I wanted to teach my students again. But a full day of classes had worn me out.

Tomorrow would be better, and the next day better still. If I got discouraged again, I'd remind myself of that unending walk in the mists of Huron Court, of a time when I'd thought I had lost everything I loved.

Footsteps approaching the room pulled me from my reverie. Jasmine peered into the room. Her eyes were red, and her makeup was smudged, blue eye shadow under her eyes rather on the lids.

"Jasmine," I said. "What's wrong?"

"Are you busy, Mrs. Ferguson?"

"No. Come in. Have a seat."

She entered the room but stood by my desk, fidgeting with her bracelet, looking down.

"Are you ill?" I asked.

"I... Can I tell you something?"

"Of course. Are you sure you won't sit down?"

"I'm okay. I was so sorry when I heard about your accident. I thought, what if you died and I never got to talk to you again?"

"Well, I didn't."

"You know how your stuff kept disappearing? Our short stories?"

I'd forgotten about them. I nodded.

"I said Slade pushed the stories into the trash." She paused. "It was his idea, but I was the one who did it. I did it all. Just to show him I could."

"I see."

She looked down again. "I wanted him to keep liking me."

"And did he?"

"Not really."

What could I say? That's all right? Thank you for being honest? You're forgiven?

"Well," I said. "People have their grades, but stealing their property, destroying their works. That's so wrong."

"Am I in trouble?" she asked.

"Will you promise me never to do something like that ever again?"

"I won't," she said. "Promise."

I believed her. She didn't have to confess, but she'd made a decision to do so.

"Then let's leave all that in the past."

"I'm glad you're back, Mrs. Ferguson," Jasmine said. "Gotta go now."

She hurried out of the room. I sat sipping my coffee. Crane would say I'd been too easy on Jasmine. Maybe I had. All the time wasted on searches, endless angst, Grimsley's displeasure... Yes, but how insignificant that was set aside the perils of Huron Court.

I'd still keep an eagle eye on my property. Once bitten, twice shy. But I thought in the future I'd have one fewer problem in fourth period American Lit.

Better times are coming.

Fifty-one

On a cold November day, we all drove to Old Resurrection Cemetery, taking Huron Court which still held ominous memories for me. But Crane was driving, and I felt safe with him.

Still, in spite of what I'd told Brent, there was no way I was ever going to go walking on Huron Court again.

We passed the pink Victorian, no longer pink but faded to its unappealing beige-gray and slowly coming apart at the seams. All of the leaves in the surrounding area were down, and I thought there couldn't possibly be a more desolate place on earth.

"Are you still going to make it an inn, Brent?" Annica asked.

"Sure am. It's going to give the Spirit Lamp Inn a run for its money."

"You have plenty of time to change your mind," Lucy said softly. "I still think the place is evil."

He didn't answer. I didn't think he'd change his mind. Brent loved a challenge.

The cemetery was indeed old. Crane told us there was a New Resurrection Cemetery north of Foxglove Corners.

"New Resurrection is where we'll all end up," Brent said.

"Brent!" Sometimes Lucy couldn't help voicing her outrage at Brent's utterances. "It's bad luck to say something like that."

"Well, there's no room for us here."

A black wrought iron gate surrounded the cemetery, and the graves were situated on an upward rising slope. The illusion that the dead were looking down at us was a bit disconcerting.

We found Violet's grave with no trouble and no need of a guide, which was fortunate as I didn't see any small building where we could avail ourselves of one.

Violet had gotten her wish. At the foot of her grave stood a small statue—a lamb holding a basket. There were no flowers in the basket, but the gravesite was well kept and an oak tree grew nearby, providing shade for the ones who slept beneath the earth.

If that mattered to her. I thought it would.

It was difficult for me to think of Violet in that grave. In a sense, I had just talked to her. She had been young and vibrant, filled with love for her collie, looking forward to teaching piano. And laughing. I would always remember her laughing.

Just last week.

Ah the voice of bygone days.

Once again I was grateful that Violet was not forever traveling on Huron Court.

"We'll never know how she died," Annica said. "Did someone kill her? Did she die from some disease?"

I contemplated the statue. Imagined it filled with fresh flowers in the spring. If no one else paid a visit to her grave, I'd come, and I'd bring the flowers. Fresh, purple violets.

I said "We may never know, but when I get a chance, I'll go back to the library and do some more research. I think maybe it was a violent death. After all, she did disappear first. It might be in some newspaper I haven't looked at yet."

In the meantime...

"Rest in peace, Violet," I whispered.

And there was nothing more to say.

Meet *Dorothy Bodoin*

Dorothy Bodoin lives in Royal Oak, Michigan, about an hour's drive from the town that serves as the setting of her Foxglove Corners cozy mystery series. A graduate of Oakland University with Bachelor's and Master's degrees in English, Dorothy taught secondary English for several years before leaving education to write full time and stay at home with her collies. *The Mists of Huron Court* is #21 in the Foxglove Corners series. She is also the author of one Gothic romance and six novels of romantic suspense

Other Works From The Pen Of

Dorothy Bodoin

Treasure at Trail's End (Gothic romance)—November, 2005—The house at Trail's End seemed to beckon to Mara Marsden, promising the happy future she longed for. But could she discover its secret without forfeiting her life?

Ghost across the Water (romantic suspense)—March, 2006--Water falling from an invisible source and a ghostly man who appears across Spearmint Lake draw Joanna Larne into a haunting twenty-year-old mystery.

Darkness at Foxglove Corners—February, 2007—Foxglove Corners offers tornado survivor, Jennet Greenway, country peace and romance, but the secret of the yellow Victorian house across the lane holds a threat to her new life. #1

Winter's Tale—December, 2004—On her first winter in Foxglove Corners, Jennet Greenway battles dognappers, investigates the murder of the town's beloved veterinarian, and tries to outwit a dangerous enemy. #3

A Shortcut through the Shadows—March, 2005—Jennet Greenway's search for the missing owner of her rescue collie, Winter, sets her on a collision course with an unknown killer. #4

Cry for the Fox—July, 2005—In Foxglove Corners, the fox runs from the hunters, the animal activists target the Hunt Club, and a killer stalks human prey on the fox trail. #2

The Witches of Foxglove Corners—May, 2006—With a haunting in the library, a demented prankster who invades her home, and a murderer in Foxglove Corners, Halloween turns deadly for Jennet Greenway. #5

The Snow Dogs of Lost Lake—November, 2006—A ghostly white collie and a lost locket lead Jennet Greenway to a body in the woods and a dangerous new mystery. #6

The Collie Connection—March, 2009—As Jennet Greenway's wedding to Crane Ferguson approaches, her happiness is shattered when a Good Samaritan deed leaves her without her beloved black collie, Halley, and ultimately in grave danger. #7

A Time of Storms—November, 2009—When a stranger threatens her collie and she hears a cry for help in a vacant house, Jennet Ferguson suspects that her first summer as a wife may be tumultuous. #8

The Dog from the Sky—April, 2010—Jennet's life takes a dangerous turn when she rescues an abused collie. Soon afterward, a girl vanishes without a trace. Ironically she had also rescued an abused collie. Is there a connection between the two incidents? #9

Spirit of the Season—October, 2010—Mystery mixes with holiday cheer as a phantom ice skater returns to the lake where she died, and a collie is accused of plotting her owner's fatal accident. #10

Another Part of the Forest—February, 2011—Danger rides the air when a kidnapper whisks his victims away in a hot air balloon, and a false friend puts a curse on a collie breeder's first litter #11.

Where Have All the Dogs Gone?—July, 2011—An animal activist frees the shelter dogs in and around Foxglove Corners to save them from being destroyed. Running wild in the countryside, they face an equally distressing fate and pose a risk to those who come into contact with them. #12

The Secret Room of Eidt House—March, 2012—A rabid dog that should have died months ago from the dread disease runs free in the woods of Foxglove Corners, and the library's long-kept secret unleashes a series of other strange events. #13

Follow a Shadow—September, 2012—A shadowy intruder haunts Jennet's woods by night, and a woman who can't accept the death of her collie asks Jennet to help her find Rainbow Bridge where she believes her dog waits for her. #14

The Snow Queen's Collie—March, 2013—A white collie puppy appears on the porch of the Ferguson farmhouse during a Christmas Eve snowstorm. In another part of Foxglove Corners, a collie breeder's show prospect disappears. Meanwhile the painting Jennet's sister gave her for Christmas begins to exhibit strange qualities. #15

The Door in the Fog—November, 2013—A wounded dog disappears in the fog. A blue door on the side of a barn vanishes.

Strange wildflowers and a sound of weeping haunt a meadow. The woods keep their secret, and a curse refuses to die. #16

Dreams and Bones—May, 2014—At Brent Fowler's newly-purchased Spirit Lamp Inn, a renovation turns up
human bones buried in the inn's backyard, rekindling interest in the case of a young woman who disappeared from the inn several decades ago. As Jennet tries to solve this mystery, she doesn't realize it may be her last. #17

A Ghost of Gunfire—January, 2015—Months after gunfire erupted in her classroom at Marston High School, leaving one student dead and one seriously wounded, Jennet begins to hear a sound of gunshots inaudible to anyone else. Meanwhile she resolves to find the demented person who is tying dogs to trees and leaving them to die. #18

The Silver Sleigh—August, 2015—Rosalyn Everett was missing and presumed dead. Her collies had been rescued, and her house was abandoned. But a blue merle collie haunts her woods and a figure in bridal white traverses the property. #19

The Stone Collie—February, 2016—Jennet's discovery of a collie puppy chained in the yard of a vacant house sets her on a search for a man whose activities may threaten Foxglove Corners' security. Meanwhile horror novelist Lucy Hazen is mystified when scenes from her work-in-progress are duplicated in real life. #20

Letter to Our Readers

Enjoy this book?

You can make a difference

As an independent publisher, Wings ePress, Inc. does not have the financial clout of the large New York Publishers. We can't afford large magazine spreads or subway posters to tell people about our quality books.

But, we do have something much more effective and powerful than ads. We have a large base of loyal readers.

Honest Reviews help bring the attention of new readers to our books.

If you enjoyed this book, we would appreciate it if you would spend a few minutes posting a review on the site where you purchased this book or on the Wings ePress, Inc. webpages at: https://wingsepress. com/